PRAISE FOR THE NOVELS OF

Jill Shalvis

"A writer of fast-paced, edgy but realistic suspense . . . fiercely evocative." —*Booklist*

"Delightful . . . Jill Shalvis rules." —*Midwest Book Review*

"Fast-paced and deliciously fun . . . Jill Shalvis sweeps you away." —*USA Today* bestselling author Cherry Adair

"Humor, intrigue, and scintillating sex." —*New York Times* bestselling author Suzanne Forster

"A fun, sexy story of the redemptive powers of love . . . red-hot!" —*New York Times* bestselling author JoAnn Ross

THE
TROUBLE
WITH
PARADISE

JILL SHALVIS

BERKLEY SENSATION, NEW YORK

THE BERKLEY PUBLISHING GROUP
Published by the Penguin Group
Penguin Group (USA) Inc.
375 Hudson Street, New York, New York 10014, USA
Penguin Group (Canada), 90 Eglinton Avenue East, Suite 700, Toronto, Ontario M4P 2Y3, Canada
(a division of Pearson Penguin Canada Inc.)
Penguin Books Ltd., 80 Strand, London WC2R 0RL, England
Penguin Group Ireland, 25 St. Stephen's Green, Dublin 2, Ireland (a division of Penguin Books Ltd.)
Penguin Group (Australia), 250 Camberwell Road, Camberwell, Victoria 3124, Australia
(a division of Pearson Australia Group Pty. Ltd.)
Penguin Books India Pvt. Ltd., 11 Community Centre, Panchsheel Park, New Delhi—110 017, India
Penguin Group (NZ), 67 Apollo Drive, Rosedale, North Shore 0632, New Zealand
(a division of Pearson New Zealand Ltd.)
Penguin Books (South Africa) (Pty.) Ltd., 24 Sturdee Avenue, Rosebank, Johannesburg 2196,
South Africa

Penguin Books Ltd., Registered Offices: 80 Strand, London WC2R 0RL, England

This book is an original publication of The Berkley Publishing Group.

Library of Congress Cataloging-in-Publication Data

Shalvis, Jill.
  The trouble with paradise / Jill Shalvis.— 1st ed.
    p. cm.
  ISBN: 978-0-425-21719-1
1. Survival (after airplane accidents, shipwrecks, ect.)—Fiction. I. Title.

PS3619.H3534T76 2007
813'.6—dc22   2007020574

PRINTED IN THE UNITED STATES OF AMERICA

10 9 8 7 6 5 4 3 2 1

To Kelsey for giving up homework time to look up iguanas in the South Pacific for me.

To Megan for doing the dishes every time I whined about my deadline.

To Courtney for sometimes cooking her own dinners of questionable nutritional value during the writing of this book.

And last but not least, to David for putting up with me since before the fall of Rome.

PROLOGUE

*Day Two on deserted island without cookies,
and it's not pretty.*

Only a week ago, Dorie Anderson's nighttime fantasies had run along the lines of, say, Matthew McConaughey, but now as she lay on the long, golden stretch of beach, staring past their shelter to the star-riddled night sky, she fantasized about chocolate chip cookies.

Make that double chocolate chip cookies.

Sorry, Matthew, but priorities were priorities. Stuck on a deserted South Pacific island without cookies? Serious suffering going on.

All around her came the sounds that people tended to buy those nature CDs for: the waves gently hitting the shore, crickets chirping, an exotic bird squawking . . .

Her stomach growling.

She put her hand on her belly, thinking she'd give her right arm for an entire bag of cookies all to herself. Maybe even her left as well.

"How's the patient?"

Ah, there he was, the bane of her existence. She knew this because just his voice made her nipples go all happy.

Damn nipples.

She felt him sit in the sand at her side but she didn't look at him. Nope, looking at him was a really bad idea because then her brain would begin that painful tug-of-war.

Want him.

Hate him.

Want him.

Hate him.

She sighed. "Go away."

"Ah. You're feeling better." He lay next to her so that his arm brushed hers, the one she would definitely sell for that bag of chocolate chip cookies.

"Question," she said.

"Hit me."

"Do you ever think about chocolate?"

He turned his head and looked at her. He was all hard, lean, sinewy lines to her soft, curvy ones. She imagined if she pointed out how different they were, he'd say he liked those differences very much. "I think about other things," he said.

"Like?"

"Things."

His arm shifted, just barely pressing into the side of her breast. And more than just her nipples got happy. *Bad. Bad body.* "I'm tired," she said, and yawned to prove it.

"Here's something to wake you up." Instead of taking the hint and leaving, he rolled to his side, facing her. "Our bet."

Oh, no. "We are not going to talk about the bet." No way.

"That's because you lost."

"You cheated."

He was silent, letting that lie live a life of its own as she remembered the details . . .

As if she could forget.

"You could just pay up," he suggested.

That thought shot tingles of excitement directly into certain areas of her anatomy that had no business getting excited. She closed her eyes, a bad idea because her other senses took over. How did he manage to smell like heaven on earth while on a deserted island? "I don't know what you're talking about."

He just laughed softly.

Bastard.

"You didn't hit your head that hard," he said. "You *know*."

"You're not going away. Why aren't you going away?" she asked desperately, knowing *exactly* what he was talking about, exactly what bet she'd made, and what she now owed him, which involved her.

Dancing.

Naked.

Beneath this very starlit sky. "If you were nice, you'd go."

He lifted a broad shoulder. "Never claimed to be nice."

Also true. *Damn it.*

"Plus we're stuck on an island," he pointed out. "Just how far away do you think I can go?"

Keeping her eyes closed, she sighed again. She really hated it when he was right.

ONE

Two weeks before,
blissfully ignorant of the hell to come . . .

Damn, it was hard to run in her cute new cork-heeled sandals, but Dorie pumped her arms and did her best as she made her way through the parking lot. She was only five minutes late for work, but the store manager of the Los Angeles Shop-Mart she worked for had fired people for less. In fact, Mr. Stryowski was on a downsizing spree, firing staff left and right, which meant it'd been a really bad morning for her alarm to malfunction.

Okay, it hadn't been her alarm. It'd been her hair straightener. But a girl had to do what a girl had to do, and that did not include going to work with frizzy hair, thank you very much.

Into the store, past the food court . . .

Faster, faster, or it wouldn't matter how good a hair day she was now having. She burst into the employee-only area, her huge, carry-everything-but-the-kitchen-sink purse banging at her side.

No Mr. Stryowski in sight.

A miracle in its own right, because nothing got past him. Last week he'd heard Kenny sneaking in late all the way from Garden Supplies.

Kenny was now on the early shift, for the rest of his life.

Dorie hated the early shift. She did not do early. But like Kenny, she was paying dues for her sins. Her apparently ongoing sins. Still running, she passed Sally. The Snack Shop clerk was pouring herself a coffee. They waved and grinned at each other, Sally's sympathetic as she made room for Dorie to get by.

"Great hair today," Sally called out.

The qualifier "today" did not escape Dorie, but truth was truth. She had a lot of bad hair days. "Thanks!"

"Why are you late? Hot date last night?"

"I wish." Nope, that phenomenon hadn't occurred in . . . yikes. She couldn't even remember. Statistically speaking, these years were supposed to be the sexual highlight of her life. So where were the highlights already?

She was a single woman in her twenties, with average looks—at least on the days when her hair straightener functioned—and some average smarts. So it bore thinking about—why couldn't she get a man-made orgasm?

Unfortunately, she had the answer to that. Whenever she got naked with a man, she tended to dwell, and when she dwelled, any self-esteem flew out the window.

Along with her hopes for that orgasm.

Panting for breath now, her tiered crinkle skirt flying around her legs, her darling new sandals already killing her feet—not a good sign with eight hours minimum in front of her—she fumbled for her time card and—

"You're *late!*"

At Mr. Stryowski's bark, Dorie squeaked like the timid little mouse she tended to be in the face of authority and whipped around. He was wearing his default expression—a scowl.

Be cool, she ordered herself, and gave him her best *Who Me?* smile. *Late? Are you sure?*

He was skinny, tall, and with his hook of a nose, could have passed for a medieval warlock, except for the bad rug hanging off his forehead. He'd gotten a new toupee last month, and frankly, he hadn't spent enough. The thing kept slipping in his eyes, making him crankier than usual. "What do you think this place is, Target?" he groused. "You owe me five minutes of your lunch time."

Dorie glanced at Sally, who rolled her eyes. Neither of them had taken a lunch break all week because he was shorthanded, especially in Dorie's particular area of expertise—the Junior Fashion area. He was too cheap to hire anyone else, but since Dorie needed her paycheck, she bit her tongue. "No problem."

Mr. Stryowski narrowed his beady eyes on her while she did her best not to squeak again. Damn, she needed to grow a pair of balls. She'd been meaning to . . .

"You had a phone call. Even though I've told you—no personal calls while you're on the clock."

She wanted to remind him she wasn't yet on the clock, but talking directly to him was like feeding a polar bear—bad for her health.

Even more interesting was the fact that someone called her here at work, and not on her cell. No one did that. At least no one she knew . . .

"Here." He shoved a pink message note into her hands.

To: Dorie Anderson
From: Peter Wells, All Continental Resorts
Subject: *Your prize*

Huh. She'd never won anything in her life. Well, except for that one time in high school, when the captain of the football team, Damian Randal, had won a fish at the carnival. She, Queen of Dorkdom, had been standing in line behind him, trying not to trip over her own tongue, when he'd turned and thrust his winnings into her hand. She'd reacted predictably, becoming socially challenged as always when in the presence of a cute guy. "I'll love the fish forever," she'd gushed, giving him her heart with every breath she took.

He'd laughed and muttered "Whatever" before walking away.

She'd woken up the next morning to Goldie floating upside down and very dead in her bowl. Dorie had been devastated, and when her mother had discovered her grandma's crystal bowl being used for Goldie's home, also grounded.

"Call him back on your own time," Mr. Stryowski said, jerking her back to the present, snatching Sally's coffee right out of her hands. "Needs sugar," he snarled after a sip.

Sally tightened her lips, and looked to be plotting his death while she shoved a sugar packet at him and poured herself another cup.

"Is it just me?" Dorie asked when he'd left. "Or does that man get sweeter every day?"

"Forget him. Call this Peter guy and see what you won."

It didn't surprise Dorie that Sally had read the message. There were no secrets here at Gossip Central. So she pulled out her cell phone while Sally brought her a coffee, complete with two sugar packets and a dollop of hot chocolate powder—the poor girl's mocha latte. Her fellow employees might be a nosy bunch, but they were also incredibly sweet.

Dorie sipped her drink, then punched in the phone number. "It's ringing."

"Ask him if he's single," Sally whispered, cheek to cheek with her, straining to hear. "And don't forget cute. You need to know because he could be some kind of desk geek with a paunch. You're too young for a paunch."

Dorie waved her hand to shush her so she could hear. "It went to voice mail."

"Don't leave your cell number. He could be a mass murderer."

"You watch too much *Law & Order*." At the beep, Dorie left her number. Two seconds later, her cell phone vibrated. With a leap of excitement, she glanced at the ID, but her euphoria quickly drained. "My mother."

"Oy," Sally said, speaking volumes in that one word. She patted Dorie's shoulder and went off to the food aisles to shelve the new stock.

Each vibration of the cell phone seemed more and more agitated, until with a sigh, Dorie flipped it open. "Hi, Mom."

"*Finally.* Where have you been?"

"Vacation in the Bahamas with a cute cabana boy."

Her mother gasped.

"Kidding. I'm kidding." She was a bad daughter. For three days her mother had been leaving messages that all started with "call your mother" and ended with "before she dies lonely, of old age because you haven't given her grandchildren to love," and Dorie hadn't yet called. The reasons were complicated, and mostly had to do with the fact that if Dorie was the Queen of Dorkdom, her mother was the Goddess of Guilt. "I *need* a vacation in the Bahamas with a cute cabana boy," she said, and sat at the rickety employee table, pulling an empty pad of paper to doodle on out of her ever present purse. Doodling always helped. Not as much as, say, chocolate, but a close second.

"So take a vacation," her mother said. "Phyllis is going to Hawaii."

Dorie's left eye began to twitch. Her sister had married a rich plastic surgeon. Going to Hawaii was a bimonthly event for her.

But for Dorie, Hawaii wasn't on the To Do List. As an overly educated Shop-Mart clerk (damn it, yes, everyone *had* been right, her degree in design was worthless without the means to actually front her own clothing line), her vacation options consisted of walking as far as her own legs would take her, or hanging out on her fire escape. Maybe if she dipped into her savings account—

Nope. No can do, not since she'd emptied it out the last time something came up. Which had been a Nordstrom's sale. Remembering, she began to sketch the skirt she'd bought there. The one she'd wanted to improve on.

But she could sketch all she wanted; the facts didn't change. She had no job prospects in the fashion industry because the economy was down, and no designers were hiring interns whose resume read: *Shop-Mart sales clerk*.

She'd like to know how the hell she was supposed to get reasonable experience when no one would hire her, but hey, she'd also like to know how to have a good hair day without two hours of prep time.

"You could tag along with your sister, Phyllis," her mother suggested. "Phyllis would pay for your flight if you watched the kids for her and Donald."

Yes, but she'd discovered she had a severe allergy to wild, sticky, loud, uncontrollable children.

"Or you could catch your own rich doctor," her mother suggested. "And then quit your job for something better."

Well, gee, she hadn't thought of that. "Doctors aren't really my thing."

Her mother sighed heavily. "What is your thing?"

Sweet, she wrote on the pad. She was looking for sweet. And kind. And loyal. If he happened to be cute, too, then so much the better. But not a distant, egotistical, workaholic doctor . . .

"There's a block mixer on Friday night at the clubhouse," her mom said. "All the single, professional men will be there. You'll come, and pick one of them."

Her mother lived in a senior neighborhood in the west end of the San Fernando Valley. The mixers there did indeed include single, professional men. All retired, all wannabe golf pros, and all hair and teeth challenged. "Thanks, Mom, but I'm busy."

"Do you know what your problem is?"

No, but she had a feeling she was about to hear it. She pinched the bridge of her nose. "Can we do this later? We'll sit around and pop some popcorn and list all my faults, promise. But for now I've really got to get to work before my boss blows a gasket."

"You're scared of commitment."

Actually, she was scared of dancing with old guys with wandering hands. She was not scared of commitment.

The truth was she was scared she'd never get a *chance* to make a commitment, not with her social handicap.

"And don't take this wrong, honey, because I have only your best interests at heart, but you're too picky."

Dorie rubbed her left eye, which was now twitching freely. "Mom, I've really got to—"

"Don't hang up—"

"Love you." With a wince for the lecture that she knew would be headed her way the next time they spoke, Dorie shut her phone, which immediately vibrated again.

All Continental Resorts.

The excitement came back in a flash, and her heart leapt into her throat, which was silly because what could she have possibly won? "Hello?" she said breathlessly.

"Dorie Anderson?"

"Yes."

"My name is Peter Wells, and I'm pleased to tell you that you've won a fabulous prize."

"Really?"

"Brace yourself now, because you're about to scream for joy."

Uh, doubtful. She wasn't much of a screamer. Sally said it was because Dorie didn't let go enough, but she thought it was mostly because she hadn't had sex in two years and she couldn't remember much about the screaming factor.

Sally believed that not having sex was bad for the skin and bad for the body, and that certain parts of said body could actually shrivel up and fall off from neglect.

Dorie didn't want to lose any parts, that was certain, but the guys weren't exactly beating down her door.

Still, she couldn't help but yearn for the occasional scream of joy—or otherwise.

"Dorie Anderson?"

"Yes, I'm here."

"Prepare yourself. This isn't just any contest win, this is a special, once-in-a-lifetime opportunity."

He was clearly reading from something, and Dorie waited eagerly for him to get to the point. Maybe she'd won a new coffeemaker. Or a blender . . .

"You've just won a weeklong, all expenses paid trip on a sailing yacht, amongst the small, intimate, beautiful islands of—"

"Ohmigod. The Bahamas?"

"Fiji."

Definitely more than a toaster. This couldn't really be happening. Could it? "You mean the South Pacific Fiji?"

"Is there another?"

"Just clarifying."

"Yes, the South Pacific. You and a handful of others will be spending most of your time on a luxurious sailing yacht, complete with a captain, chef, and crew hand, and in return all you need to do is attend a seminar on the joys of resort sailboat ownership—"

Ah, there it was. The scam. How disappointing. "Look, thank you, but if you have a toaster or a coffeemaker—"

"You don't want to go to Fiji?"

"I don't want to buy anything, not today."

"No purchase required, Dorie Anderson."

Okay, his use of her full name was beginning to creep her out.

"You filled out a form at Roger's Gym last week, correct?"

She had. Her sister had bought Dorie a membership for her birthday. She'd taken a yoga class where everyone but herself could balance on one leg with their other wrapped around their neck like a pretzel.

Dorie, on the other hand, had fallen flat on her face.

Lying there humiliated on the mat, amongst a few snickers and some pitying looks, she'd decided she was better off dressing to hide the extra few pounds rather than make a fool out of herself again.

"Take a week off and pack your bags, Dorie Anderson, because the South Pacific awaits you! A dream come true!"

It did sound like a dream. She pictured pristine white beaches, with gorgeous cabana boys serving her drinks . . . "So this is completely one hundred percent free?"

"That's right!"

At least he didn't say her full name again.

Mr. Stryowski poked his head back in the door, still wearing his favorite expression, which could scare a ghost. He tipped his freakishly big nose down at her, which caused his toupee to slide down his forehead. Slapping a hand on it, he pointed at her with the other. "You're clocked in but not working. What's wrong with this picture?"

She covered the mouthpiece of her phone. "Apparently I just won a week's vacation in the—"

"I don't care if it's on the moon—"

Of course he didn't.

"Get your butt to work."

"Dorie Anderson?" Peter said in that eerily cheerful voice. "Are you interested in this fabulous opportunity, at no cost to you?"

Hands on his too thin hips, Mr. Stryowski looked about ten minutes past annoyed, and in that moment Dorie realized something— he was truly and completely sucking the soul right out of her.

So was her life.

New goal—no more letting anyone suck on her soul. No more letting anyone suck anything . . .

Unless it was that cabana boy.

"Hang up," Mr. Stryowski demanded.

She held up a finger, but he kept coming.

Oh boy.

He was going to take her phone and close it. But she wanted the prize. She *needed* the prize. "I'm interested," she said quickly to Peter Wells, and turned her back on her soul-sucking boss. "Very, very interested."

Behind her, Mr. Stryowski snorted his disapproval, but she didn't care. For a week, for one entire week, there'd be no bullying, no working her fingers to the bone for too little pay, no wondering when her life would kick itself into gear and become the adventure she'd always dreamed of.

Because it just had.

"Peter Wells? How soon can I leave?"

TWO

Day One—Kicking Life into Gear Day.
Or Finding a Cabana Boy Day.
Pick one. Hell, pick both.

Dorie had done it. She'd packed a suitcase—okay, two—and flown for a day and a half, first to Australia (ohmigod, Australia!) then onward to Fiji, specifically Viti Levu, and the international airport there.

She got off the plane and into a bright green taxi without windows. On the console sat a humongous parrot, singing along in falsetto to Cher's "Do You Believe in Life after Love," the warm, salty breeze ruffling its feathers. Dorie joined in, and at the harbor, got out and stood on the dock, grinning from ear to ear at the beauty around her. Let the adventure begin!

More of that light wind rolled over her, rustling the stiff fronds of coconut palms edging the streets and beach. There were people everywhere, in all colors and sizes, speaking a myriad of gorgeous-sounding languages with delightful accents.

She'd wondered if she'd fit in, and she had to say, she did. She was wearing one of her own designs, a white sundress, with brand-new heeled sandals—her cruise splurge—which gave her more height and confidence than practicality. But she figured the confidence was more important at this point.

At anchor on the bay sat a dozen gleaming sailboats, their hulls slashes of white on a backdrop of startling blue so bright it almost looked like a painting.

I'm in the South Pacific . . .

So hard to believe, and she took a moment to soak up the ambiance. That, and the fact that this whole Kicking Life into Gear thing felt good, really good. Following the directions she'd been sent, she walked to a slip at the north end of the docks, where she stared up at a very large sailboat. A very large sailboat that looked like something right out of one of the history books she'd done her best not to read while in school; tall, proud and . . . sinkable.

Gulp.

The *Sun Song*.

She knew from the info that Peter had sent her that the sailing yacht had been made in France, was eighty-two feet long, and was a ketch, whatever that meant. The exterior was made out of welded aluminum alloy, which sounded good and well and extremely water worthy, but it was nice to see the safety raft strapped to the side in case of emergency.

Although come to think of it, she didn't know if she wanted to think *emergency* in the same sentence with the words *sailboat vacation* . . .

Nope, no negative thinking. She'd gotten the week off, and to do so she'd only had to promise Mr. Stryowski she'd work Christmas Eve, New Year's Eve, and Easter—for the rest of her life. But it was done, and she would enjoy herself. After all, it was her new mission statement.

That, and to not think of Mr. Stryowski, or her slowly wasting away life . . . not once.

The plank to get on board was flat and wide enough, assuming she was very careful, and she planned to be very, *very* careful. There were chain handholds on either side, protecting her from the long fall to the water below, but her age-old fear of heights gripped her hard, making nerves flutter in her tummy.

Or maybe it was the king-size candy bar she'd consumed on the plane over here. As she stood there, frozen by her own shortcomings, she contemplated the plank, and how long it seemed. From above, what seemed like miles of white sails seemed so pristine against the azure blue sky.

"Helluva lot of sheets up there, huh?"

At the southern drawl, Dorie turned in surprise and got an even bigger one. A man stood next to her. Correction, a magnificent Adonis of a man.

He was dressed in clothes he definitely hadn't bought at Shop-Mart. Nope, she recognized those pants and shirt as Hugo Boss, and the fashionista in her sighed. There was nothing more attractive than a man who knew how to dress.

Not even a Nordstrom's sale.

His pants were khaki, his shirt a stark white linen, artfully shoved up at the elbows. His luggage—a gorgeous leather saddlebag—hung off one seriously broad shoulder. So broad that he nearly blocked out the sun. He had sun-kissed blond hair and stunning warm hazel eyes, topping about six feet of solid hard body, the kind one got from a most earnest commitment to the gym.

Unlike her own, not-so-earnest commitment.

Turning his head, he looked at her. "A real beauty, don't you think?" he asked in that Texas accent.

She tried to respond, but her tongue was swelling. Good to know she was still a socially challenged idiot. Any second now she'd start drooling—an unfortunate side effect of the swollen tongue.

"Hello?"

Heat zoomed up her face to the tips of her ears, undoubtedly lighting her up like a Christmas tree. *Perfect.* She bit her tongue and managed two words. "A beauty."

He smiled, and the sheer wattage nearly knocked her to her knees, but she did her best to return the smile. Given her nerves, and the fact that she'd stopped breathing the moment he'd started talking to her, she probably only bared her teeth. *Smooth.* She was so smooth.

He pulled a pair of designer sunglasses from his pocket and put them on, covering up those decadent eyes. "You going on board, too?"

"Yes." Assuming she managed to cross the plank.

"Excellent." He held out a big, strong hand. "Andy Hutchinson."

"Dorie Anderson." His hand, warm and callused, swallowed hers whole. She was so distracted by his hotness factor, she almost missed the fact that he was looking at her, clearly waiting for a reaction.

"Baseball," he drawled, and did the big wattage smile thing again.

She really needed to get on board and away from him so she could commence breathing before brain damage occurred, but she was nothing if not polite. "Baseball?"

"You're wondering where you know me from. I play for the Astros. First base."

She thought maybe he paused there for adoration, but he was wasting his time, because all she knew about baseball was that the players looked cute in their tight uniform pants.

Besides, she already adored him.

From far above, up on the ship, voices rang out, and then laughter. Baseball Cutie looked up, clearly eager to board. "You ready?"

"Oh. Sure."

He gestured for her to go first.

"Uh . . ." Once again, she eyed the plank, then let out a nervous laugh. "You know what? I'll just . . ." She took a step back to make room for him. "Meet you up there—"

Only she never got to finish that statement because she tripped over her luggage, still on the ground behind her, and went ass over kettle right there on the dock, hitting hard enough to rattle her teeth.

Sprawled flat on her back with her legs draped over her own two suitcases, she stared up at the brilliant blue sky with the solitary white puffy cloud shaped like a pair of lips grinning down at her, and wondered if it was possible to die of embarrassment.

"Jesus. You okay?"

Was she? Well, that depended on his definition of *okay*. She moved to sit up, but froze at the unmistakable sharp prick of a splinter—in her butt. As she contemplated this unwelcome turn of events, Andy's gorgeous face appeared, that easy smile now twisted into a worried grimace as he leaned in close. "Dorie? Talk to me, darlin'."

Well, if he kept calling her *darlin'* in that slow, southern boy speak, she'd be juuuust fine. "I'm good."

"You sure? Because that was a doozy."

Yeah, she knew. She'd been there.

"I mean, I haven't seen such a good landing since we beat the Yankees at home last season."

Terrific. She was more entertaining than a nationally televised baseball game. As she dwelled on this, a breeze hit and her vision became momentarily hampered by . . . oh yes, perfect . . . her own gauzy white sundress. This was because the hem of it flew over her head.

Which meant she was showing parts of herself to Baseball Cutie that shouldn't ever be shown before a fifth date.

Okay, maybe a third. Not that she'd been on a third date lately . . .

Horror and embarrassment warred for first place. Slapping down her dress, she sat up and tried not to look directly at him, as if that could possibly help the fact that he'd just gotten an upfront and personal look at her Victoria's Secrets.

How long had she known him? A minute, tops? This was a record, even for her, making a fool of herself in less than sixty seconds. But he was gentlemanly enough not to mention it, though his eyes sparkled. He simply offered her a hand and another of those brain-cell-destroying smiles.

Okay, so he was cute and sweet *and* kind. Three out of the four characteristics on her list. Too bad she was such a blathering idiot. She let him pull her to her feet, only to go very still. Forget the splinter in her tush, she'd hurt her ankle.

"Everything all right?"

"Peachy." She'd never admit otherwise. Nope, after the show she'd just given him, she'd rather die.

"You know, Dorie, it's going to be fun getting to know you better," he murmured in that slow honey of a voice.

Sure. But would he still want to get to know her better if she'd had on her granny laundry-day panties?

"Dorie?"

Oh, boy. Now she had to look at him. Trying not to wince, she tilted her head up, but apparently there was a God, because someone from on board called down to him, waving wildly, holding up a drink.

Andy waved back and shot the guy a thumbs-up. "That's Bobby," he explained. "The crew hand."

Dorie waited for Bobby to come down and help them board, but he didn't. "A friend?"

"Ex-friend, actually. He owes me big bucks and can't pay up, so here I am, taking it out in trade. Not a bad deal, huh?"

"Not at all."

Andy nodded, clearly already on board in his own head. She'd lost him. Not a new feeling for her, and thankfully her tongue began to revert to its normal thickness.

"So, you're okay?"

"Oh me? Great. I'm great." She attempted another smile and hoped she pulled it off. "You just go ahead."

"Sure?"

"*Positive.*"

He moved to the plank with his smooth, elegant gait and her heart gave one last little sigh. All men were definitely not created equal.

When Andy didn't fall into the brink, she let out a shaky breath. Now all she had to do was figure out how to do the same with her healthy fear of heights, her two heavy suitcases, a sprained ankle, and a splinter in her butt. She grabbed her luggage, and with a combination limp/hopping motion, staggered closer to the plank, attempting to walk on the toes of her right foot to keep the majority of her weight off the ankle, all while not looking down—

"*Excusez-moi,*" a man said from behind her, crowding up close, trying to get around her, probably since she was moving at the pace of a geriatric snail.

Don't look. Just keep going.

"If I could please just get around you."

"Yes," she said to the French accent, carefully not eyeing anything but her goal—the end of the plank. "I know. Just a minute—"

"I have an onboard emergency, so if you don't mind . . ."

Actually, she did mind. She understood he was in a hurry, she really did, but there was the ocean, just waiting to swallow her up. Holding her breath, she did her best to turn to allow more room for him to pass her, expecting . . . well, she didn't know what she expected. Given his impatient tone, Mr. Stryowski, maybe, complete with a hooked nose and beady eyes and a tight mouth. Maybe a pitted face, and thinning hair. Definitely he'd have a paunch belly.

Not. Anywhere. Close.

Long and leanly sinewy, he was built like an athlete, with golden skin that suggested he spent a good amount of his days outside. He had dark waves of hair that curled up around the edges of a baseball hat and around the collar of his black polo shirt, which was untucked over a pair of Levi's that were clearly beloved old friends with his lower body.

No pitted face, no hooked nose in sight.

No paunch either.

But if Andy-the-Baseball-Cutie had been all smiles and flirting, this guy was his polar opposite—tall, dark, mysterious, and brooding, which was good. Dark, mysterious, and brooding were so not her thing. Nope, her tongue wouldn't swell here.

Not that he seemed to care. He didn't so much as look at her, still attempting to get between the chain handrail and her body. In fact, he couldn't get past her fast enough, and though he sucked in a breath, they still brushed together, his warm, hard chest and arm sliding against her much softer form, and at the contact, *she* sucked in a breath. She didn't really know why, it just happened, but at the sound she made, a sort of involuntary breathy gasp, he looked at her, finally meeting her gaze with those killer stormy gray eyes.

For some inane reason, she thought about her list: cute, sweet, loyal, and kind. This guy wasn't cute. More like bad boy edgy, dangerous. Certainly not sweet or kind. A relief—because it meant she got to keep her wits about her. Good thing, too, because she needed every single one of them.

"Do you need help with your luggage?"

Huh. She might have to revise her assessment on the kind thing. "As a matter of fact—"

"Wait here. I'll get help for you." He moved onto the boat ahead of her, his stride easy but purposeful, not once looking back.

Dorie let out a long breath, surprised to find herself a little pissy. And intimidated. "He's not so different from you," she reminded herself.

Well, except for the confidence.

Oh, and the penis.

That warm, salty breeze nudged at her. Letting go of one of her suitcases in order to shove the hair from her eyes, she reached back for the suitcase again, but it wasn't there.

Because it was now rolling backward on its own, down the plank, slipping right beneath the chain handrail, snagging by its handle so that it hung off the side of the plank, only slightly better than splashing into the water. "Hello?" she yelled up at the ship. "Help?"

Two men appeared out of the woodwork. "Hi," she said, feeling ridiculously inept—not an unusual feeling for her.

One of the men took hold of her arm. He wore a billowy white shirt and loose navy pants low on his hips, with his long, silvery blond hair pulled back by a strand of leather. He looked like a pirate. A really good-looking pirate.

Was everyone on this boat gorgeous?

He smiled, his eyes revealing a good amount of trouble—the kind that drew women like flies.

Uh-oh. And there went her tongue, swelling away.

"I'm Denny McDonald, the captain." He jerked his chin toward the other guy, the one rescuing her suitcase. "And this is Ethan Erle. Our burger flipper."

"Chef," Ethan corrected mildly, also incredibly good-looking, wearing the same navy pants Denny was, with an apron over the top. Cute as he was, he looked as if he was still in school.

Middle school. His youth was probably the only thing keeping Dorie's tongue from further engorgement.

"I'm a chef," Ethan said again, looking at Denny over Dorie's head. "Unless maybe you'd like to be called an oar specialist, Captain?"

Denny merely arched a brow. "Oar specialist?"

Ethan smiled. Seriously, he looked twelve. "*Chef?*" she repeated.

He laughed, his baby face crinkling in good humor. "I'm older than you think."

"Thirteen?"

"Twenty-five," he corrected, still smiling. "Old enough to be experienced. I can promise you, just one of my meals will make you feel like you've died and gone to heaven."

Okay, now *that* sounded promising. "Well, food is one of my favorite things."

"Do you cook?"

"I can toast a Pop-Tart."

He laughed. "Then you're in for a treat."

"You have your ticket?" Denny asked.

"In my purse." She patted the purse slung around one shoulder, which as always, carried just about everything she could ever need.

Except good sense. That she seemed in short supply of.

"Purse?" Ethan eyed it. "That thing is the size of a suitcase."

"No, *those* are my suitcases," she said, taking a few limping steps toward the luggage, including the one hanging off the plank.

Denny was frowning down at her ankle. "What's up with the limp?"

"Nothing. It's nothing."

He didn't push, but he did rescue her luggage, then guided her on board, where she looked around in awe.

The *Sun Song* was impressive, with the sail poles high and proud in the sky above.

"Enjoy," Denny said, and left Dorie with Ethan, who gave her a tour of the ship from bow to stern. It dazzled her. The interior, polished teak and accented with bright, welcoming colors and fresh flowers and gorgeous prints, was surprisingly spacious and luxurious.

Despite her pain, a frisson of excitement coursed through her. She was really doing this, really sailing off into the sunset and the South Pacific, among over three hundred islands made of coral and dormant volcanoes covered in rain forests.

They walked (Ethan walked, she limped) through the large galley, a place stuffed to the gills with all kinds of mouthwatering food piled high on trays. "Oh my God." She nearly moaned. "You did all this?"

Clearly very proud of himself, he nodded. "For the Meet and Greet. It's in twenty minutes."

The adjoining salon was more gleaming teak and held a bar, a gorgeous dining booth, an entertainment center, and a spiral staircase leading up to a lookout deck above. Everything dripped elegance and sophistication, and for the next week, she got to belong in this world.

Belowdecks, her state room was as glorious as the rest of the ship, done in beautiful wood and brightly colored accents, clearly made for comfort and privacy. Ethan left her with a complimentary bottle of champagne, and she toasted herself. "To no more tripping, falling, or stumbling," she said to her reflection in the mirror over her dresser. "To confidence. To having fun." She finished off her glass and then, just a little bit overwhelmed, went to sit down on her bed.

Bad idea.

Sitting down reminded her that she had a splinter in a very vulnerable place. Leaping up in response reminded her of her other problem, her ankle, which had gone from some discomfort to unmistakable throbbing, accompanied by a lovely mottled blue bruise—not her color if she said so herself. She needed ice. Grabbing her purse, she hobbled to her stateroom door, thinking to find Ethan again.

In the hallway, she ran into a different crew member, as extremely good-looking as the rest of them. He was the same guy she'd seen waving to Andy while on the dock. In his early twenties, he wore the same navy cargo pants and white shirt as Denny and Ethan, and oddly enough, a grumpy frown that rivaled Mr. Stryowski's. Along with that frown, he wore an Astros baseball cap backward on his head and carried a tray of what looked to be iced tea, along with a small stack of glasses, and was sending off enough waves of irritation to make her wonder what could possibly be so bad about working on a boat in the South Pacific. *Try Shop-Mart, buddy.* "Houston," she said. "We have a problem."

"Oh, I'm not Houston," he said. "I'm Bobby."

"Well, yes. I was just making a joke— You know what? Never

mind," she said at his blank expression. "Look, I'm sort of injured." She felt so stupid for adding her problems to his clearly already bad day. "I twisted my ankle, and then got a—" *No.* She was not going to tell him about the splinter. Her bottom could just fester and fall off before she'd tell a single soul. "I just need—"

"The ship's doctor?"

She blinked. "Do you have one?"

"Christian's part of the sailing crew, but also an MD." He eyed her ankle over his tray. "Can you walk?"

"Yes." To prove it, she took a step, but her ankle gave out entirely and she fell right into him.

And his tray.

The iced tea fell over, and dumped down her front, soaking into her pristine white sundress. *Oh, yes, right on track to having fun.*

Bobby, his Astros cap askew now, eyed the front of her dress, which was drenched through. *"Shit on a stick!"*

"I'm so sorry." She pulled her dress away from her skin, because wow, the tea was *iced.*

"Shit," he said again, and handed her the small linen napkin draped over his forearm.

She dabbed at the damage, but it was like plugging Niagra Falls with a tampon. Worse, she realized she had a sort of wet T-shirt effect going. "Next time I'll wait until you've got something warm," she tried to joke.

"This is bad." Bobby was trying to look away, but his eyes were drawn to her breasts like magnets. "Oh, God." He covered his eyes. "I'm going to get fired. *Again.*"

"No, it's my fault, not yours—"

"It's never the guest's fault," he said miserably, as if he'd had this phrase repeated to him more than a few times. *"Fuck!"* Then he put a hand over his mouth.

"What?"

"And I'm not supposed to swear in front of you either. Oh, God, I'm toast. Burnt toast."

"No, you're not. Look, we'll just forget about the tea, okay?"

His expression went to sheer disbelief. "You're not going to tell on me?"

"Of course not. It wasn't your fault."

"Really?"

"Really."

He let out a long breath, then nodded, as if trying to reassure himself. "That's good. That's great." Bending, he began to clean up the glasses on the ground.

"Um . . . Bobby?"

He glanced back.

"Maybe I could get some ice? For my ankle?"

"The doctor." He slapped his forehead. "You need the doctor." He reached for her, but eyeing her wet dress, he pulled his hands back, shoving them in his pockets. "Uh . . ."

"I can walk—" Trying to prove it, she took a step and stumbled. Looking like he might prefer facing the guillotine, he bent to scoop her up in his arms, but he was thin, lanky, and she was . . . not. He staggered back with her and hit the wall behind them, where both of them crashed to the floor in a tangle.

Leaping up, he shoved his hands into his hair. "Listen, just kill me," he begged. "Do it quick. Before Denny does."

"No, it's okay. I'm not hurt." She stood, then couldn't control her grimace at the fire in her ankle. "Well, I'm not *more* hurt. Just give me your hand."

Looking miserable, he moved to her side, acting as her crutch, helping her down the hall, both of them dripping iced tea. "Doctor's quarters," he said, and opened the last door. "Wait here."

Then he hightailed it out of there so fast her head spun.

She hopped inside. The room was small but high-tech, with all sorts of medical equipment on shelves against the far wall. There was a patient bed, a sink, and a cart with more supplies.

Dorie eyed a set of tweezers and her bottom actually twitched. Still dripping iced tea, she picked up a medical journal from the counter and was reading about the latest bird flu theories when the door opened.

To her vast disappointment, it was Tall, Dark, and French Attitude, still looking . . . well, tall, dark, and attitude-ridden.

"*Bonjour,*" he said, those pale eyes cool. "What are you doing here?"

"I'm waiting for the doctor."

He looked at her, and not at her tea-soaked body either, but straight into her eyes, as if he could read her without her saying a word, and wasn't exactly thrilled at what he saw.

"So . . ." She tried a smile. "Is he coming?"

He sighed, somehow sounding very French without saying a word. "He's here."

THREE

Still Kicking Life into Gear Day
(aka Life Kicking Dorie Day).

You're the doctor?"

At the question from his dripping wet patient, Dr. Christian Montague sighed from the depths of his irritated soul and strode across the small room to the sink. This was his second patient before they'd even set sail. The first, his so-called "emergency," the one that had gotten him on board a half hour early, had suffered from—stop the presses—a paper cut. She'd turned out to need nothing more than a Band-Aid, though her eyes had wanted something else.

Him.

He was used to that. It had nothing to do with ego and everything to do with the fact that he worked on a boat that catered to the extremely wealthy, which often equaled spoiled. He was a single man, a doctor to boot, surrounded by exotic, lush landscape that inspired certain emotions, one of them being lust.

But Christian didn't mix business and pleasure. Ever.

At least this bedraggled patient wasn't coming on to him. She seemed to be in honest distress. She wasn't drop-dead gorgeous as Brandy had been. She wasn't smooth, suave, or sophisticated as their guests often were.

Instead, she stood there, her dress stained and wet and dripping on his floor, wearing a tote on her shoulder that was nearly as large as she was, looking uncertain, with her wide chocolate eyes broadcasting her naivety.

Didn't she know what that doe-eyed, innocent expression did to most men? Turned them into assholes, that's what. The transparency of her drenched dress didn't help. She was a walking please-take-advantage-of-me waiting to happen.

He couldn't have said why this annoyed him, it just did.

Because you don't want to be here.

Oh yes, there was that. He flipped on the tap at the sink and scrubbed his hands. "I'm Dr. Christian Montague," he said, and yanked out a paper towel, turning to face her as he dried off.

"Dorie Anderson."

Okay, he *could* say why she annoyed him. It was those devastatingly dark eyes that gave away her every thought. He wanted to tell her to close them, before he took advantage of what she didn't even realize she was offering. "What can I do for you?"

"Uh . . ." Her wavy, somewhat wild flyaway brown hair was half out of its clip, and she lifted a hand to shove it away from her eyes, her fingers shaking.

"Are you sick?"

"No."

"Hurt?"

When she didn't answer, he attempted to curtail his irritation. "What seems to be the problem here, Ms. Anderson?"

He knew what *his* problem was. This room was small. Make that tiny, postage stamp tiny. They were within two feet of each other without even trying.

"Dorie," she whispered. "You can call me Dorie."

She smelled like lemon. Lemon iced tea to be exact. Not a scent he'd have considered a turn-on by any means, and yet he couldn't seem to stop looking at her, or breathing her in. The woman barely came to his shoulder. She was drenched. And there were those eyes, those drown-in-me, heal-me, I'm-so-sweet-I'll-kill-you-slowly eyes . . .

Not his type, not even close.

"My problem," she finally said, "is that I tripped on the dock." Her cheeks went pink. "I nearly lost my luggage, and then I spilled iced tea—"

"You don't need a doctor for any of that."

At the base of her throat her pulse beat like a hummingbird's wings. He found his gaze trapped there.

"I hurt my ankle."

Okay, now they were getting somewhere. He gestured to the bed. "So have a seat."

Dragging her teeth over her lower lip, she glanced at the bed. "Um." She slid her hands behind her, over her bottom, and winced. "I prefer to stand."

"I can't look at your ankle while you're standing."

"I—" The boat lurched. She gasped, and her arms flailed out, and so did the huge bag over her shoulder, which smartly connected with his jaw.

The thing must have rocks in it, because he actually saw stars.

He also saw her falling, damn it, and grabbed her as those huge pools of melted chocolate landed on him.

"What was that?" she asked.

"We've just left the dock."

Pressed against him, hair wild, eyes locked on his, her dress soaking into him, she took in the unmistakable sensation of the boat moving over the water. "Oh. Right. I didn't think. It's . . ."

Scary. Sickening. Unsettling. He waited for her to say any of those words, or a dozen others, but after another beat, she let out a surprised smile. "Lovely."

She had a smile on her, he'd give her that. The kind of smile he didn't see every day—real. He tried to back away, but she had a grip of steel on him.

"I hit you." She touched his jaw. "Or my purse did." She let the bag slip to the floor, where it landed with a loud *thunk*.

Definitely rocks. Unfortunately he couldn't think about that because her warm, soft curves were pressed against him, and he became so hyperaware of that, nothing else penetrated. For all the people he came in daily contact with, for all the people *he* touched during the course of his work, he was rarely touched in return.

"I'm sorry," she said softly, hands still on him. "I have a terrible habit of doing that."

"Hitting people?"

"No." She laughed nervously as he untangled himself from her. "Being clumsy."

"Speaking of that . . ." When he pulled his wet shirt, it came away from his chest with a sucking sound. "What is it, tea?"

"Yes. Iced." Reaching out, she brushed a hand over his chest, but he stepped back, free of her touch.

"Sorry," she murmured, her gaze flying to his. "That's going to stain. I'll pay for it, of course—"

"Forget it." Needing a change of subject, he patted the bed. "Sit already."

"Oh. Um—"

She shut up when he lifted her to the bed himself, where she winced big time. "I thought it was your ankle."

She blushed. "It *is* my ankle."

"And . . . ?"

"And nothing."

Nothing, his ass. Or, more accurately, *her* ass.

But she suddenly became fascinated by something on the floor. *Fine*. She didn't want to talk about it. He couldn't care less. Shifting to the end of the bed, he put his hand on her lower leg, over her wet dress, determined to get this over with.

But at his touch, she sucked in a breath. A low, husky sort of sound really, but similar to the sound she'd made on the plank, and as it had then, it zipped right through him. He ignored it. This touch was about healing.

Not sexual.

Yet she'd brought an innate sensual earthiness right into the room, like a third person. Almost against his will, he looked into those huge eyes, and was seriously leveled.

Not good.

He still had his hand on her leg. The material of her dress was soft and gauzy, thin. He could feel the heat of her body beneath. "I need to see the ankle."

When she nodded, he pushed the hem of her dress up a bit, and was blinded by brilliant pink toenail polish. Sliding the dress hem up a bit more, he revealed her legs from the knees down. She did indeed have a contusion and swelling around the ankle, and he slid a hand beneath her foot.

"Ouch."

"Yes, it's a good one."

"I think the dock's uneven."

"And I think it's the silly shoes." He unbuckled her ridiculously high-heeled sandal and slipped it off. "You did realize you were going to be on a boat, right?"

"Yes, but I was thinking *Love Boat*, not *Gilligan's Island* boat. And these sandals, they're made by—"

"They could be made by God himself, I don't care. Your feet weren't made for four-inch heels, no one's were."

"Tell that to Jimmy Choo."

"Who?"

"Not much of a shopper, I take it?"

He found himself letting out a laugh. "I live on a boat, remember?"

"Well then I can admit that these aren't really Choos." A quick smile crossed her lips. "They're Shop-Mart specials. I got them with my employee discount."

"No Shop-Marts around here."

"I know." She went quiet while he studied her ankle some more. Her skirt had slid up to her knees, revealing her pale legs. She was not used to being in the sun, as evidenced by how dark his tanned hand looked against her lily-white skin.

"Your life must be fascinating," she said softly, and when he looked at her, she smiled. "At least to me it is. I'm a clothing designer working at Shop-Mart, I don't get to the South Pacific much."

He ran his fingers over her bruise, doing his damnedest not to notice her skin was the softest he'd ever felt. Or that his touch had given her goose bumps up her legs.

And her arms.

He absolutely wasn't noticing that her nipples—visible through her now sheer dress—were two pebbled peaks. "Maybe you should try designing a more practical shoe for women."

"Did I break it?" She whispered this, her voice husky and low.

"Hard to tell without an X-ray, but I don't think so." He was whispering, too, and he had no idea why, so he cleared his throat and forced himself to look her in the eyes. "You need to ice it and stay off it for a few days." Relieved for the excuse to turn away, he reached in a drawer for an ACE bandage. "I'll have ice sent to your room."

He had to put his hands back on her to wrap up the ankle. He didn't like the fact that her breathing had changed, or that in the deafening silence, his breathing sounded loud and choppy as well. He tucked the ends of the bandage into itself and tried not to look into her eyes. *"L'aspirine?"*

"What?"

His French tended to come out when he was ruffled, and for some reason, he was definitely ruffled. "Painkiller?"

She managed a smile. "You have something for my klutziness?"

"Sorry."

"Oh well. I have my own aspirin, thanks." She pointed to her bag. "In my purse."

"That's not a purse. That's a weapon."

She laughed. "Just inside is a small leather pouch . . ."

Reluctantly, he crouched by the bag. The mysterious depths of a woman's purse had always terrified him, but steeling himself, he opened it. The thing was filled to the gills; brushes, makeup, a wallet, hair bands . . . Damn it—tampons, right on top of an opened sketch pad featuring a pencil-drawn sundress that he'd seen before—on his current patient.

"The pouch is peach," she said from the bed.

He dug past the tampons and found a big box of . . . "Condoms."

Her gaze swiveled to his, her cheeks red. "I like to be prepared."

He hoisted the mega-box. "Just how many guys did you think would be on this cruise anyway?"

"The peach pouch," she reminded him.

He set down the condoms and resumed his search. "Peach is a fruit."

"A light pumpkin sort of color, then."

"Also a fruit." But he kept digging.

"There," she said, looking over his shoulder and pointing. "Right there."

Orange. Why hadn't she just said orange? Tossing the thing to her, he straightened and went to the small refrigerator in the corner, because suddenly he was thirsty, dying for a drink. Something stiff would be best, but he grabbed two bottles of water, one for his patient, except she'd already dry swallowed the pills like an old pro. Then she wriggled to the edge of the bed and tentatively hopped down, gingerly putting weight on her right foot.

"What about your other injury?"

"What?" She slid her hands to her butt. "I don't have another injury."

He let out a low laugh. "Did you fall on it?"

Looking away, she sighed. "Yes."

"Bruised? Or even . . . cracked?"

Her head whipped toward him, and at his raised brow, she rolled her eyes. "I'm okay."

She didn't look it. She was in real pain, and some of his amusement faded. "Maybe I really should take a look—"

"No!" She blew a stray strand of hair from her face and forced a smile. He knew it was forced because it was short of the sheer volume of her real smile, which could single-handedly knock him off his feet.

"It's fine," she insisted, and hobbled to the door. "Really. Thank you. Thank you so much. Just let me know how much I owe you—"

"Nothing. My services are on the house."

"Oh." Her eyes were doing that thing again, that killing him slowly thing. "Well that's incredibly kind of you."

Kind? *No.* Necessary? *Unfortunately.*

One year.

He had one year left of being nothing more than a glorified indentured servant on this gig, and then he was free to live his life how he wanted. He'd be free to go home to his native France if he chose, to ER work, back to everything he'd left behind. No more nomadic lifestyle, no more bandaging paper cuts and twisted ankles.

He could get back to *real* medicine.

"Well." Dorie flashed a small smile. "Thanks again." Then she backed right into the door. Jumping, she blushed again, fumbled with the handle, and then quickly left.

Christian moved after her, sticking his head out the door to see if anyone else was waiting for him.

And ended up watching her walk away.

Actually, she was limping away, yet not all of the limp was from her ankle. She had one hand on her ass.

A very nice ass, most definitely, but hurting. He shook his head. *Women,* he thought, just as another one passed Dorie and sauntered right toward him.

"Well, hello," she purred.

Brandy Bradelyne, paper cut victim.

She lifted her Band-Aid-less finger. "I could use another fix, Doc."

Most men would not have objected. She was built like a supermodel and looked like one, too, with her artfully messed golden hair and lean, willowy, tanned limbs exposed in a pair of tiny denim shorts and an even tinier red halter top.

She was island-ready.

He had a feeling she was also *man*-ready.

"Tough job you have here." Putting a hand to his chest, she pushed him into the room, then followed, kicking the door closed behind them. "Not as tough as my job, mind you . . ."

"What is your job?"

"Me?" She strutted around the bed. "I'm a dancer in Vegas."

"Dancer."

Her eyes filled with good humor. "You're wondering if that's code for stripper."

"I'm just standing here."

"Standing there wondering."

Maybe a little. She had the walk. And certainly the talk. As she trapped him in the corner and rubbed that hard "dancer" body against his, he knew she also had the moves. Blindly, he reached behind him, opening a drawer, feeling for and grabbing a Band-Aid.

She stared at it, then sighed and took it. Instead of moving away, she shifted closer, so close that she could have checked him for a hernia by coughing herself. "Aren't you going to ask me if I need anything else?" she murmured.

"You don't look like it's a doctor you need."

She sighed. "My date stood me up. And you're obviously not interested either"—she pushed her hair from her face—"I guess I'm feeling a little off, sorry. And alone."

That he understood. "You're not alone, they're three other guests booked for this cruise."

"Yes, but I'm a woman who likes to have *personal* companionship." She was still close, close enough to make sure all her good spots touched all of his. "Well, thanks for the Band-Aid—" She rubbed her body to his. *"Huh."* Her gaze went to his. "Is that a stethoscope in your pocket, Doc, or are you just happy to see me?"

He *would* be seeing her, daily. Hourly. The boat simply wasn't that big. He could take what she was offering, but there was that whole not mixing business and pleasure thing.

That wasn't what had stopped him. Nope, that came from something else, something even more unsettling. If he gave up his own decree and went after a hookup on this trip—which he wouldn't—it wouldn't be Brandy he wanted, sexy as she was.

Nope, it'd be another woman entirely—the naive, completely unaware of her own sexuality Dorie.

Which cemented it, really. After two years out here, he'd finally lost it.

Dorie limped away from the doctor's quarters, managed the climb up the spiral staircase to the deck level, and leaned against the hull to stare out at the sea. They'd left the island far behind. It was just a distant blur now, the curving golden sand lining the semicircular bay long gone. As far as the eye could see lay the azure ocean, dotted with whitecaps that sparkled in the slowly sinking sun. The sky, all long strips of pink and purple, was darkening now to blues.

Stunning.

Everyone she'd met so far had been stunning. And so sure of themselves. Baseball Cutie Andy, the pirate captain, the hot stuff chef . . . the gorgeous grumpy doctor. Yep, they all seemed to know exactly what they were doing.

Especially Dr. Christian Montague with that accent, that relaxed and self-assured air as he'd wrapped her ankle, his steely eyes not missing a thing.

God, what she'd give for a fraction of that confidence.

Beneath her feet, the water seemed choppy, and though the rise and fall of the boat didn't make her feel sick, she was extremely aware of how they sped over the water, as if they were flying. She stared at the whitecaps, unable to see into the depths of the water, but knowing all that separated her from the sea life—especially the sharks—was this boat.

Yeah, definitely not in Kansas anymore. Definitely out of her comfort zone as well, away from all things familiar. Behind her was a wall of snorkel equipment and other fun-in-the-sun toys, and a full-length mirror that she did not appreciate.

Her reflection was a mess.

Her sundress, which had started out with such promise, was now wrinkled and stained by the tea. The material sagged loose and soggy around her breasts, and yet clung persistently to her belly, emphasizing the fact that she'd neglected her sit-ups.

In summary, she looked like one big Fashion Don't. *Terrific.*

"Shh."

She turned around, but saw no one.

"Did you hear that?" came the voice again.

Okay, who was talking? She turned around again. Still no one.

"Never mind, it's nothing," that no one said. "Listen, we have to settle this now."

Dorie searched all around her, but could see nothing and no one but her own bedraggled reflection. "Hello?" she whispered. "Who's there?"

"The deal was seventy-five/twenty-five."

Someone answered this ghost's statement, but so softly, Dorie couldn't catch the words.

Then "*Fine*, fifty–fifty, but *you're* taking care of the mess."

Dorie gripped the railing. "Hello?"

The voices—low, probably male, but with the wind and the water hitting the sides of the boat, she couldn't swear to it—went silent.

She strained her ears but could hear nothing. Real or Memorex? After all, she'd had that glass of champagne, and her brain had been scrambled by Cute Guy Overload Syndrome. Maybe she'd return to her room, change for the Meet and Greet, and ice her ankle. Maybe sip some more champagne. Turning back the way she'd come, she limped down the stairs.

"Shh, goddamnit."

She hadn't imagined that. She went still. *"Hello?"*

Nothing.

Creeped out now, and just barely managing not to break her neck, she hurried, heading for . . . she didn't know, except she needed to see another human being. She headed back to the last person she'd seen.

Grumpy Gorgeous Doctor.

Given that she'd clocked him in the head and spread iced tea all over him, he wouldn't be happy to see her. Even without those things he wouldn't be happy to see her, because she hadn't made much of an impression.

No problem. He didn't fit her qualifications either. Hell, she wasn't even entirely sure he was human—which in no way explained why she was heading straight for him, bursting into his office without knocking.

He stood there, being swallowed whole by a tall, leggy, buxom blonde that even on a very good day for Dorie, which this was most definitely not, would have made her feel extremely inferior.

At her sudden extrance, both the beautiful hottie and the grumpy hottie looked up. The beautiful hottie had a canary-eating smile on her face. Dr. Christian Montague had lipstick all over his jaw.

So much for kicking her life into gear.

Four

Definitely Life Kicking Dorie Day.
Damn it.

Dorie stared at the couple for one beat before she managed to come to her senses. "I'm sorry. I should have knocked."

The woman smiled. "No problem."

Dorie whirled, hightailing it back down the hallway.

"Dorie, wait."

That French accent made her name sound so exotic. She moved faster. Not easy with the twisted ankle and splinter in her tush.

"Damn it," she heard him mutter, which only fueled her into moving faster. "Ow, ow, ow . . ." Painfully aware of him catching up, she grabbed her butt and limped as fast as she could. At least her tongue wasn't swelling, but she could feel her ears flaming and her left eye began to twitch as she made it back to her room. *Alone.*

The champagne was warm, which was a damn shame because

if ever there was a need for a drink, it was right now. She took a deep breath and told herself to relax. Everything was going to be fine. *Fun.*

Or it would be, but first things first. The splinter had to go. She limped into the bathroom, where she searched the fathomless depths of her purse and pulled a pair of tweezers from her first-aid kit. Now all she had to do was reach the damn splinter, which wasn't exactly in the most accessible place. She stripped out of her still wet sundress and undies, and then eyed the mirror over the pristine, sparkly sink.

Too high.

She had to climb on top of the closed toilet, twisting around, just barely managing to catch sight of her own pale behind.

Make that *two* splinters. With her handy-dandy tweezers she actually managed to get one. Holding it up in triumph, she did the pretzel twist again to reach the other, but no matter how she bent, she just . . . couldn't . . . get to it—

She broke off trying at the knock on her stateroom door. She stared at herself in the mirror, naked except for her bra.

The knock came again.

"Uh . . . just a minute!" Hopping down, she limped to her bed and dug through her suitcase for a fresh pair of panties—

Another knock, this one more firm. "Dorie?"

Gorgeous Grumpy Doctor. Was Sailing Barbie with him? "Yes?"

"I need to talk to you."

His French accent made him sound so formal, yet beguilingly intimate at the same time. "I'm a little busy." *Where were her panties?*

"Come on, open up."

Okay, forget her underwear, she had no time for underwear. She snatched another skirt and shoved her legs into it. "Now's really not a good time." She found a matching tank top, pulled it on, and hopped to the door, opening it just as Christian was lifting his hand to knock again. "Hi," she said, breathless.

"*Salut.*" His gaze settled on her face, which she knew had to be beat red from the wild exertion. Not to mention the no-panty thing. He held a bag of ice in his hands. "You okay?" he asked.

"Fine. Why?"

His eyes narrowed. "Because you look like you have a fever." He pushed his way into her room without waiting for an invitation, dropped the ice next to the champagne, then turned to face her.

She stood her ground in that small space, her skirt brushing her hips and legs . . . and various other parts that weren't usually so intimately brushed against. "Perfectly fine."

He arched a brow, silently reminding her of how she'd just burst in on him in his own office as if there'd been a fire on her tail, so how fine could she be.

"Okay, not so fine," she admitted, letting out a long breath of air. "But I'll handle it, thanks."

Please go.

He was quiet a moment, just looking at her with those eyes that seemed to see far more than she liked. "I was with a patient—"

"Yes, I could see that."

"I think you misunderstood what you saw—"

She lifted a hand. "None of my business."

"Clearly you needed something."

She'd needed comfort. Now all she needed was underwear. "No. It was a mistake, that's all."

A silly mistake. So she'd overheard a strange conversation. A *really* strange conversation. *Big deal.*

"Coup de grace, huh?"

"What?"

"I've irritated you to the final straw, and now you're done talking."

"Oh. Well . . ." Not irritated exactly.

He scrubbed a hand over his face so that she could hear the rasp of his day-old beard. Then he pulled off his baseball cap and ran his fingers through his hair, which was several weeks past a badly needed haircut, and yet somehow the long dark waves looked right on him. Slightly scruffy.

Edgy.

Dangerous.

Thanks to his fingers, his hair stood up a little, but he either didn't realize or didn't care. She voted for option number two, and when he jammed on his hat again and looked at her with frustration brimming from that steely gaze, the oddest thing happened.

A frisson of heat coursed through her.

Uh-oh.

Where was this coming from? She didn't know, but it was going to stop. He was clearly involved with Sailing Barbie. She gestured to her door.

With a long look that she couldn't even begin to interpret, he moved—but not out. He came right toward her, stopping only when he was so close she could see his eyes had black flecks swimming in the flinty gray. So close she could smell his soap, or shampoo, or whatever it was that smelled woodsy and cedary and really quite amazing. Close enough so she could see that although his mouth wasn't smiling, his eyes were, a phenomenon that did something to her, something that definitely hadn't happened when Andy had smiled at her, or any of the other men.

Not that she wanted to think about what *that* meant.

"One thing," he said, lifting a hand to the wood above her head, then leaned in even closer. His long, lean, rangy form surrounded her now, his every exhale brushing the hair at her temple. He had a scar that bisected his left eyebrow, and her finger inexplicably itched to touch it.

He apparently itched to touch, too, because he stroked a stray strand of hair from her cheek.

"What?" she asked, sounding as if she'd just run a mile. Uphill, in the snow.

"The Meet and Greet is in the salon." His gaze dropped over her body before meeting hers. "You might want to change one more time before you go."

"What?" Was that her voice, all soft and whispery and very Marilyn Monroe–like? It couldn't be. She cleared her throat. "Why?"

"Because if you're going to go commando, *Cherie,* you need a thicker skirt. Something not quite so . . . sheer."

Oh, God. She felt her mouth fall open, felt the heat once again claim her face. *He could see through her skirt.* "Um—"

A hint of a smile bloomed into a full-blown one, and holy cow. If she'd been attracted to him, the pure heat from that smile, the heat that said he knew exactly how to make a woman melt into a boneless heap at his feet, might have knocked her right off her feet. Good thing she wasn't attracted to him. *Much.* "Um—"

"You say that a lot." He shifted just a little closer. "Do I make you nervous, Dorie?"

She managed to snap her mouth shut. "Of course not. Don't be ridiculous."

He didn't make her nervous. Not compared to, say, every other man on this yacht. At least with him, she could swallow past her own tongue!

But he did make her . . . frustrated. Annoyed.

Hot.

As if he knew, he laughed softly and stroked a finger over one of her burning ears.

And just like that, her nipples got happy. Her thighs trembled. *What was happening here?* Besides a train wreck waiting to happen. "Good-bye, Doctor."

His lips quirked. "Good-bye, Dorie." He turned to the door, then turned back. "You know, you didn't strike me as the commando type."

"Maybe it's laundry day."

"On the first day of your vacation?"

She caved like a cheap suitcase. "I wasn't finished changing."

"Ah." The look he gave her was smug, as if he knew her, knew her type.

"Hey, maybe I go without all the time."

He full out grinned. "Do you?"

He didn't believe her, and she pretended not to care. "Yes."

At that, he laughed, and after he left, she didn't move for a long breath. She was being cool. Cool as a cucumber. That only lasted so long; after a minute, when she was sure he wasn't coming back, she raced to her suitcase and pulled on a slip.

But not underwear, damn it. No way. She had a point to prove.

And a life to start living.

*   *   *

A new application of lip gloss and one self pep talk later, Dorie limped her way out of her stateroom. Out of necessity, she wore flip-flops instead of the heeled sandals, but was still commando. Climbing up a spiral staircase, she found herself at the bow of the ship, all by herself, looking at the last sliver of sun as it sank beneath the horizon.

Very by herself.

Leaning against the railing, into the wind, giving herself a little *Titanic* moment, she wondered at the odd sense of loneliness. Probably if she had Leo DiCaprio standing behind her, she wouldn't feel so alone.

Actually, it didn't have to be Leo. She'd have settled for Baseball Cutie Andy. She bet he never made a fool out of himself in front of a woman. He was always sweet, kind, and loyal. She let herself go with the fantasy for a moment but since her tongue swelled in his presence, she had to be real. Tongue swelling could really pose a problem on, say, their honeymoon.

Out of the corner of her eye she caught a movement. Unbelievably, Andy stood there, hands in the pockets of his very expensive linen pants, his equally expensive shirt billowing in the wind. Catching her eye, he smiled, and right on cue, her tongue began to swell.

Damn.

"Hey," he drawled, his eyes filled with an easy-going good humor and a huge dose of dazzling sex appeal. "How about it. You ready?"

Ready? If he meant for that *Titanic* moment she'd just been fantasizing about, where she would face the setting sun and spread her arms and let him support her from behind as they sailed off into the sunset, then *you betcha.*

Maybe they'd go to his room, where he'd slowly strip her out of her clothes, or maybe not so slowly. He'd ravish her, giving her what she hadn't gotten in way too long . . .

"It's already started."

Yep, her engine was started, too.

"There's food."

"Food?" Was she missing something, because—

"Looks amazing. They went all out for the Meet and Greet."

"Oh." Yes, definitely missing something. *Her brain.* "The Meet and Greet."

He cocked his head. "What did you think I was talking about?"

Wild sex. "Nothing." Best not to respond, she decided. Instead, she turned and tipped her face up and studied the spectacular puffy cumulus clouds chasing after the nearly gone sun—

Andy pulled her around to face him. "Did you think I meant something . . . sexual?"

Oh, God. Why couldn't he just ignore her? She closed her eyes. "Listen, I'm—" *Stupid. Socially challenged. Inept. Pick one.* "Really in need of food, apparently."

"Don't worry." He smiled. "Women often get all tongue-tied around celebrities. It's okay, I'm just human."

Well, human was good. She hadn't understood that he was a celebrity, but she couldn't mention that because he'd just put his hands on her hips and was looking the part of the Baseball Stud, and he stepped even closer, and then her heart was attempting a half gainer right out of her chest. She closed her eyes to enjoy the moment, but her tongue filled her entire mouth. If he kissed her now, she'd suffocate. So would he. She'd go to jail for accidentally causing the death of a national treasure. "Andy, I—" She opened her eyes, startled to see that someone had just come up on the deck as well, and was standing right behind Andy.

Dr. Christian Montague.

Tall, Dark, and French Attitude arched a brow, managing to convey buckets of cynicism in that one small gesture. *So who was misunderstanding who?* his sarcastic gaze asked.

"Excuse me," she said, pulling free of Andy. "But I really think I need that food. Now." She walked—limped—past both men, hoping she still had a shred of dignity left.

Andy followed right behind her. "I thought it was your right ankle," he said in that slow, southern voice that was just dreamy enough to make her sigh.

"It is." She didn't look to see if Christian followed her as well.

"But you're hobbling on both legs," Andy said.

Damn splinter! "I'm fine."

"Are you sure?"

"*Very!* Listen, tell me there's chocolate at this event."

"Sure is, darlin'. Lots of it."

"Perfect."

Christian entered the salon just behind Dorie and Andy, who clearly believed he had a shot with her.

For all Christian knew, he did.

The salon was filled with people and tons of food. Dorie moved directly toward the large platters and began piling her plate high, a look of glee on her face, as if she'd hit the jackpot. A woman who liked food. He liked that.

Unfortunately, he liked her. But he wasn't the only one. Andy was following her around like a puppy on a leash.

A horny puppy.

Oblivious, Dorie caught Christian watching her and blushed, but didn't look away. There was most definitely something about her, something which Andy clearly sensed as well because the baseball star shifted a little closer to her. "Want a drink?"

"Oh." Dorie flashed Andy a small smile. "You don't have to babysit me." She began to stack up a second plate now, speaking with a slight speech impediment, almost as if her tongue was suddenly too big for her mouth. "I can get it."

"I'm not babysitting." Andy was really pouring on the southern charm. "I enjoy your company. What'll it be?"

"Um . . . Soda?" Her plates had reached Mt. Everest proportions, but she kept piling the food on.

Christian eyed her petite frame. Where the hell was she going to put it all?

"How about something with a kick?" Andy asked her.

Ah, Christian thought. Let the alcohol-plying begin. But Dorie wouldn't fall for that. She was sweet and naive, but not that naive. Nobody was that naive.

It's not like you have to drive home." Andy leaned in, waggled a brow. "And afterwards, we could dance."

Her plate wobbled and Andy steadied it for her.

"I'm not a very good dancer," she murmured.

"All that matters is that you do it." Andy shot her the smile that probably got him laid nightly. "Come on, Dorie. Live a little."

Come on, Dorie, slug him a little.

But Dorie nodded. "Yeah. You're right. Okay, I'll take that drink with a kick. Your pick."

Christian shook his head. Unbelievable. She had fallen for it.

"Atta girl." Moving to the bar, Andy looked over the display of pine coladas, bushwhackers, daiquiris, choosing two rum punches, no doubt for their potency and potential seduction aid.

Christian's jaw hurt and he realized he was clenching it. Andy moved back to Dorie, taking one of her plates so she could drink.

"Here it goes," she said. "Liquid courage."

"What could you possibly need liquid courage for?" Andy asked.

Christian wondered the same thing. Dorie sucked down her drink, then set both her empty glass and her second very full plate on a nearby table. Drawing a deep breath, she tipped her head back to look up at the baseball player. "I'll have that dance now. If you still want it."

With a smile, Andy pulled her in close, sliding his hand low on her spine. Then a little lower . . .

Christian frowned.

Dorie squirmed.

Andy grinned.

"I know what you're thinking," Dorie muttered.

"Do you?"

She blushed adorably. "I was in a hurry when I got dressed."

Andy laughed. "Are you somehow apologizing for not wearing panties?"

"It's just that—"

"Can I see you later?"

She looked up at him, extremely cute, and extremely flustered, and Christian had the inexplicable urge to pull her away from Andy.

Crazy.

"See me?" Dorie repeated. "As in go out with me see me?"

"Yep," Andy replied.

"We're on a boat."

"In the South Pacific. Nothing more romantic than that."

She blinked, slow as an owl. "You want to be with me."

"Say yes, Dorie."

Say no, Dorie.

"I have to use the restroom," she said, and hightailed it out of Andy's arms.

Finally.

FIVE

The rum punch had gone straight to Dorie's head. Or maybe that was just amazement that she was really here, on a sailing yacht, out of her comfort area.

Make that a couple of time zones out of her comfort area.

Baseball Cutie wanted to be with her. Boggled the mind, it really did. In the bathroom just off the galley, she looked at herself in the mirror. "I'd love to go out with you, Andy," she told her reflection.

See? How hard was that?

How was she going to do this whole living life thing if she couldn't talk? Well, she'd be a mime if she had to, because this was an opportunity of a lifetime. *He* was the opportunity of a lifetime.

She touched up her gloss and headed back to the salon, looking around at the beautiful boat as she did. The interior gleamed with obvious care and pride in every nook and cranny, and the view . . . unbelievable. She was used to tall buildings, smog, and traffic twenty-four/seven. Here there was nothing but glorious open water.

And gorgeous, tongue-swelling inducing men. Remembering that odd conversation she'd overheard, she stood there a moment trying to put faces to the voices she'd heard.

But couldn't.

Captain Denny was talking to Christian near the door. Gorgeous Grumpy Doctor had lost his baseball cap, and now his dark hair tumbled loose and free. He hadn't changed those faded, well-worn Levi's, and surrounded by elegance and sophistication, he looked like the last holdout.

His gaze snagged hers, and she couldn't help but notice he seemed rough and tumble and . . . trouble, pure trouble. Before she could look away, he cocked a brow, and slowly dropped his gaze down the length of her.

Then again, it might just have been her rum punch.

Yet he did it again, definitely eyeing her skirt. *Looking to see if she'd put on panties?* Something went through her at that. A bit of daring. Bravery. And because of it—and the slip she'd added—she executed a little curtsy, spreading the material of her skirt out with her fingers, inviting him to do his best to try to see through it.

An invitation he freely took.

His gaze traveled slowly down to her toes and back up, and by the time his eyes landed on hers, they were two scorching balls of pure flaming heat.

Yowza.

She hadn't realized the full potency of the serious sex appeal he was packing behind that edgy, dangerous front. So much so that she nearly staggered back a step. She actually had to look away to breathe, and then, unable to help herself, she turned back.

He was still looking at her.

She swallowed hard, suddenly unsure of even attempting to play, because unlike Andy, who probably ran bases during a World Series game looking relaxed and easygoing, Christian was one long, lean line of tensed muscle.

Ready.

But for what, she hadn't a clue. Just thinking about the possibilities did the oddest thing—it heated her from the inside out. Interestingly enough, her tongue didn't swell.

It made sense, she supposed. The men in her life had mostly been safe and sweet and kind. Fun and easygoing. Her father. Her sister's husband. Her own too few and far between boyfriends. She *liked* fun and easygoing. In fact, it was what drew her to Andy. Fun and laid-back counterbalanced all the stresses in her life, such as working at Shop-Mart when she really wanted to be designing clothes.

But, and this was something she'd never really admitted to herself until she'd won this cruise, something had been sorely missing.

What, exactly, she wasn't yet sure. Sex? *Definitely.* But if she could just get her nerves under control—and her tongue—she could have that. No, this went deeper. Maybe she needed adventure. Excitement. Danger.

A brooding rebel.

Another peek at Christian assured her that she was the only one still thinking about this because he and the captain were deep into conversation, both looking . . . extremely uptight? In fact, there was a tic in the captain's jaw, and Christian's eyes were still hot, but no longer sexy hot.

Temper hot.

Huh. Maybe things weren't as comfy cozy as they seemed,

which was a disturbing thought considering they were in the middle of the ocean.

Denny stepped onto a platform, and Dorie realized it was some sort of observation deck, and that he could control the boat from right here. Good to know.

He called Bobby to his side. Bobby tugged on his baseball cap. Whatever Denny said made the three of them look even more tense. Unable to help herself, Dorie shifted closer.

"The weather could go south," Denny was saying. "Hard and fast. I want that storm jib checked."

"We're not going to hit bad weather," Bobby said. "They've been calling for this supposedly big storm for days now, and we've gotten nothing."

"Check the fucking jib."

"But—"

"Look But-Boy, I sign your checks. I can stop signing your checks."

Without a word, Bobby turned away.

Through the large windows, Dorie scanned the horizon but saw no signs of a storm growing. Surely they weren't in any real danger or Denny would turn back. *Right?*

"Care to join us?"

She turned. The two other women on the boat were seated at the bar, smiling at her. The dark-haired woman wore capris and a blouse open over a tank top. Casual clothes, but worn with a look of easy elegance that spoke of wealth. Dorie recognized it because she'd never looked that way in her life.

The other woman was Sailing Barbie, who'd been trying to eat off Christian's face in his office. She wore a different pair of shorts, stark white, with a matching itty-bitty halter that barely contained her, with carefully perfect makeup that couldn't quite hide a hardened soul. She smiled though, a genuine one actually, as she scooted over to make room for Dorie. "Brandy," she said, holding out her perfectly manicured hand—with the exception of her thumb nail, which was chewed down to the stub. She caught Dorie looking at it and laughed easily. "That's my nerve nail. Have a seat."

Dorie had no idea why such a gorgeous creature would ever need a nerve nail, but her handshake was warm, and in spite of wanting to hate her for looking like a goddess, Dorie couldn't. So she sat.

"Cadence Powers," the other woman said, and offered her hand as well, which was much smaller, but strong and callused. "We're just figuring out what we're going to do with ourselves out here in the middle of heaven on earth."

"Whatever we decide," Brandy said, "I plan to do it prone, while soaking up the sun, with any or all of the onboard stud muffins oiling up my back."

"No prone for me," Cadence said with a shake of her head. "I came for adventures."

"Honey, there's plenty of adventure to be had while prone." Brandy waggled her brow at Dorie. "We've already had two drinks, each, and have jabbered for an hour. Let me put you on the fast track. Cadence here? An artist. In spite of that, she's practical and pragmatic, and always in a hurry. Has a big problem with a little thing called relaxation."

Cadence nodded. "True. And don't leave out the part where I tend to make bad decisions when it comes to men."

Brandy patted Cadence's arm. "We all do that. Now tell her about me."

Cadence considered. "You're tough and jaded on the outside, but soft and gushy on the inside—"

"Soft and gushy?" Brandy repeated in shock.

"A woman with a big heart," Cadence insisted. "I saw you tip Bobby fifteen bucks just for getting you another drink."

"Trying to improve his attitude. He's in the South Pacific, for God's sake, and scowling like that. Can you imagine?"

Cadence smiled. "See? Soft and gushy." She turned to Dorie. "She's a dancer in Vegas."

Brandy nodded, and Cadence continued. "Oh, and you like to eat bad boys for dessert."

Dorie choked out a surprised laugh. She'd seen her doing just that with Christian.

"It's a metaphor," Brandy told her. "Although"—she looked over at the crew—"I'd gladly eat anyone on this boat. Anyone with a penis, that is."

Cadence blinked. "You're also very honest."

"Yeah, most people don't actually find that a bonus."

"I do," Cadence said. "How about it, Dorie? Give us the Cliffs Notes version on you."

"Um . . ." Dorie tried to think. "I'll go with the soft and gushy thing. I'm soft and gushy on the inside and the outside."

"What do you do for a living?" Brandy asked.

"I'm working at Shop-Mart instead of starting up my own clothing line."

"Oooh, you design clothes?" Brandy asked excitedly. "I love clothes. How about men? Are you good at them?"

"Good? Uh, no." Dorie shook her head and smiled at Cadence. "I don't choose the wrong men, I just don't ever seem to choose at all."

"You batting for the other team?" Brandy asked.

"What? Oh, no. I just haven't had much luck in the long-term department, that's all."

"Join my club." Cadence looked out at the water. "Hey, I have an idea. Let's go for a sunset dip off the swim platform."

"See? Relaxation issues," Brandy said to Dorie.

Cadence defended herself. "I just have a hard time sitting, that's all."

So did Dorie, thanks to her splinters.

"Well, I happen to enjoy sitting." Brandy eyed Ethan as if maybe he were a lollipop and she was a sugar junkie. "It's too bad *he* bats for the other team."

"You mean . . ."

"Gay as a two-dollar bill, I'm afraid. Not that there's anything wrong with that. I just think it's a waste of a good package, is all. And he's quite the package, isn't he?"

Dorie took in Ethan. He was medium height, slim and trim, and to Dorie, he still looked twelve, albeit an extremely good-looking twelve. But how to tell if someone was gay by just looking, she had no clue. "How do you know?"

"Oh, I have the radar." Brandy fluffed her already perfectly fluffed hair. "He's gorgeous, immaculate, fit . . . They don't make 'em straight like that, which is a real shame, let me tell you. Maybe I can convince him."

Dorie blinked, then turned to Cadence. "Swimming sounds good."

"What about sharks?" Brandy peered out at the ocean, a frown puckering her brow. "I hear they can sense you from twenty-five miles away. Aren't you worried?"

Well, she was now. Given the look on Cadence's face, she wasn't alone. "Okay, so no swimming. I probably couldn't anyway. I twisted my ankle earlier."

"Right. When you fell on the dock." Brandy nodded. "The crew was talking about it."

Great. She was already infamous.

Cadence pulled her napkin out from beneath her drink. "Anyone have a pen?"

"Me." Dorie fished through her purse and found one of her charcoal sketching pencils. "Here. This'll work."

"I'll make our lists," Cadence said.

Brandy looked over Cadence's shoulder at the napkin. "You mean for which guy we want?"

Cadence laughed. "Uh, no. For our activities. I was thinking we could wind-sail tomorrow, see the whales and feed the turtles the next day, possibly parasail . . . And the captain said he'd show us this amazing coral reef . . ."

Brandy looked at Dorie and raised a brow.

"Oh." The pencil slowed as Cadence looked up. "I'm doing it already. Impulsive organizing. Sorry. It's just that I've never been on a vacation like this, in the South Pacific of all places. It's unimaginable to me. We have to take advantage of it."

"I've never even been out of Vegas." Brandy lifted a shoulder when they both stared at her. "Born and raised to be a dancer. That's my whole world, never ever even thought about making it bigger, or that I could and why are you looking at me like that?"

"It's just that you look so . . ." Cadence trailed off.

"Worldly," Dorie finished diplomatically.

Brandy looked startled, then pleased. "Worldly? Really? That's the nicest thing anyone's ever said to me."

Dorie thought that if that was true, then maybe Dorie wasn't the only one who had some living to do.

Brandy glanced at Denny, who stood at the control pad with a deep look of concentration on his face. "I do like the idea of him teaching us to sail. Actually, I could get behind him teaching us anything."

"Yeah." Cadence sighed dreamily, also looking at the captain.

Dorie nudged Brandy, who took in Cadence's expression and shrugged.

"You take him, honey."

"Oh," Cadence said, looking shocked. "No, I couldn't. I'm not here for that. No more men. I'm on a penis embargo."

"One more won't hurt you."

Cadence bit her lip, then shook her head. "No. My grandma just died, and I've been feeling a little . . . lost, I guess. I wanted a vacation, to clear my head, to try to relax."

"No better way to relax than some good sex."

Cadence choked on her drink.

"If I hadn't won this cruise in a contest, my vacation would have been babysitting my sister's kids," Dorie said, patting Cadence on the back. "This saved my life. So count me in on the relaxing. With or without good sex."

"We need to toast to that." Brandy lifted her drink. "To making the most of this trip."

Cadence and Dorie lifted their drinks. Brandy tossed hers back, then set her glass down on the bar and grinned. "But we have to do more than toast. We have to actually *do* it. Make this trip amazing. Who's first?"

Dorie and Cadence looked at each other, then shook their heads.

Brandy laughed. "All right, me then. Watch and learn, girls." She tugged on the hem of her halter so that it revealed a bit more cleavage. Not enough, apparently, because she tugged again.

Once more, Dorie thought, *and there won't be anything left to conceal.* "Um, you're getting sort of close to a situation there."

Brandy patted her breasts like beloved old friends. "Let me give you a little tip on making the most of something." She leaned in and whispered, "Know your audience."

"I thought you already had your audience," Dorie said, and when Brandy looked confused, she clarified. "I saw you with Christian."

"Oh, that." Brandy smiled. "He gives good Band-Aids, but he's not interested." Standing, she tossed back her hair and sauntered toward Bobby and Andy, who were talking to the chef.

"Not shy, is she?" Cadence murmured.

Dorie was having a hard time getting past "he's not interested." "When you look like that, I guess there's no need."

They watched Brandy cozy up to Bobby. The poor guy looked as if he'd won the lottery.

"Well, she's right about one thing," Cadence noted. "There is some serious eye candy on this boat." She was looking at the captain, who stood hands on hips, his long legs planted firmly apart, his loose clothing nicely showcasing a lean, hard body as the sun sank below the horizon behind him. His face was deeply tanned and rugged, his long hair still held back by a strap of leather. "I mean look at him. There's just something about that billowy pirate shirt and that long hair . . ." She laughed at herself. "Oh well."

"Not oh well," Dorie said. "Go for it. We just toasted to going for it."

"Oh, no. No, no, no. I wasn't kidding when I said I always go for the wrong guy. I have absolutely no radar when it comes to the losers. No men for me this week, thank you very much. I was serious about the penis embargo."

"I'm perpetually under a penis embargo," Dorie said.

"Then *you* must break routine. Which one would you do?"

"*Do?*"

"Oh, sorry. Didn't meant to sound like the stripper—er, excuse me, dancer."

Dorie laughed. "She might really be a dancer, you know."

"Uh-huh. And I'm the Tooth Fairy." Cadence's dark eyes were shiny with laughter. "Look at her. Lapping him up. And then there's the Cowboy. He's something, too, isn't he?"

"Andy?" Dorie looked at him, so big and strong and beautiful. "Actually, I think he asked me out."

Cadence's eyes widened. "You think?"

"It doesn't matter. He's cute, and my tongue swells near cute guys."

"Sounds problematic."

"You could say so."

"Go for it anyway," Cadence suggested.

"I'll suffocate."

"I know CPR."

She *should* go for it. She'd planned to.

Except her gaze strayed to Christian, who stood at the far end of the salon, in front of the bar, eyeing the drinks.

He didn't take one.

"Talk about dark and smoldering," Cadence said, seeing where Dorie's gaze wandered. "Nice choice."

"What? Oh, no. No, not him. No. He's too . . ." *Everything.* "He's not my type at all. No. Not him."

Cadence was smiling. "Me thinks the lady doth protest too much."

Dorie nibbled on her lower lip, and Cadence laughed. "See, you want to bite him. I think you should."

"Cadence."

"Sorry. It's the free alcohol." She downed the rest of her drink. "Goes straight to my head. He's curious about you, if that helps."

"Based on . . . ?"

"Based on the fact that he keeps looking at you."

Dorie peeked again. He stood there, enigmatic and brooding. And indeed looking at her.

He was out of her league. *Waaaay* out of her league. "Problem."

"Is your tongue swelling?"

"No." Which was extremely curious in its own right. "He's . . ."

"Fabulous?"

"Grumpy. Sort of offsets the whole fabulous thing."

His gaze captured hers, held it prisoner.

And the oddest thing happened. Time sort of stuttered to a halt. Her body flashed hot, her heart kicked hard, and she began to sweat, but one thing did not happen—no tongue swelling.

What did that mean?

"He's still looking at you," Cadence whispered. "And oh my, but he's hot. How's the tongue?"

"Still behaving," she said, shocked.

"Maybe it's a sign."

No, it couldn't be. Clearly she was still suffering the effects from traveling halfway around the world, and then having champagne and a rum punch, because she couldn't have a crush on him, she just couldn't. Even without her social awkwardness, it was a supremely bad idea all the way around. Unfortunately, she seemed to make it her mission to follow bad ideas.

SIX

Cadence came back from the food table. "The buffet is going to be tricky."

Dorie eyed Cadence's full plate with envy. She'd given Andy her plate, damn it. "Why?"

"Because I'm going to be big as a house if you let me eat all this by myself. Dig in," she ordered, setting the plate between them.

Worked for Dorie. Behind them the moon began its nightly rise, glittering over the water. The breeze cooled her as the sailboat gently rose and fell on the easy swells.

"He's looking again," Cadence whispered.

Dorie turned her head and met Christian's hot gaze.

"Boy, oh boy, he's something."

"Yes." The doctor sure was something. She just wasn't sure what.

"It's going to take a really together woman to keep him entertained."

"In light of that alone, I should stick with Baseball Cutie." Her chances were better, seeing as Andy had actually expressed interest, something Christian had not. Besides, she wanted Andy. She did.

Or she wanted to want Andy . . .

"Honestly? You really can't go wrong either way. Look at Brandy."

Brandy had positioned herself in front of the wall of windows so that the moonlight fell over her like a spotlight, where she held court with the captain, Ethan, and Andy.

"She's a man magnet," Dorie said in envy. "So confident."

"I've heard that if you fake it, it sort of sticks."

"Yes, but I've never really gotten the hang of faking it."

Cadence's eyes sparkled with good humor. "As women, we were born with the ability to fake it."

Dorie laughed.

"Maybe she could teach us," Cadence said, watching Brandy toss back her head and let out a low, throaty laugh at something the captain said.

Apparently it was infectious, because all the men laughed, too.

Dorie let out an admiring sigh. "Something tells me she never fakes a thing."

Off to the side, Christian took a bottled water from the bar, uncapped it, and tilted it up to his mouth. After he drained half of it, he wiped his mouth on his arm and once again locked gazes with Dorie. An indefinable *zing* hummed through her system.

Cadence nudged her shoulder. "Here he comes."

But Christian hadn't moved an inch. He wasn't smiling; he wasn't doing anything except looking at her. "No, he's not."

"Cowboy," Cadence whispered. "At one, two, *three o'clock*."

Dorie broke eye contact with Christian as Andy came close.

"Hi, ladies." He still wore those designer duds, looking like a million bucks as he smiled at Dorie.

Whose tongue promptly began to swell and stick to the roof of her mouth.

Oblivious, he sat down next to them at the bar. "The captain said we're snorkeling tomorrow."

"Snorkeling?" Cadence's smile congealed. "Oh. Is that an entirely underwater sport do you think?"

"Unless the fish are flying through the air."

Cadence looked at her list. "No. Snorkeling is not on here, sorry."

"Are you kidding? We're in the South Pacific. The fish are huge. Denny says they swim right up to your face mask and bump into you."

Cadence lost some of her color. "On purpose?"

Andy laughed. "That's right." He turned to Dorie. "Sound like fun?"

"Ith nether thn—" Ruthlessly, she bit her own tongue, then tried again. "I've never snorkeled."

"There's a first time for everything, darlin'." His smile said that maybe snorkeling wouldn't be their only first.

In response, Dorie's tongue twitched. Panicked, she looked at Cadence.

Cadence shook her head. "Sorry, but I have a fear of putting my face in the water. Totally and ridiculously juvenile, I know, but snorkeling is *not* happening for me. You're on your own."

Andy smiled at Dorie. "No problem. We go in pairs anyway. How about we partner up?"

"She'd love to," Cadence said for her.

Andy lightly tugged on a strand of Dorie's hair. "Don't worry, you'll be in good hands."

Dorie looked at his handsome face, and thought of him in a bathing suit. "Fun," she agreed.

He smiled the smile of a man charmed. A man who knew he was on his way to getting lucky.

She just had to decide if that was going to be true. And if she could sleep with him without swallowing her own tongue.

Night One—No cabana boy yet but still working on it.

Dorie slept in soft, lush bedding that wasn't from Shop-Mart and woke to the sound of the wind whipping at sails. From her window she could see an incredible blue sky, so bright she needed sunglasses to look at it. She showered and winced anew at her unreachable splinter, but it didn't look infected so she wasn't going to worry about it.

Much.

Her ankle felt better and was no longer swollen. She pulled on the bathing suit she'd designed when she'd promised herself to lose ten pounds, which had never happened because barbeque chips had gone on sale at the store and she'd bought an entire carton. Not a single bag, but a *carton*. Now the suit was a little tight, but the top gave her breasts a nice lift, which was a fun bonus. Unfortunately, the shorty bottoms exposed more than they covered.

Damn BBQ chips.

She pulled out a wraparound skirt, tied it on, and called it good.

Up on deck, she was momentarily staggered by the huge, yawning sky and even huger, yawning ocean, both in that brilliant blue, with only the occasional whitecap to break it up. The air was warm, with a soft breeze that felt like heaven. Far above, the sails soared and cracked in the wind like fireworks.

"An amazing way to wake up, isn't it?"

She turned and smiled at Cadence, who sat on a lounge. "Beats the L.A. smog, that's for sure." Despite the warm air, Cadence had her sweatshirt zipped up to her chin, and Dorie gestured to it. "You cold?"

"No. My bathing suit is all screwed up. I think it shrank." She grimaced. "Okay, that's a lie. It didn't shrink, I got bigger."

"Let me see."

Cadence looked around carefully for other eyes, then unzipped her sweatshirt. Dorie took in the bikini top, which was so tight it had Cadence's barely size B breasts looking like C-pluses.

"It's hopeless."

"I can fix it." She pulled Cadence off the lounge and around the corner, to the relatively secluded corner of the boat where she'd stood yesterday having her fantasy *Titanic* moment. "Take it off."

"Here?"

"Trust me. A designer, remember?" Which felt incredibly good to say. She wished she could always say that instead of "Shop-Mart sales clerk." "Take it off and turn it upside down." Dorie showed her what she meant, and then retied the strings.

Cadence looked down at her breasts, which now fit into the material, still snugly, but not X-rated-ly. "That's amazing."

"Just a little trick. Hungry?"

In marvel, Cadence cupped her breasts, adjusted. Smiled. "Starved."

"I bet Ethan cooked something good."

"I don't know. He was busy busting Bobby for being a lazy shithead. A direct quote."

They entered the galley. Busy bickering or not, Ethan *had*

cooked something good, and they ate a breakfast spread fit for kings, served with a scowl by Bobby under the supervision of Ethan, who was wearing spotless, wrinkle-free trousers and an immaculate white shirt.

Dorie took a bite of her food and moaned. Ethan might look like a pretend chef but there was nothing pretend about the fabulous food he could produce.

So much for losing ten pounds.

"I'm going to have to replace my bathing suit with a muumuu," Cadence said, stuffing her face.

Brandy joined them, wearing a minuscule bikini and an iPod tucked in between her breasts, looking like a supermodel.

Ethan came over. "A mimosa?"

"Oh, no thanks," Brandy said. "I don't drink in the mornings. Unless it's straight caffeine."

"Food then?"

"I don't eat in the mornings either."

Ethan laughed. "What *do* you do in the mornings?"

A wicked light came into her eyes. "Guess."

Ethan arched a brow. "To each his own."

Brandy grinned and dragged Cadence and Dorie out on deck, where they stretched out on lounge chairs. They slathered themselves in suntan lotion and soaked up some of the tropical sun. Well, Dorie and Brandy did. Cadence stood on the deck doing exercises.

"Crazy," Brandy decided after watching her new friend sweat.

But Dorie understood Cadence's restlessness. The idleness felt strange to her, too. As long as she could remember, she'd had a long list of things to do at all times. The list never seemed to go away, mostly because she was disorganized and could never actually find the list. This just lying here thing, it was definitely decadent. After awhile, she brought out her drawing pad, and inspired by the ocean, by the sails snapping high overhead, spent an hour designing beachwear cover-ups.

"Nice," Brandy said, looking over her shoulder. "The long lines are gorgeous and slimming." She pointed to Dorie's own wrap-around sarong skirt. "I want one of those."

Dorie glanced over at the table Ethan had used to set up drinks for them. It was covered with a long, thin, silky cloth in bright red and yellow. She pulled it free. "Stand up," she said to Brandy, then folded and stretched the material, wrapping it around Brandy's hips. "There."

Brandy strutted past Cadence—now doing yoga—looking like a runway model. "It's perfect. I could go from beach to nightclub in this thing. A tablecloth."

"I beg your pardon, that's an Anderson original."

Denny came up on deck, took one look at Cadence executing some complicated yoga pose, and laughed. "Relax, mate."

"Not so good at that." But she tried to sit, managing to stay seated for oh, thirty seconds. "See? Can't do it."

Denny, standing at the observation deck, offered to teach her to sail. "Come on, come up here."

Cadence grinned at Brandy and Dorie, then joined him. She put her hands on the wheel, and was content until a whipping breeze jerked the boat. Denny yelled at Bobby—working on the sails—to make some adjustments, but Cadence shook her head and backed up. "That's enough for me."

Brandy tried next. She stood at the helm of the boat in that sexy bikini and new sarong skirt, an equally sexy smile on her face, feet planted firmly and confidently apart. "*God*," she said, holding onto the wheel, tipping her head back. "The power. It's glorious."

"You know it." After another sharp gust, Denny turned on Bobby. "What the hell are you doing? Hoist sail!"

Bobby, face impassive, set about the chore.

"My momma always said to think big, live big, and love big," Brandy said, grinning. "I'm sure doing all three right now!"

Dorie absorbed that and decided that Brandy's mother had some good wisdom. "What did your mother do?"

"Oh, she was a hooker. And at least twenty cents short of a dollar, but she was the best of the best on the street. Dorie, you've got to come give this a try."

Dorie took the wheel. She could feel the swell of the ocean beneath her feet, the speed of the boat, and appreciated the authority. With the wind whipping at her and the control all hers, she felt dangerous and better yet, important. She could imagine she was a pirate on a raid, all-empowering, but then she hit the tip of a swell and the boat rose so high she screamed.

Just behind her, Denny laughed wholeheartedly.

"What if I capsize us?"

"You can try, but we're tougher than you think."

Good. Tough was very, very good. "What if I run into something?"

Denny took in the view. There was a faint line of islands in the distance, but other than that, nothing was out there, nothing at all.

"Good luck finding something to run into," he said.

So she kept at it, in charge of the helm, with the wind giving her a rush. She was grinning from ear to ear when she finally turned to give the control back over to Denny—

And found Christian standing there, watching her.

"I was pretending to be a pirate," she said.

"Ah." He didn't smile, but she'd have sworn his eyes warmed.

A chink in the armor. She was wondering if there was some sort of trick to getting him to say more than a word or two at a time, when Andy showed up in designer board shorts and a vintage T-shirt, snorkeling mask in hand.

"Hey, partner," he said to Dorie, looking as if he belonged on the cover of *Sailing Today*. "Ready to snorkel?"

Her tongue jerked once and promptly stuck to the roof of her mouth. "Um—"

Not noticing her handicap, he pointed to the stretch of tiny islands that lay scattered like a handful of emeralds cast upon a shimmering blue tabletop. "I bet we can move closer, maybe go exploring."

Alone on a deserted island with a sexy baseball cutie. It should have thrilled her. Instead, she found herself glancing back at Christian.

But with one inexplicable glance, he was gone.

Snorkeling turned out to be a fairly painless adventure. Brandy joined them, and they even coaxed Cadence into the water—up to her neck, that is.

"You gotta relax, girl!" Denny yelled out to her from the boat. He stood at the platform, long hair flowing behind him, eyes covered behind aviator sunglasses, shirtless, tanned, weathered, looking like he'd been born to the sea. "You're in the South Pacific for God's sake!"

Cadence nodded but didn't look like she relaxed any.

Andy was in the water with Dorie, putting his hands on her as required. Which seemed to be fairly often. Every time he touched her, he was smiling easily, innocently.

Sweetly and kindly.

She tried to relax and enjoy the fact that Baseball Cutie *wanted* to touch her, but her tongue wouldn't cooperate, and as a result, she was having a hard time relaxing herself.

The crew took turns taking quick dips, including Christian, who dove off the top deck wearing nothing but a pair of black board shorts low on his hips. He swam hard and fast, straight out until he vanished, and then straight back, pulling himself out of the water in one sleek motion, collapsing on the deck to catch his breath.

"Mmm-hmm," Brandy murmured softly, for Cadence and Dorie's ears only. "Ladies, I can almost feel the man-made orgasms as I lie here."

Dorie, who'd just taken an unfortunate sip of soda, choked.

Brandy just smiled. "Much better than battery-operated toys."

Dorie coughed some more while Cadence let out a shocked laugh.

Andy scooted closer. "What's so funny?"

"Nothing," Dorie said quickly.

He nodded but didn't shift away, using his new closeness to get extra attentive, lotioning up Dorie's back and shoulders, and taking his time about it. Not that Christian seemed to notice or care. Nope, as soon as he dried off, he simply pushed up to his feet and vanished.

Without a word.

Which worked for Dorie. Really, it did.

That night they ate Ethan's fresh salmon and beef tenderloin with French onion soup served by an even surlier than usual Bobby, as the setting sun tinted the sky lavender and orange. For dessert they consumed homemade ice cream to die for, then listened to

Denny's pitch on why they should buy into time-share sailing on the next luxurious sailing yacht the owner of the *Sun Song* was having built.

Afterward, they danced beneath a darkening sky as clouds moved in with shocking speed, blotting out the moon and stars, churning up the night sky. Even the air changed, chilled, and from far off to the east, lightning flashed.

"Bumpy seas ahead," Denny called out.

Dorie grabbed her drink just as it would have sailed across the table. "He's not kidding."

The boat lurched again, and Cadence gripped her hand.

"Uh-oh." Brandy went an interesting shade of green. "I like to sleep off all unpleasantries. Time for me to hit the sack." She went through her purse, pulling out a bottle of pills, shaking a few out in her hand. "Nope, not those"—she fingered through them—"No, not that one either. Ladies, never, ever, take a sleeping pill and a laxative in the same night . . ." She looked up. "Oblivion, anyone?"

Dorie shook her head.

Cadence did the same.

"Suit yourselves." She popped a sleeping pill, while the boat continued to rise and fall with sharp precision.

Bobby appeared at their side. Though the night had cooled considerably, he was sweating. "The captain wants you to go down to your rooms for the night."

"Why?" Cadence asked.

"I'll take the nasty storm that wants to eat us up for a hundred, Bob," Brandy said, still looking green.

Dorie kept her gaze on Bobby, who wasn't looking happy. Not that he ever did, but tonight he seemed especially grim. "Are we in danger?"

"There's a storm moving in. It's . . ." He looked away. Adjusted his cap low on his head. "Unexpected."

No, it wasn't. Denny had warned him yesterday to check something—the storm jib?—but Bobby hadn't wanted to.

"A big storm then?" Cadence asked worriedly.

He grimaced, not very effective at hiding his feelings, which at the moment included frustration at having to deal with them when he clearly had other things to get to. Like checking the storm jib. "Can you just go below please?"

"I'll get seasick below," Cadence said, just as the boat pitched hard to the right.

Dorie gasped and grabbed onto the table to steady herself.

"Look at the sky," Cadence said in a low, fear-pitched voice.

The sky was black, huge, and menacing as the storm clouds roiled above them. Earlier, Dorie had looked at the view with awe. It'd seemed so impossibly big, so all encompassing. She was still filled with awe, but horror-filled now, because this sky seemed bigger, and *more* all encompassing. Ready to gobble them up.

"Ohmigod," Cadence gasped.

"Relax." This from Denny, at the helm. "It'll blow over by morning—"

The boat pitched harshly. They all grabbed their things.

"Go on down now," Denny called. "We'll have a day for the memory books tomorrow. Parasailing, whale watching . . . tons of fun, I promise. But go now."

Brandy leaned into Dorie and Cadence. "Yeah, that whole buying a time-share thing? Doesn't look so good."

They all laughed a little, but it felt weak as they stood and got a glimpse at what they were sailing into. A billowing, churning sky, and huge, tumbling waves.

"What if a wave knocks us over?" Cadence asked in a small

voice. "I didn't really listen when they were going over the safety procedures . . . oh, God. I'm going to die."

"No one's going to die," Brandy said. "Not yet. Not when I haven't gone to confession in fifteen years. Hey," she called to Christian, who'd come to stand next to Denny. "You aren't by any chance a priest, too, are you, Doc? I need to confess before I kick the bucket."

"No one's dying," Ethan said, coming out of the galley, but he looked uncustomarily ruffled. "Going below is simply for your own safety."

"*Absolument.*" Sounding extremely in charge and extremely French, Christian moved forward, his eyes right on Dorie, as if planning on taking her by the arm to escort her below himself if he had to, which definitely didn't qualify as sweet but reached her anyway.

"*Tous ensemble,*" Christian said. "Together." But before he got to her side, Andy stepped between them, reaching for Dorie himself. "I'll get them below."

Christian simply changed course as if it mattered not in the least to him, but he did give Dorie a long, almost daring look that she couldn't have begun to interpret.

Nor did she understand the funny feeling still sizzling in her belly, sort of like hunger but not.

More like *lust. Really?* She asked herself. *Now?* She decided to ignore it and looked at Andy to see if she got the same feeling when he looked at her. He smiled, but all that happened was that her tongue threatened to swell. *Damn it.* She bit it, then jumped when Denny yelled.

"Jesus, look at that! Sixty knots, and counting! Bobby, hoist that storm jib, goddamnit!"

"I'm trying!"

Christian leapt to help Bobby, his expression tense as he effortlessly climbed up the equipment in the face of the storm, the wind battering him as he did, without any sign of fear for his own safety while he ensured hers. Dorie stared at him, knowing she'd never forget the sight of him silhouetted against the terrifying sky. "Get below," he shouted at her roughly. "Jesus, Andy, do it. Get the women belowdecks."

"Come on." Andy grabbed Dorie and Cadence, who was holding on to Brandy. They moved to the stairs, and then hesitated, staring belowdecks. Nothing but pitch darkness.

"Whoa," Cadence said, hands out for balance as the boat rocked and rolled.

Andy flipped on the running lights, which illuminated the stairs but not much else. Still, they headed down. At the bottom, they were galvanized by a sudden drumming sound.

"What's that?" Brandy gasped as it grew louder and louder. "A pack of angry bees on crack?"

"Rain." Andy sounded grim. "Torrential rain."

They stood belowdecks, huddled together in the middle of the dimly lit hallway. When the boat pitched again, Brandy gasped and grabbed the closest person—Andy. "Sorry, hon, but my pill is kicking in. Take me to bed, sailor?"

Andy glanced at Dorie, clearly torn, which was incredibly sweet. *Sweet* was on her list. She liked her list. "We'll be okay," she assured him.

"I'll be right back." He slipped an arm around Brandy and steered her toward her room.

"I don't like storms." Cadence said this very quietly to Dorie. "Especially when I'm on a boat in the middle of the ocean."

Dorie thought of the men above deck. Particularly Christian, putting his life on the line. "Me either."

They could hear the shouts of the crew. "Bobby, wrestle down the reefed mainsail!" This from Denny, clearly taut and angry. "Jesus, get the number *three* jib! Speed it up!"

More drumming rain, even louder if that was possible.

"Shorten sail, shorten the fucking sail, Bobby!" Denny yelled, and then Ethan's voice joined his. "Come on, man, get with it!"

Dorie swallowed hard. "Sounds . . . intense."

"And not very encouraging," Cadence whispered.

"Oh, you know sailors." Dorie smiled, trying to be brave. "They make everything sound so dangerous."

The boat rolled. They crashed into each other, where they remained together, hugging tightly. "So you don't think . . ." Cadence started.

"No. Absolutely not." But in spite of herself, Dorie's cheerful tone faded just a little bit as around them the wind howled and screeched, the rain continuing to come down at deafening decibels. She thought about the boat sitting on the churning, swirling, massive waves, being flung about like a bath toy, and wasn't comforted.

Every few seconds it seemed they'd hear something crack or crash, and would wince in tandem.

Was the sailboat falling apart?

She didn't want to think about what would happen if they did just that, because it would mean getting onto a ten-man raft out on that sea.

If the eighty-two foot *Sun Song* couldn't survive the seas, how could a raft?

That, in a crux, was the source of panic balled in her throat. "Stay calm."

"Calm," Cadence repeated. "Right. I'm calm."

"Actually, I was talking to myself." They held on to each other like orphaned baby monkeys as they pitched up and down and every which way.

"We're going to capsize," Cadence whispered.

"No. No, we're going to be fine."

"How do you know?"

"Because I didn't finish living yet." Truth be told, she hadn't really even started. "Just stay positive. That's the trick. Stay positive."

That's when the lights went out.

SEVEN

Forget the cabana boys,
send out the Coast Guard.
And chocolate . . .

Are you still thinking positively?" Cadence whispered.

"Yes." *Or trying anyway,* Dorie thought.

"I really don't want to be a statistic."

"We are not going to become a statistic." Not as certain as she'd needed to sound, Dorie's voice wobbled just a little bit on the last syllable. "The key is the whole positive thinking thing."

"Not my strong suit. The positive part, that is. Not the thinking."

Dorie felt a smile at that. "Okay, humor is good. More of that, please."

"I'm fresh out."

It was up to her. *Great.* Positive thinking . . . well, there was the food. The food had been good. And—

The boat swayed. *Hard.* Cadence whimpered in terror, and so did Dorie at the sensation of floating on choppy water while not being able to see a damn thing. With the electricity out, there was utter and complete darkness such as she'd never known; no city lights, no glow from a computer screen or cell phone.

Nothing.

Cadence let out a small sob as panic gripped her, and Dorie felt her heart squeeze. "I know!" Fumbling through her purse in the dark, her fingers finally closed over what she'd been looking for.

Her penlight.

She clicked it on, and a small beam of light cut through the dark.

Cadence threw her arms around her. "I love you!"

Dorie laughed and hugged her back. "It's the bag. This baby has everything we need." She flicked the light down the narrow hallway just as the boat tipped and listed hard to the right. With no warning, they both went flying against the wall, as did Dorie's purse, which flew out of her hands, slid down the floor, and emptied out everywhere.

Dorie went crawling after it on all fours, and Cadence went after her. But then the boat rocked to the left, and to the left they all went; Dorie, Cadence, and brush, dental floss, sketch pad, charcoal, sugar packets, box of condoms . . .

They landed in a tangled heap at the end of the hallway, and slowly, a little dazed, used the light to stuff the things back into the purse.

"Good thinking," Cadence said, holding up the condoms.

"More like wishful thinking." Dorie put the box in the bag. "They were on sale."

"You bought a box of condoms because they were on sale?"

"Yes. You can see why I needed this cruise." Dorie slung the strap of the purse over her neck and shoulder, tucking it against her back. "You okay?"

"As long as you have that light."

"Want to know something pretty pathetic?"

The boat swayed and dipped again, and they grabbed each other, huddled there on the floor in the hallway. "Yes," Cadence said, sounding desperate for a diversion.

"I even have a spare flashlight."

"That's not pathetic, that's just smart. Oh, God."

"What?"

"My motion sickness patch isn't working."

The boat did some more of that horrible shimmying, and Dorie gulped hard. "It's going to be okay." *God, please let it be okay.*

"I wanted a kick in the ass," Cadence said. "But I wanted a *change* in my life, not death. I don't even have a will."

Dorie let out a weak laugh. "Me either. But I hereby will all my worldly possessions to you. How's that?"

"Oh, Dorie," she said, sounding unbearably touched.

"Don't get too excited, all I have is a portfolio of designs."

"If I die, you can have my stuff, too. It's just my art, and my fish Sparky, who sleeps upside down, but he doesn't eat much."

Dorie didn't know whether to laugh or cry. "Better idea. Let's not die."

"Yeah, that's my first choice, too."

"Hey, you guys okay?"

Dorie lifted the light and revealed Brandy and Andy, both crawling back out of Brandy's room. Brandy was pale, still green, and yet somehow managed to look like a gorgeous actress playing the part of the distressed victim. "I think fear has overridden my sleeping pill. I needed to see if you're okay."

Andy's face was taut with all sorts of emotions one didn't usually experience on a dream vacation. But he looked big and strong and capable, which Dorie had to admit was a comfort. "We're okay."

"Sure?" He peered into their faces with sweet concern.

They both nodded, and he pulled them in close, giving them a warm hug. "Hold on," he said, tightening his grip on them. "Another wave."

Once again the boat tipped, accompanied by a horrendous sound of something tearing, breaking. They all gasped, and as before, slid down the hallway, hitting the wall in unison.

Dorie braced herself, terrified that Christian and the others on deck wouldn't have the same luxury.

"Hard to believe I was safer at my damn job," Brandy said with a groan as she sat up and untangled herself.

Then Cadence asked the question they were no doubt all thinking. "Do you think the ship's okay?"

"Don't know," Andy said quietly. "But I'm going to find out. Stay here."

"No. Andy—"

But he was gone, making his way through the dark and up to the deck above, leaving Dorie sick with worry.

Brandy pulled a flask out of her pocket. She took a deep pull. Her eyes watered and she coughed, then passed the flask to Cadence.

Cadence shrugged and drank, choked, then passed it to Dorie, who took a swig and then nearly died as flames burst down her esophagus. She dug into her purse for gum. "Always prepared for the worst, you know."

"Hopefully this is the worst," Cadence said.

They all looked at each other as that somber thought sank in.

"Hey, it's better than a lot of things," Brandy decided.

"Like?" Cadence asked.

"Prison, for instance."

Cadence gaped at her. "Have you been to prison?"

"Oh, just the once."

Cadence blinked. So did Dorie.

"I blame my wild youth," Brandy said.

Cadence looked at Dorie, then closed her eyes, looking like she was concentrating on not getting sick.

"What are you all doing down here like this?"

Everyone turned at the French accent coming down the stairs.

Dr. Christian Montague, of course, and Dorie nearly leapt toward him to throw her arms around him for still being alive. He was drenched, frowning, and intense, and far more edgy than she could have even imagined, but he was breathing, and breathing was good.

Just behind him came Andy and Bobby, who looked as overjoyed as always. "You should be hunkered down in your bunks," Christian said, shining his flashlight over them. "Trying to sleep through the storm."

"As if we could." In contrast to Christian, Andy sounded extremely Texan as he looked at the women. "We're blowing out sails left and right. There's only one left."

"Andy," Christian said in a warning voice. "That's not really—"

"You were yelling at the captain." Andy turned to Bobby. "I heard you."

"Not yelling," Bobby corrected. "More like . . . talking loud. We do that when things are going bad."

Everyone looked at him in horror.

"Bobby," Christian said softly.

"Hey, things go bad at sea. It's the nature of the beast."

"Not exactly helping, Bobby." Christian turned to Andy. "And what you heard was a private conversation."

"The outcome of which affects us." Andy looked at the women. "There's a problem with the storm sails, specifically something called a gale sail."

"Problem?" Cadence asked weakly.

"Yeah. As in we don't have one."

"Oh, God."

Dorie's stomach dropped like a two-ton weight. "Maybe we don't need it."

"We don't," Christian said, his gaze running over her with what she wanted to think was warm approval. "Not when there's a hanked-on storm jib."

"And we have that?" Cadence asked.

Christian hesitated.

"Do we?" Cadence's voice shook.

"We did."

"*Did?*"

"We lost it twenty minutes ago," Bobby informed them. "But—"

Whatever he might have said was lost under everyone talking at once, until Christian stepped in the middle of them and let out a sharp whistle. "Listen up," he said when everyone looked at him. "Under the right circumstances, the force of the wind on the hull and rigging can generate enough force to propel the craft with or without a sail."

Brandy let out a laugh that held no real amusement. "But do we have the right circumstances?"

"No," Bobby said.

"Goddamnit," Christian murmured, and sent him a sharp look. "*Fermez l'enfer.*"

Bobby's mouth tightened.

"What did he say?" Cadence whispered.

"He told me to shut the hell up," Bobby said.

Christian drew in a long breath.

"So it's true. We're all going to die." Cadence staggered back until she bumped into the wall, as if desperately needing the support.

Andy moved closer to her. "Breathe," he said quietly, because she wasn't, and appeared perilously close to passing out.

"Why don't we have a gale sail?" Dorie dared to ask.

"Actually, we did." Christian sent Bobby a scathing look. "But it didn't get inspected as it should have, and has been abused by the elements. It was no good."

"Ohmigod." Dorie pushed down her rising panic.

Brandy covered her mouth. "I didn't drink enough for this."

"All you need to do," Christian said. "Is stay belowdecks until this blows over."

"I need an escort." Brandy sounded incredibly subdued. "I think my pill worked after all . . ."

She weaved and Christian grabbed her arm, pulling her over to Bobby. "Take her to her room, get a life vest on her now. There're life vests under each of your beds," he said to everyone else. "If the captain rings the emergency bell, you need to put them on. Immediately."

Bobby gestured for Brandy to walk ahead of him, but she slid her arm in his. "Dizzy," she said, and set her head on his shoulder.

His Adam's apple bounced hard. "Okay, then." After a hesitation, he put his arm around her and led her to her door. "Here you go."

"Need more help than that." And she tugged him in after her. The door slammed shut.

Christian turned to Dorie. "Now you. Andy, get Cadence."

Andy was looking at Dorie, too, making her feel . . . was it wrong to say . . . elated? Never in her life had she had two men looking at her. And now here were these two, these gorgeous sexy men, definitely looking right at her—God.

"Andy," Christian repeated. "Cadence."

Andy looked as if maybe he wanted to argue with this. His

brows slammed together, his mouth tightened. He was eyeing Dorie with a hint of possessive intent that she could admit gave her a sort of thrill, if not a definite twitch to her tongue. "I'll be right back."

He'd be right back. She glanced at Cadence, who gave her a "you go girl" look.

Christian did not look amused.

And the keep-the-peace woman in her reared its head. "I'll be okay."

"I want to make sure you get to your room okay."

"I'll get her there."

This, of course, from Christian, who reached for her. It was unbelievable, it was like a dream, one of those really great ones, where she got to be the popular girl.

A definite first.

Andy opened Cadence's door and nudged her inside.

Christian reached for Dorie. He took her light, then slid an arm around her waist. A warm, strong arm.

She looked up at him, torn between her body's undeniable reaction to him and horror. But before she could say a word, Christian silently pulled her toward her room.

While she couldn't help but wonder what they'd do when they got there.

EIGHT

The boat pitched and rolled as Dorie stepped into her room, but before she could go flying face-first into her bed, a hard arm hauled her back against an even harder chest.

"Careful," Christian murmured in her ear. "You don't have your summer fling here to protect you."

She had to repeat the words to herself because the feel of his long, sinewy body so close to hers kept them from penetrating into her brain. "Summer fling?"

"Andy."

His arm still held her tightly to his chest, and although the sensation was the furthest thing from amusing she'd ever felt, even bordering on shockingly erotic, she laughed.

He dipped his head slightly, his jaw grazing hers.

The oddest thing happened.

Her knees actually buckled. Good thing he hadn't let go of her. "Um."

Again his jaw brushed against hers.

In happy reaction, her nipples hardened. Her thighs tightened. And most baffling yet given that she was apparently getting turned on . . . her tongue still didn't swell.

What did that mean? She turned to face him. "I'm not having a fling."

"No? It's what he's looking for. It's what you're looking for. Man-made orgasms."

"I didn't say that," she said, ears flaming. "Brandy said that."

He laughed softly, and the sound scraped low in her belly. *Bad body.* "Really? So you didn't divide up the men on this cruise, thinking we could give you those man-made orgasms?"

No. Okay, yes. But she wouldn't ask if he knew how to give her one, not when the answer was all over his face. It always was, all damn day long as he moved with an ease and confidence that baffled her because she'd never had either. "You're not exactly in a position to make fun of summer flings."

His brow arched in silent question as the boat lurched.

"Brandy?" She clutched at him for balance, not too busy in conversation to notice how good his hands felt on her hips or how hard his chest felt beneath her fingers. "I saw you kissing her yesterday."

"Did you?"

"Yes, in your office . . ." She trailed off when he just looked at her. "Okay, I didn't actually *see* a kiss. Not exactly."

"If you want to know what you *did* see, why don't you ask me?"

She opened her mouth to do just that, while he waited with a smug expression that made her shake her head. "Never mind."

That little smile still curving his lips, he shrugged. Fine with
him.

Good. Great. Fine by him. God, he smelled amazing. Why was
she still holding on to him? And why did she not want to let go?
She closed her eyes but that just made the sensations stronger, and
the situation even more intimate. "How about me? Do you want
to know anything about me?"

"None of my business. I'm going to leave now."

"Right."

But neither of them moved. Christian let out a slow exhale near
her ear and her entire body shuddered. In response, a sound escaped him, a low, rough one that seemed to awaken every single
erogenous zone she owned.

Get it together, Dorie. Let go of him.

Instead, her body seemed to disconnect from her brain without
permission, allowing her hands to slide up his chest. Beneath her
fingers, he was corded with muscle, muscle that quivered at her
touch. "You should know," she said a little shakily. "I'm not looking to be *anyone's* fling."

Liar, liar, pants on fire.

Catching her wandering hands in his, he arched a brow. "You
sure about that?"

She snatched her hands free. "Yes."

"Might want to inform Andy."

"I don't need to explain anything to him."

"Don't take this the wrong way, but I don't think you're quite
as insightful as you think, not when it comes to men."

"What are you saying?"

"I'm saying"—again he exhaled—"be careful."

Concern? Was that concern from the man she wasn't yet entirely convinced was even human?

Another wave rolled beneath them, making the boat shudder and groan and creak, and she again clutched at him.

"Helluva storm. Denny's navigating the waves at an angle to prevent slamming into the back side of the next wave, but he's missing a few."

His hands were back on her, his head bent low to hers. She pressed her jaw to his, taking comfort in his nearness. "Are we going to be okay?"

"Time will tell."

Brutal honesty. She had a feeling he'd always be that way, no matter what, which might be refreshing—if they were on land.

As if fate wanted to drive home the point, the boat tipped hard to the left, and she wrapped her arms around his neck and squeezed.

"Need to breathe here."

"I could use some bedside manners right about now."

When he didn't respond to that, she tipped her head back and looked into his eyes, which were tense, even for him.

"Dorie—"

"Oh, God." Had she just admired his brutal honesty? Because she could see that brutal honesty in his gaze, and suddenly she wanted a lie. "The boat's going to break apart, isn't it, and we're all going to die." Her throat closed at the thought, her eyes burned, and when she spoke, her voice broke. "I'm too young to die, Christian. Way too young."

"Hey. *Hey,*" he murmured, and stroked a hand down her back. "I've been in worse storms, and I'm still breathing."

The boat rocked to the right now, but Christian had his legs spread for balance, and still holding her as he was, they didn't go anywhere.

And there, surrounded by the hell of her reality, she felt . . . safe.

Maybe the shock of that had her feeling other things as well, such as the way her breasts were smashed against his chest, or how the button fly of his jeans pressed into her belly—

Again the boat shifted hard, groaning and creaking under the strain. His arms tightened on her, and she turned her face into his shoulder. The motion arched her spine, just a little, and tore another of those low, rough sounds from his throat.

Needing to see his face, she looked up.

His gaze slid to hers, though he didn't say a word, or move so much as a muscle.

"I did not consume enough alcohol for this," she whispered, lifting a hand to her head, which was spinning. "Or maybe the opposite is true."

"You only had two."

He's been watching? "I'm a real lightweight," she admitted. "A cheap date."

"Dorie." He pressed his forehead to hers. "You're not supposed to tell me that."

"Why not?"

"Because I could take advantage, that's why." He glanced at her bed. "Big advantage."

Her erogenous zones went on high alert. "Are you that kind of man?" *Did she want him to be?*

He closed his eyes briefly. "You need to go to sleep."

Yes. Yes, she did. "I'm scared, Christian."

"Don't." He scrunched his eyes shut. "Don't tell me that either. Don't tell me anything. Hopefully this'll all be over by morning, and everything will be back to normal."

"Which would be you being distant."

He stared down at her for a long beat, and she became incredibly, intimately aware of their position, and how she'd glued herself to him. But he wasn't an innocent bystander. His hand was low on her spine, low enough that his fingers were within reach of her splinter.

Not commando tonight . . .

He didn't say a word but she knew he was thinking it, and she realized there was something pressing into her belly, and it wasn't just the buttons on Christian's Levi's. She licked her dry lips. "Um, are you—"

"Yes." His voice was a low, rough whisper. "How's that for distance?"

Because she was weak, oh so weak, she arched against him. Nearly every bone in her body melted at the feel of him, at the sound that escaped him, one that might have been part laugh, part groan. She felt his fingers spread wide on her bottom, as if trying to touch as much of her as he could. "Bed." He sounded strained. "You need to go to bed."

Yes, she knew. *Bed.* But if she went to sleep right now, and if the worst happened and the boat broke apart before dawn and they all drowned tonight in their sleep, she was going to die knowing she hadn't yet accomplished her goal for the trip. Heck, her goal for the rest of her life.

Live life to its fullest.

She glanced out her porthole, where the black night and blacker storm had whipped the sea into a frothy, frenzied, terrifyingly lethal state.

Dying was a possibility, no matter what he said. Pretty damn final, too. No more chances to do what she'd always figured she had time to do. At the thought, regrets filled her, nearly choked her, but she ruthlessly bit them back. She was going to live to tell this tale, and starting right this very minute, she'd allow no more regrets, no more stalling.

As Brandy's mom had said—think big, live big, and love big. *Now.* Because *now* was all she might have. In light of that, she was going to do something she'd never done before. "Christian?"

He looked at her warily.

For the first time in her life she made the first move, reaching up, fisting her fingers into his hair, tugging his mouth to hers.

He allowed it, until they were only a fraction of an inch apart, and then he went very, very still.

Holding back.

Huh. She sort of thought he'd take over from here, which would be helpful since she really didn't know too much about seducing a man.

He didn't move.

So she opened her eyes and stared into his stormy ones. "Aren't you going to kiss me?"

"No."

Turning her back, she hugged herself. "I'm good now. You can leave."

"Dorie—"

"Please."

"All right."

She waited. She heard him open the door, and then shut it, and she smacked her own forehead. *"Idiot."*

"You, or me?"

She froze. He hadn't left. Of course not. Because apparently she hadn't yet made a big enough fool of herself. "Me," she said, not opening her eyes. "I'm definitely the idiot."

"There's something you should know, Dorie."

She cracked one eye, thinking if she squinted, it'd somehow be less embarrassing.

"I don't mix business and pleasure." He said this softly, with genuine regret in his eyes. And this time when he opened the door, he really left.

NINE

Day Three
on the Not-Quite-the-Love-Boat Cruise.

The next morning Dorie opened her eyes and became immediately aware of two things. One, the daylight barely peeking into her porthole looked gray and dingy, nothing like the brilliant sunshine she'd experienced until yesterday evening.

And two, the boat was still pitching like a roller coaster ride gone bad. She sat up in bed and felt extremely grateful not to be experiencing seasickness, though vertigo was another thing entirely. Taking a shower was an exercise in stamina, but she managed, then dressed—wearing panties today, too, thank you very much. No more commando, even if the material rubbed the splinter. No matter how much it irritated her, it'd just have to stay put until she came up with a solution that didn't involve requiring outside assistance to remove it.

Because the only outside assistance she could think of came in the form of a man who'd rejected her kiss, and that was just a bit too humiliating to contemplate.

What the hell had she been thinking, trying to kiss Christian?

Well, she hadn't been thinking, that had been her problem. She'd have to correct that immediately. Note to self: THINK at all times.

She could do it.

She just wouldn't look at him again. Not for the entire trip.

But Andy, sweet, kind, sexy-as-hell, Texas Andy . . . him she could look at all she wanted, she promised herself. Because she'd bet that he wouldn't have rejected her kiss!

She grabbed her purse and opened her door. The hallway was empty, but walking it with the boat rocking wildly was no picnic. She made it to the stairs and got halfway up before she heard something from below her, a sort of muted hushed whisper.

The hair on the back of her neck rose as the sense of déja vu hit her. *Enough with the mysterious conversation!* "Hello?" she called out, turning to try to see behind her, though unfortunately she couldn't see past her own tush.

While she was twisted, the boat jerked, and she hit the wall. *Ouch.* She began climbing again. She felt off balance, inside and out, which is probably why, when the boat lurched, she lost her grip on the railing entirely, flying straight backward—

Into a hard wall.

A hard wall that went "oomph."

Then that hard wall gave, and she was sailing down the way she'd come—

Landing in a pile of limbs, half of which did not belong to her. *"Fuck."*

Since that single oath was muttered in an unmistakable French accent, with both irritation and resignation, she knew exactly who it was before she even opened her eyes.

The bane of her existence, of course.

The boat pitched again, and together they went sliding across the floor. Dorie gripped her purse with one hand and him with the other, and watched the hull wall come directly at her. She closed her eyes and winced in anticipation, just as Christian tucked her beneath him.

She still hit, but not the wall.

Nope, Christian did that for her, and then she hit him.

Hard enough to produce stars in the daylight.

Flat on her back, she opened her eyes and groaned.

Christian leaned over her. "You okay?"

"I think so." For such a long, lean, hard body, he was quite the cushion. "Thanks."

He frowned and held her down when she would have sat up. "Make sure."

She must have hit her head or something, because the way he was bent over her, eyes narrowed, mouth tight, jaw bunched, he looked concerned.

And hella sexy with it.

Definitely, she'd hit her head. She lifted a hand to it but it didn't hurt. *So far so good.* She rolled to her back and winced at the splinter in her butt.

Still there.

"What is it?" Without waiting for her to answer, he began running his hands down her limbs. Arms first, all the way to her fingers. She was so shocked she just stared up at him as he shifted his attention to her legs, his warm, firm hands checking her ankles, calves, knees— "Hey!" Finding her senses, she slapped at his hands.

"Checking for broken bones."

"You're copping a feel!"

"If I were 'copping a feel' as you say, I'd have my hands somewhere else entirely." He leaned back on his heels. "Good news. You're fine."

"I know!"

"Unless . . ."

"Unless what?"

"Unless you want me to look at your ass."

"*What?*"

"You hurt it that first day, and you're still hurt."

"I said I was fine!"

"I'm a doctor."

She got to her feet, hands on her bottom. "I'm not showing you my splinter!"

His brow shot up so high it all but vanished into his dark, wavy hair. "Splinter?"

She looked away. "It's nothing."

He pulled her around, and this time he wasn't thinking about smiling. "It needs to come out."

"Uh-huh. And when it does, naturally, you'll be the first to know."

He stared at her, apparently—and correctly—gauging her determination and stubbornness as nonnegotiable. "Okay, but when you get infected—"

"It won't."

"It *will.*"

He was deadly serious, and she swallowed hard. "I'll be fine. I *am* fine." Staring up at him, she realized that while she was fine, he was not. His mouth was bleeding, and before she could stop herself, or remember last night's humiliation, she put a finger to his lip. "I hurt you when I fell on you."

He lifted a hand to his mouth, looked at his bloody fingers. "It's nothing."

"So we're a fine pair then, aren't we? You need some ice."

"Is that your professional opinion?"

"Hey, I'm the aunt of two very agile, slippery, weasely nephews under the age of five. I know my first aid."

"Is that right?"

"Absolutely."

"Good." He nodded. "You're so eager to be up and about, you're hired."

Hired. To doctor him up? An incredibly inappropriate vision of doing just that came to her, of slowly stripping him down to skin to play doctor—

"*On n'est pas sorti de l'auberge.*"

"Translation?"

"We're not out of the woods yet. This storm isn't just a stubborn bitch, it's a hurricane. Winds at ninety miles an hour, and the waves are topping at thirty-five feet. People are *mal de mer*. Seasick."

So he didn't mean play doctor with him. *Damn.* "How did this happen?"

"The low pressure system hit a jet stream and just like science, here we are."

She crossed her arms. "You have such a way of making me feel better."

"No time for coddling. Wear your life vest if you come above deck."

"Why?"

"No one goes up there without one until further notice. Let's get going. You'll need some supplies." He pulled her down the hall and into his quarters. "The others are on their deathbeds. Just ask them, they'll be happy to tell you. I think Brandy's probably the sickest, so check on her first. Keep rotating through the rooms."

"Where will you be?

"Helping Denny."

Outside. Vulnerable to the elements. In danger. "Why can't we go back?"

"To Fiji?"

"Yes."

Something crossed his face at that, a shadow, a grimace, whatever, but it caused a terrible foreboding to seize her, from the inside out. She took a step toward him and gripped his shirt. "Christian? Talk to me."

He looked at her hand fisted on him. "There are some technical difficulties."

"Skip the cryptic. I hate cryptic."

"We were hit by lightning last night."

She gasped. "My God."

"Several times. And then there are the thirty-five footers. Some of our equipment's been damaged."

"Damaged," she repeated carefully.

"Actually, gone."

"Explain, please."

He seemed to weigh his next words carefully, but gave her the truth she'd asked for. "The blast of lightning bent the steel deck of the compass room, wrecked the compass, and swept some of the equipment onto the main deck where it was washed overboard."

She just gaped at him, trying to understand.

"The oiler's door on the starboard side was smashed in by a rogue wave, and some of the windows on that same side have been blown in as well. Is that enough?"

"There's more?"

"We're taking on water, and without functioning sails, we're not in control of our direction. We're off course, way off course. How about now? Enough now?"

She swallowed hard. "Are we drowning today then? Because if we are, I should schedule in my panic attack."

"There is good news."

"I'd like that please."

He slid open a supply closet. "The storm is losing strength."

She stared at his broad shoulders, shoulders that took on so much. "So are we drowning today or not?"

"Well, it's not on my agenda, no."

"Even without the storm, if we're damaged beyond control . . ."

He turned back, acknowledging that with a slight bow of his head.

She drew a shaky breath and gave up on trying to get promises. There were none to be had, and she didn't want false ones anyway. "Okay. Let's—"

The boat jerked, nearly sending her flying against a wall, but Christian reached out, snagged her by the shirt, and hauled her to his side, saving her from more bruises and who knew what else. When she could stand on her own, he grabbed a bag and handed it to her, filling it with things she might need from his shelves: ice packs, Band-Aids, aspirin . . .

She watched him work quickly and efficiently, and when he caught her staring at him, he stopped. "What?"

She dug into the supplies he'd just given her for gauze, and then shifted close, dabbing at his lip.

He hissed out a breath.

"Baby," she murmured.

His gaze slid to hers, surprised. "*Baby?* As in infant?"

"That's right. You can dish it out, but you can't take it."

"Trust me, I can take anything you've got."

Oh boy, if that didn't start her engines. "Sorry, but you relinquished that right last night."

"My loss."

Did he really feel that way? The boat rocked, and she reached out to balance herself against him, her hand settling on his chest as if it belonged there. She found her fingers sort of stroking over him, and stared at the motion.

Stop touching him.

But beneath his T-shirt, he was warm, solid. Her fingers glided over his pec, a nipple. It pebbled, and she did it again.

"Playing with fire, Dorie?" he asked softly.

Lifting her head, she stared at him. Her heart had sped up. He could pretend he was unaffected, but she felt his heart do the same, thumping with increasing velocity beneath her hand. She opened her mouth to say so but he put his fingers over her lips, making them tingle, making every part of her tingle.

"Stick with Andy."

She shook her head. "What?"

"You heard me. And you know why."

"Actually, I don't."

Turning away, he took a few more things from the shelves, and dropped them into a backpack for himself. "You need to make sure they're drinking plenty of liquids—"

The boat pitched again and she put out her hand to brace herself against the wall.

He simply spread his legs and remained steady. "They'll need you to remind them to keep drinking. If anyone turns nonresponsive, come find me."

She studied his broad shoulders, and the invisible weight there. He either didn't want her, or didn't want to want her. She voted for option number two. "You must get tired of this."

"Being a doctor?"

"Babysitting passengers. Storms. Not having your own space."

He looked at her for a long moment. "Most people assume my job is the best job on the planet. Sailing for a living. Taking care of the occasional seasickness. Or splinter."

She ignored that because he was most definitely *not* taking care of her splinter. "I would think that this job might be a bit . . . claustrophobic for you."

He turned away, but not before she saw the truth in his gaze.

Why did it he do it? Why did he stay? "Did you mean it when you said I should be with Andy?"

"I mean everything I say. Always."

TEN

Christian made it up to the deck, then leaned against the hull, eyes closed, body tight. His body had been tight ever since he'd first laid eyes on Dorie, but he could get over that.

What he couldn't get over was the way she'd gotten inside him. Just looking at her, with those wide, expressive eyes, all that untamable hair, that sweet expression, which said she might be a little naive but was willing to try anything . . .

He wasn't used to such conflicting emotions. There hadn't been many in his life he'd let get to him. His mother, yes. She'd been the center of his universe, but he'd lost her so young he could scarcely even remember being held by her. After that he'd been sent from his native France to live with his father, who'd been a traveling medic, a man not much for warmth and affection. Later there'd been women, even a few Christian had found himself attached to, but no one who'd made him want things.

Until now. He wasn't sure what it was about Dorie, or what he wanted exactly. She had a way of opening him up and laying him bare, even while being so damned annoying he wanted to wrap his fingers around her neck and squeeze.

No, that was a big, fat lie. He wanted to wrap his arms around her, and his body.

And his tongue.

Even more unsettling, he wanted more, more than he'd wanted in a long time. She'd made him feel this way with a single glance of those soulful eyes, the ones that always gave her away; gave away her insecurity, her vulnerability, her sweet, loving nature.

Her attraction to him.

An attraction he'd all but told her to give to Andy instead. Definitely that was for the best. The two of them would enjoy their vacation, and then go on their merry way.

And Christian would still have one long year left in his own personal hell . . .

He could hear someone swearing—Denny. The winds and rain had lessened slightly. One thing in their favor. Now if they could survive the seas, limp into the next port, and get the passengers safe on land . . .

"Goddamn piece of shit scuppers, fuck me if they won't goddamn work." More from Denny, who was slapping at his instruments—those that were left. "Hell, fuck, shit—"

"You kiss your *maman* with that mouth?"

Denny didn't laugh, or make some smart-ass comment in return, which had Christian taking another good long look at him. They'd worked together a long time now, and though there was an ease, a familiarity, there was not a kinship. They were too different for that, but it didn't take close kinship to see Denny was overly pale, and not pissed off as Christian had first thought, but something far worse.

Scared.

"Shitty day, mate," Denny said without looking at him. "I'm running warps and using the drogue. But the waves are traveling faster than the boat, breaking over our stern. Pushing us sideways. We're going to broach."

"Let's loop lines on the port primary winch—"

"You think I haven't tried that?" Denny shoved his wet hair out of his face. "We're out of gear. We have to switch to passive techniques, no other choice."

Passive techniques meant giving up and hoping for the best. Christian had never been good at passive. Never. Spending his younger years traveling Africa, South America, wherever his father had been needed, they'd gone, all the while gathering life skills. Those years had been exhilarating, adventurous, and educational as well as exhausting, but had left him with a certain sense of invincibility.

Yet he didn't feel so invincible now.

Another wave hit them hard. The deck became a graveyard as things washed overboard.

"See?" Denny yelled over the mountainous seas slamming into them like a battering ram. "Screwed."

"The storm's weakening." In fact, he could see the edge of it on the far horizon, just beyond the swirling gray massive clouds.

Blue skies.

"Hope it's not too late."

It wasn't like Denny to be such a defeatist, and Christian took another good look at him, noting the deep gash above his left eyebrow. "What happened?"

"Bastard wave. I hit the helm. While I was down, the water carried away the front of the mainsheet and block, and tore things loose by the tiller. Almost tore me loose as well."

Christian moved directly in front of him and studied his eyes. He looked okay. "You need to take a few minutes off, give your brain a rest."

"Well, fuck me."

"I'll pass. You need a few stitches."

"Later."

Christian set his backpack down between his feet, where he could make sure it didn't slide away. He pulled out gauze as Dorie had done for him, and straightening, he dabbed at the cut. "Where's Ethan and Bobby?"

"Checking out another little problem."

"Which is?"

Denny's mouth tightened even more, his gaze remained straight outward, at the storm raging. "We're taking on water. Can't radio for help either, not with the radio trashed by the lightning strike. Our spare and all our spare supplies in the raft are gone as well."

"Well, you radioed yesterday, right? So someone knows we're out here."

"Storm blew us off course. Way off course. Truth is, I have no clue where we are, and neither will anyone looking for us."

Christian's stomach sank. *Definitely not so invincible now.* If they'd already been off course when the distress signal had gone out, there was no telling how long help would be. "I'll take over for a bit, you need to rest."

It spoke of exactly how bad off they were that Denny let him. He took the helm, or what was left of it, and tried not to think about anything other than keeping them afloat.

Dorie found Brandy sick as a dog. Cadence wasn't in much better shape. Convinced they needed sustenance, she put on her life vest and attempted to make her way to the galley, thwarted by the heavy rocking of the boat. But she was far too determined to let a little wind and water stop her, and finally, bruised and battered, she made her way up the stairs.

If Christian caught her, he'd probably be pissed off, but he was the one who'd put her in charge of the patients, so really he had no one to blame but himself.

She didn't see Christian. She didn't see anyone as she fought her way to the deck, where for a moment she just stood, holding on to the railing for dear life, staring at the bow of the ship as it lifted and fell, making her feel as if she stood on a seesaw. Worse, she knew it was daytime but the skies were so dark and stormy, it could have been before dawn for all the light the day was giving off.

Rain pelted her, the wind whipped at her, and the dark, misty gray air seemed to take on a life of its own, swirling around her, almost swallowing her up.

With the fog and mist so dark and heavy, she couldn't even see five feet in front of her, and she began to rethink this whole needing food thing, even more so when she heard the haunting voices again.

"Not again," she said to herself, trying to blink the fog away. "I'm not hearing things—"

"It ends here . . ."

Or that's what she thought she heard, and frustrated by her lack of vision, she rubbed her eyes as if she could rub the storm gone. Blinking hard, she tried to focus—

"Ohmigod," she whispered to no one, staring ahead at the shadowy silhouette of two men, locked together against the railing. She couldn't tell if one was trying to help the other, or—

The shadow on the right collapsed and tumbled over the railing.

Vanishing from sight.

The boat pitched, and she went flying into the hull, hard enough to rattle the teeth in her head, and when she scrambled to her feet again, she was alone on deck.

No shadowy figures at all. She shook her head, rubbed her eyes, and looked again. Still nothing.

Real, or Memorex?

Racing back downstairs, she burst into Cadence's room, only to find Brandy and Andy there as well. Dripping all over the place, she counted heads.

"You just missed Ethan," Andy said, munching on a chunk of cantaloupe. "He and Bobby put together a feast for the stowaways."

Brandy lifted her head from her prone position on the bed. "And since Christian took over for Denny for a bit, the captain popped his head in on his way to get some shut-eye. He thought the storm would blow over by afternoon, but he promised to make it up to us."

Dorie stared at them. Everyone was accounted for. Which meant not only was she hearing things, she was now seeing things. No more hitting her head, she decided, sinking wearily to a chair. Her brain couldn't take it.

Christian helmed the boat for hours, which took all of his brain power so he couldn't think of anything else. Finally, at some point in the late afternoon, Denny came back on deck, not looking so rested, but fit enough.

Christian left him to hit the galley for food.

Ethan sat at a table, studying a map.

They'd been in tight situations before, the tightest actually, and through it all, Christian had never seen the chef look anything but perfectly put together. Now Ethan didn't look perfectly put together. His hair was wild, and so were his eyes. He was covered in sweat or rain, or maybe both, and when he saw Christian, he shook his head. "We're kicking the bucket. Jesus Christ, we're really kicking the bucket."

"Not necessarily—"

"Denny's not pulling this one out of his ass, not this time."

"Where's Bobby?"

Ethan lifted a shoulder. "Haven't seen him in awhile."

"Is he sick?"

"Probably just lazy."

Denny yelled for them then, and they ran on deck. When he saw them, Denny shook his head and called. "Prepare the raft."

Christian took one beat to stare at Ethan while the horror sank in, and then he whipped around, back the way he'd come, down the stairs to get to their guests.

To Dorie.

He found her, always with Brandy, Cadence, and Andy, all together in Cadence's bunk, playing cards. Cadence and Brandy sat on one side of the bed, Andy and Dorie on the other, so close their thighs were touching. In fact, Andy had his hand braced on the mattress, extremely close to Dorie's ass.

"I'm winning," Dorie told Christian. "They wanted to play—" She stopped talking at the look on his face and slowly rose to her feet, holding on to the wooden frame of the bed for balance. "What's the matter?"

"We're going to have to go up on deck."

"Why is that?"

How to tell someone with eyes like a soulful river that she was in danger, more danger than she'd ever been in her life?

"Christian? You're scaring me."

Outside of being in bed with a woman, he'd never been much of a toucher. It seemed too personal, too . . . close. But he reached out now and squeezed her hand. Maybe he did it to see if there'd be that odd charge of current between them—there it was—maybe he did it to see if he could get her to look at him the way she sometimes did, with wonder and anticipation.

She did that, too.

Suddenly he wished he'd found a way to be alone with her, to strip them both down to skin and go for it, just to see if this crazy thing would go away. "I'll explain on the way." He moved forward and helped them all off the beds. They'd already put on their life vests, and were as ready as he could get them. "Let's go." He pushed Cadence and Brandy toward the door, then Andy.

Dorie pulled on his arm until he looked down at her. "The storm isn't over yet."

"No."

"Then I can only think of one reason to go up on deck." Her breath caught. "Do I need to be freaking out, Christian? Because I'm about an inch away from it right now."

He looked into her eyes and thought about missed chances. Too damn many of them. "The object of heavy weather tactics is to avoid capsizing, and believe me, Denny is a master of heavy weather tactics."

"But the waves are high."

True enough. And he knew that if they were non-breaking waves, they couldn't capsize a conventional boat with good stability, and the *Sun Song* had great stability.

But the waves in the wake of this storm were breaking, and therefore could capsize them if high enough. A skilled crew had to maneuver the boat under reduced sails or bare poles, which was good because they were down to bare poles. "It's going to be okay. Denny's up there, he'll tell you what to do."

"What about you?"

"I'm going to get Bobby." He pushed her to the door. "We need all the hands we can get."

"Where is he?"

"Not sure. He vanished a while back."

Dorie paused, a look of concern coming over her face. "You haven't seen him?"

"No."

"What if he went overboard?" she whispered.

"He's too experienced for that. He might be sick in his bunk."

The others were already out the door and moving up to deck level, but Dorie held her ground. "Christian—"

"You're going. I mean it."

"Earlier, I thought I saw two men on deck, near the front of the boat, at the railing. They were hugging. Or fighting."

"What were you doing on deck?"

"Getting food. It was so foggy and misty, I couldn't be sure, and then when I blinked, they were gone, so I figured I imagined it."

"You probably did."

"Right." But she didn't sound convinced. "I'll wait here while you go look for Bobby."

"No."

She'd dressed for an island adventure in a gauzy shirt and tank top, that ridiculous purse over her shoulder, her eyes just a little too shiny, and he thought, *Hell, if she loses it now* . . . but she didn't. Instead, she did something completely unexpected.

She cupped his face. Her gaze dropped to his mouth, and he felt a shock of anticipation churn through him to match the storm outside.

"There's just one thing I have to do first," she said.

Before he could ask what, she closed the gap in one jerky motion that had her purse banging into his side, and kissed him.

Definitely not what he'd have expected from her. What he expected was that after last night, she'd keep her distance. But he'd underestimated her, and he sure as hell underestimated what her kiss would do to him.

It made him forget. Made him forget he was unhappy, trapped. Made him forget the storm, that their life was in danger, made him forget everything but her, this. Her lips on his felt like the simplest, sweetest, warmest, most moving kiss of his entire life. Because of it, he didn't have a chance in hell of keeping his own distance, so he gave up and hauled her closer, sliding his tongue to hers, running his hands down her body and back up again, an event that created another first—an instant tidal wave of heat within him.

He could feel her heating up, but then, far before he was ready, she ended the kiss.

"I didn't want to regret not doing that," she whispered. "I don't want to leave with any regrets at all."

Her cheeks were red, her mouth still wet, and though he knew it wasn't easy for her, she met his gaze straight on.

She was the bravest woman he'd ever met.

"No regrets then," he agreed. His voice came out all low and rough and just a little bit hoarse, as if he were ill.

And he was, he had to be, given what he did next.

He yanked her back up against him, swallowing her little cry of surprise with his mouth. He figured the rough movement would either terrify her or piss her off, and he half waited for her to gut check him with that ridiculous purse, maybe drop him to the floor.

But she didn't.

Instead, she let out the sexiest little murmur he'd ever heard, and shrink-wrapped herself to him. He heated up even more. If he got any hotter, their clothes were going to spontaneously combust and fall off. Her fingers were in his hair, her tongue in his mouth, and he lost himself in the sweet, hot, giving feel of her as she arched against him, panting for air as if maybe she hadn't come in far too long and he was the only man on the planet who could get her there. Some half-baked idea began to take root, that he *was* that man, that he could take her right here, right now, and show her.

Before he could, she once again pulled free and stared up at him, breathing like a wild woman, weaving slightly.

He wondered what she saw when she looked at him like that, as she slowly brought her fingers up to her swollen, still wet mouth, as if shocked to the core that she'd let him kiss her like that.

That she'd wanted it.

"Dorie." He didn't say anything else, just her name, because it occurred to him he really had absolutely no idea what to say.

Turned out, it didn't matter, because she turned and walked away. She moved toward the stairs, her hair wild, her orange life vest not matching her pink tank top, her purse hitting her side with each step, her slight limp doing something to make his stomach hurt like hell.

Truth be told, it wasn't his stomach, but his heart.

ELEVEN

Dorie sat with the others in the wind-ravaged salon, pretending that half the windows weren't blown out along with all the loose furniture, and that they were all fine.

Dark had fallen hours ago, which didn't lessen the sense of helplessness. But with the loss of sight, her other senses kicked in.

And so did the memories.

She tried like crazy not to think about that big old smackeroo she'd given Christian, but holy crap, it'd been a helluva kiss.

The mother of all kisses.

She looked over at Andy, who sat there big and strong, worried, looking a little worse for wear because of it, and felt a stabbing sense of guilt even though she hadn't once been able to have a decent conversation with him without her tongue swelling. The fact was, he'd expressed an interest in her and she'd led him to believe she shared that interest.

She'd *wanted* to share an interest, but she hadn't been able to keep her mind—or her lips—off Christian.

The wind whipped through, bringing the rain with it, but they were all already as wet as they could get.

Just outside the door sat the life raft; Christian was going to prepare it as soon as he found Bobby.

The implications of that made her feel sick, so she went back to thinking about the kiss. The wow kiss. She covered her burning cheeks and glanced at Andy again.

A little rumpled, a little unnerved, he turned to her and smiled, concern in his eyes, along with his affection for her.

She'd definitely lost her mind.

But she had to set aside the thought because she had a more pressing one—drowning. She was having some trouble getting past the mind-numbing certainty that each breath could very well be her last. She really wanted to close her eyes and pretend she wasn't here. Wanted to go to sleep until the nightmare ended. Wanted to bury her head in the sand and be a coward.

After all, that's what she did, she let life go by.

She was damn good at it.

How else to explain being nearly thirty and having nothing to show for it but a box of sketch pads? Why had she put off her hopes and dreams in order to play it safe?

"Think the water's cold?" Cadence asked in a small voice.

Dorie forced a smile. "Nah. The South Pacific waters are notoriously warm."

At that, they all turned their heads and looked out the window at the churning ocean. Though the rain and wind had begun to let up, everything was still black; the water, the sky, the spray in the air . . .

Despite her reassuring words to Cadence, Dorie shivered,

because it all looked cold as hell. "I think it's getting better out there."

Cadence gulped. "I think I'm going to be sick."

Andy slid his arm around her. "Keep your eye on the horizon, remember?"

"Hard to do when the horizon keeps bouncing up and down like a Mexican jumping bean."

"I wonder exactly where we are?" Brandy frowned out at the darkness.

Dorie opened her purse and pulled out a map of the South Pacific.

"You carry a map in your purse." Brandy shook her head. "You really needed this vacation, didn't you?"

"You have no idea." She spread open the map, and they all stared at the multiple groups of islands off the coast of Australia, which were really hundreds of individual islands.

"So . . . we're near here?" Brandy put her finger on Fiji.

"Not necessarily." Andy shook his head. "I heard the captain say we're *way* off course."

Again they all took in the myriad of islands.

"We could be anywhere," Cadence said quietly.

True. Dorie's finger ran over the clusters: Polynesia, Micronesia, Melanesia . . . "Maybe we're close to Tahiti." She tried to sound cheerful. "I always wanted to see Tahiti. We'll probably land somewhere really cool and laugh this whole thing off."

"Yeah, like Bora Bora." Cadence's voice sounded weak and uncertain. "I heard Bora Bora is exciting."

The boat creaked and let out a loud, seemingly human groan as the ocean rock and rolled beneath them.

"It's going to fall apart," Brandy whispered.

"Oh, no. No falling apart. I'm not ready to die." Andy drawled this in a normal tone, as if by doing so he could make everything right again. "I have lots of baseball left in me, and next year, a contract renewal."

"Money isn't going to matter to you if you're dead," Cadence pointed out.

"Money always matters." This from Brandy, of course.

"It's not the money," Andy told them. "It's the security of knowing I can play for at least five more years."

Dorie understood. She'd always appreciated security. A regular paycheck. But now, out here, floating in what seemed like a mortally wounded sailing yacht, Shop-Mart and any dubious security it offered her seemed very, very far away.

But not her dreams. She touched her lips, the ones that had kissed Christian. Yep, her dreams were right here with her, unfortunately going down with the ship.

From just outside, she could hear Denny yelling, shouting directions to Ethan. She pictured them out there, in the wild elements, fighting the losing battle against the equipment they had left, trying to keep them safe. "We need to help them."

"I tried," Andy said. "They want us to stay here, it's safer."

Dorie had a feeling "safer" was all relative at this point. "Then let's help Christian look for Bobby."

"He's fine," Andy said. "He's probably sleeping."

"But what if he's not?" Dorie stood up, gripping the table for balance.

"Honey, Christian told us to stay here," Brandy reminded her. "It's too dangerous to do anything else. The boat could pitch and you could fall and hit your head."

"I'm not going to hit my head." She fought her way to the door, then turned back to find them all staring at her. Yeah, she was surprised, too. She rarely took charge. Okay, she never took charge. There'd always been others to do that. But she was done letting others take over. "No, stay," she said when Andy began to rise. That's what fear did to a person, made them bossy, apparently. "I'll just go downstairs and make sure Christian doesn't need any help. Maybe Bobby hurt himself or something."

Andy shook his head. He still looked green, and more than a little shaky, but he stood. "Not alone, you're not."

Telling him he would only be a hindrance wasn't the way to make him stay. "You have to be here for Cadence and Brandy."

"It's dark—"

"I have a flashlight. Besides, Christian's down there, I'll be fine."

And with that, she turned and made her way to the stairs. Taking charge felt good, she decided. It overrode her fear.

Almost.

She hopped down from the stairs and—

Landed in water. It splashed over her ankles, halfway up her calves, and damn it, it was colder then she'd imagined it could be.

But not even that mattered in the face of the bigger picture— they were taking on water, and lots of it. Too much. "Bobby?" she yelled. *"Bobby!"*

Nothing except the whistle of the wind and the creaking and groaning of the boat. Well that, and her own panicked breathing, not to mention the thundering of her heart in her ears. She fought her way down the hallway, *fought* being the key word. The water made movement difficult, as did all the debris floating in it. Halfway, she thought she heard someone behind her, and whipped around.

No one.

Oh, God, she was really losing it. "Bobby?" She turned the corner toward the crew's quarters, where it was even darker, and became grateful for her flashlight, meager as it was.

"*What the hell are you doing?*"

She nearly had a coronary as she whirled again. "My God." She sagged back against the wall and stared at Christian, highlighted by her flashlight. "You scared me."

"How did you get down here?" He was drenched. "Which part of *stay on deck* didn't you understand?"

He was wearing the frown she'd rarely seen him without—until the kiss, that is. He definitely hadn't been frowning when she'd kissed him.

Or when he'd kissed her.

Had he thought about it? How good it'd been? Make that amazing. Off-the-charts amazing.

"Damn it, Dorie. You're not safe down here."

He definitely wasn't thinking about the kiss.

"*What?*" he asked in disbelief, making her realize she'd spoken out loud.

"Um, nothing."

"You're thinking about the kiss, *now*?"

"Yeah, and that I have the brain capacity left to do so baffles even me, trust me."

He continued to look at her as if she'd lost her mind, and she had to admit, she clearly had. "It's just that with you my tongue doesn't swell."

"You hit your head?"

"I wondered about that, too, but no. I know, it sounds crazy, but my tongue swells whenever I'm around a cute guy. Which is why it swelled with Andy, making it hard to talk to him—"

"But not with me, apparently, since you manage to talk, a lot."
He fought through the water to come closer.

"No. Not with you—"

That was all she got out before he hauled her up against him
and covered her mouth with his, probably just to shut her up; as
a quieting technique, it worked for her. He made the most of the
next few seconds, kissing her so thoroughly that when he let go and
stared into her face, she staggered back and might have fallen on
her poor beleaguered butt if he hadn't held her steady.

"So I'm guessing," she whispered. "We're *both* thinking about
the kiss, and—"

"And we can both get over it."

He needed to get over it? "*Can* you? Get over it?"

"*Oui.* Absolutely."

"How?" she asked, wondering if there was some secret.

Before he could answer, the boat pitched and rolled. Just as
she lost her grip and would have gone flying, he snagged her close
again. She slid up against that warm body for longer than necessary, and she was able to ascertain that, oh boy, no matter what he
said, he wasn't yet over it.

"Working on it," he said grimly, reading her mind.

"Do you have to?"

"Yes. *Jesus.* Now stop . . ." He waved a hand, searching for the
right words. "Distracting me."

She was distracting. She'd never been accused of that before,
and it made her grin from ear to ear.

"No," he said. "Don't do that." He pointed to the stairs. "Go.
Get up there."

"I'm helping you look for Bobby."

"No."

"But if we have to get into the raft"—please God, don't let them have to get into the raft—"he's going to get left behind. We can't leave him behind."

"No one's getting left behind. Just go back up."

"What if I saw him go overboard?"

"You said you saw two men hugging."

"Or fighting," she reminded him.

"And then they vanished," he said. "You said they vanished.

"Yes."

"But two men aren't missing."

Only one. "What if one tossed the other over?"

His jaw tightened. "Go up."

She shook her head and followed him down the hall, where he looked in every room. "I should have called my mom more often. I'm a bad daughter, Christian."

He made a low, rough sound. "I don't believe that."

"I wish I'd told her I loved her before I came on this cruise. Instead I got annoyed because she told me to find a rich husband while I was here."

He let out a short laugh that told her he understood, and checked another room.

"Do you have regrets? Do you get annoyed at your mother, too?"

"Used to."

Used to. Didn't tell her much. She yearned to know more about this enigmatic, charismatic man she couldn't seem to stop thinking about. "Are you close?" she asked breathlessly, trying to keep up.

With a sigh, he slowed, and reached for her hand. They splashed through the water that was up to their calves as he towed her by the hand, his grip ruthless as if he was afraid to let go. She appreciated the diligence. She didn't want him to let go.

"My mother's been gone a long time," he said.

"Oh, I'm so sorry."

"Like I said, a long time ago."

"Did your father raise you? In . . . France?" she guessed.

"No. My mother was French. After she was gone, I left France to go live with my father, who was an Irish medic with an international charity organization. We stayed in Ireland, Africa, India . . . wherever his job took him."

"Wow. So you've been helping people all your life."

"You make it sound like a hero thing."

"It is."

"No." He shook his head. "My father gave his life to it, at the cost of anything personal. That's not heroic, that's obsessive."

"He had you. That was personal, right?"

"I was more a responsibility than a son."

"And yet you became a doctor."

"Because going away to college was my escape from poverty. Just like being here is paying off that debt." He tried to open the door to the room Bobby shared with Ethan, but couldn't.

"Debt?"

"Now who's thinking out loud. Forget it, okay. *Bobby?*" He banged on the door.

"What debt are you paying off?"

He sighed again. "It's expensive to become a doctor. My father helped me get the loans I needed. Now I'm helping him."

"Which is why you're here."

"For one more year. Then I'm free to go back to France. Now that you have my entire life's story, will you get your pretty ass back to the others?"

He thought her ass was pretty. Apparently she wasn't suitably terrified because that warmed her more than it should. Although, in truth, his talking about his life warmed her more than his nice ass comment.

The man *was* human, and she'd just gotten proof. Looking into his chiseled, rigid features, she felt like she could finally begin to understand both his discipline and the walls he kept around himself. "What if you need help with Bobby?"

"He'd never risk his neck to do the same for you."

"But if he's hurt—"

"Then he's the responsibility of the crew."

The boat pitched suddenly, more violently than before, and they both hit the door. Dorie lost her footing and went down, and for one horrifying second, her face was underwater.

Then she was jerked to her feet, where she promptly coughed up icky, salty ocean water.

"You all right?"

She blinked the water out of her eyes. Christian had hauled her upright, against him. Her feet weren't even touching the floor.

But they were touching water. *"Christian."*

"I know," he said hoarsely as she tossed her wet hair out of her face. She was cold, much colder than she'd thought possible, and she shivered with it.

Christian swore again, and ripped off his shirt. "Here."

"Maybe we're just being Punk'd," she said, teeth chattering as she slipped his shirt on, hugging it close for the warmth he'd left in it, not to mention that it smelled like him. "Any second the camera crew is going to jump out at us."

"Punk'd?"

"You know, MTV? Ashton Kutcher . . . ?"

He shook his head, and she sighed. "Never mind. Not even Ashton would be this cruel. I shouldn't have come."

"Damn right. You should have stayed up on deck."

"I meant on the cruise."

He glanced at her, and some of the frustration left his face as he sighed. "None of this is your fault, you know that."

"I know. But if I'd stayed home, I'd be—" *Safe*. Still dodging Mr. Stryowski, true enough, but safe.

And she'd never have gotten the kick in the ass she'd needed to get herself going.

"The storm's a fluke. Without it, you'd be swimming and flirting with Andy right this minute. Having the time of your life."

"I can't even talk to him."

"No worries. He doesn't have talking in mind."

She gaped at his back, bared now that she wore his shirt. A very tanned, smooth, sleek, strong back, the kind that said he was no stranger to hard, physical labor. "You're . . . no. You're not jealous."

"Don't be asinine," he said, sounding extremely French. "I've never been jealous a day in my life."

"Good."

"*Good.*" He fought with the door handle. "*Bobby!*"

"Because being jealous," she went on. "Well that would be . . . what did you call me?" she asked, much more politely than she felt. "*Asinine.*"

"I didn't call *you* asinine. I said being jealous would be asinine."

"Yeah, well, now I'm calling *you* asinine."

This caused a completely baffled expression to cross his face. As if no one, especially a woman, had ever insulted him before. She found that extremely hard to believe, given his bedside manner.

He gave up on the handle and glared at her. "Why am I asinine?"

Because he didn't meet the criteria on her list. "You know what? Ignore me."

"If only it were that easy."

She rolled her eyes and vowed to think much more quietly in the future.

"What else?" he asked, slapping his pockets and coming up with a set of keys.

"What else what?"

"What else am I besides asinine?"

"Arrogant. Cocky."

He blinked. "Cocky."

"Yes. And a tad bit difficult." So much for keeping her thoughts to herself. She closed her mouth before more words could escape.

"Oh, don't stop there," he said softly. "You're just getting started."

"Well, I don't really know you well enough to continue," she demurred.

"I think you know me plenty. But let's do you, shall we?"

"Oh, no thanks. I have my mother for that." She reached for the door, as if she could budge it when he hadn't been able to.

The boat was lilting to one side. Undoubtedly the weight of the water held it closed. Christian put his shoulder to the door and shoved again. The tendons in his neck stood out in bold relief, the muscles in his arms and shoulders straining as well.

"Christian," she said, putting her hands on his bare back. "Stop, you'll—"

The door gave away.

He fell in, and she fell on top of him. "Sorry," she gasped, coming up to her hands and knees in the water. He did the same and pulled her in closer to steady her. Or maybe just because.

"Têtu," he said. "You're stubborn."

"Yes, I know."

"And bullheaded."

"They're the same," she pointed out.

"Obstinate."

"Again. The same."

"Beautiful."

Honestly, that French accent should be outlawed. She tried to catch her breath. "It's a shame then that you don't want to be with me."

"What I said was that you were better off with Andy."

She looked into those stone gray eyes that were not in any way cold.

His gaze dipped to her mouth. Lifting a hand, he slid his thumb over her lower lip, which had her mouth trembling open.

"I make you nervous," he noted, his voice low and French and silky soft.

Nervous. Crazy. *Aroused.* She lifted her chin. "Don't be—"

"Asinine?" He smiled tightly, then took a step away from her to look around.

Behind his back, she let out a breath and put her hands to her heated cheeks. It was like playing with fire. He was bad for her, very bad, and yet she remained mesmerized, because when he looked at her, when he touched her, when he so much as breathed in her general direction, her body reacted in a very specific way.

"Bobby," he called out, flashing his light into the room. It was dark here, dark and dingy. Things floated past them; a brush, a cell phone . . .

Christian moved toward the bunk beds.

"Has anyone ever gone overboard?"

"Yes, but always on purpose, and never a crew member."

"But it's possible, right?"

"Not likely."

Then where was he? Moving into the doorway of the bathroom, she used her light and heard herself gasp in horror. *"Oh my God."*

"Don't freak out on me now," Christian called from the bedroom. "We'll find him."

"I—" *Oh, God.* She was going to be sick. "I think I found . . . some of him."

TWELVE

The sound of terror in Dorie's voice stopped Christian's heart cold. He tried to rush toward her, but rushing through this much water was all but impossible, and half swimming, half running, he felt like he was moving in slow motion.

Jesus, why hadn't she listened to him? Why wasn't she safe with the others? When he made it to the bathroom door, she was staring at the sink and counter, at the mirror, all of which were spattered with blood, and he lunged to her side. "Are you hurt?"

"It's not my blood." She turned her ashen face to his. "Bobby's?"

"I don't know."

"It's everywhere!" Her eyes were glassy, and she was breathing as if she'd just run a marathon. Her entire body shivered. Recognizing the signs of shock, he pulled her close.

Over her head, he eyed the blood. Bobby had been young and

lazy as hell, and had definitely pissed off just about everyone he'd ever met, especially those he'd worked for, but Christian had a hard time picturing someone wanting him dead.

She pulled free. "There's not that many of us on this boat. And one of us—" She clapped a hand over her mouth. "Ohmigod. Did one of us do this?"

"Dorie, listen to me. I need you to—"

"No. I'm not leaving you."

No, she wasn't. No way in hell was she leaving his sight. "Sit down," he ordered. "I need you to sit down before you fall down."

She sat right there on the floor, right in the water. "You were in here. Earlier, right? Looking for him."

He met her gaze. "What are you saying?"

She looked away. "Just asking. You didn't see this?"

"No. We're going upstairs now, where we'll figure out our next step."

"I vote for a helicopter ride back to Fiji, and getting the authorities involved."

That was the best case scenario. He didn't know how to tell her that it wasn't likely to happen that way. If they could have gotten a helicopter evacuation, they would have by now. Unfortunately, they had no way of communicating with anyone on any shore. The truth was, their lives were in grave danger without this added complication.

Given the way she was looking at him, she'd already figured that out. She knew, and she was holding it together. She had guts.

She also had mascara running beneath her eyes, and her clothes plastered to her body. Her hair had completely rioted into a frizzy mane around her head, and she was shaking like a leaf.

Her eyes filled. "Do you think he's . . . dead?"

"I'm hoping he's up on deck, whining about the extra work."

A tear spilled over and slid down her cheek, and something deep inside him cracked open.

"Not yet," he said. "Don't fall apart yet."

"Okay." She hugged herself tight. "I'll just postpone that until later, say, when we sink like a stone. Does that work for you?"

"Yes."

She let out a shocked laugh.

"Look, Dorie, I need you to be strong here. You can do it."

"Is that how you get through life? Holding on to anger instead of dealing? Is that how you stay so completely calm, so cold?"

He nearly flinched at the accuracy of the accusation.

Her mouth tightened as he helped her up. "You're missing out on life, you know. Living it this way, without feeling."

Okay, he felt plenty. In fact, he felt so much right now he thought maybe he would explode from it. Rage at Denny for not turning back at the storm warnings. Sick for whoever'd been hurt here. Gut-deep fear for Dorie and her safety. He clamped his hand on hers and pulled her to the door.

"What—"

"Come on." There was no time to preserve the crime scene—and this sure as hell looked like a crime scene. The boat wasn't going to make it. Eyeing the rising water, he checked Dorie's life vest, checked his, and then took her back into the pitch-black hallway.

His beam of light did little to alleviate the darkness, but the sudden cry from up on deck seemed to cut right through it.

"*Cadence,*" Dorie gasped, and lunged for the stairs. She got a few steps up before Christian managed to grab her, sending them both sprawling to their butts in the water.

As it soaked into their clothes and splattered in their faces, he kept a hold on her. She was in his lap, scrambling to get up, and he was holding her against him. Even there, in the midst of hell, he wanted to pull her close and bury his face in her hair.

"Let me go! She might be in trouble!" Squirming, she fought him like a wild cat, *nothing* like the meek woman he'd once believed her to be.

"No," he said, but she fought dirty, and put a knee in his crotch. When he doubled over, she surged to her feet to make her escape.

"Goddamnit." He grabbed her calf and tugged her back to him. "You don't know what's up there!" he hissed, then shoved her behind him so he could reach for the railing. "Stay," he commanded her coldly, wanting her good and pissed so he had a chance she'd actually listen. "*Wait.*"

"Why?"

Jesus. "Because I said."

"Christian—"

"What are you going to do, rush out there and protect her with your big, clunky purse?"

"Yes, if need be!" Then she shocked the hell out of him. She lifted her foot, the one with the ankle he'd wrapped himself, and stomped down on his foot.

"*Son of a bitch!*"

Slithering out of his loosened hold, she beat him to the stairs.

Gritting his teeth, he went after her. Had he actually thought she was brave, even for a second? She wasn't brave, she had a freaking death wish!

He was behind her on the stairs in a flash, where he realized several things at once. First, Dorie was definitely wearing panties today—pink silk as a matter of fact.

And second, the storm *finally* seemed to have ended. It was still raining, drizzling really, but the wind was all but a memory. Given the slightest lightening of the sky due east, it was somewhere near dawn.

But too little too late, because Ethan had lowered the raft, while Denny spoke to Brandy and Cadence; whatever it was seemed to be making them very unhappy.

"I'm not leaving without Dorie!" This from Cadence, in a panicked cry that matched the one they'd heard.

It looked like panicked chaos to Christian, nothing close to the orderly evacuation they'd always drilled in. Then suddenly Andy twisted around, locked his eyes on Dorie, and seemed to deflate in relief.

With a hoarsely drawled "Thank God," he reached for her. "I thought—"

"I'm fine," Dorie whispered, and walked right into the cowboy's arms.

Good, Christian told himself ruthlessly, searching the seas as far as he could see, which wasn't far. No sign of anyone in the water.

Andy was still holding Dorie. Yeah, right where she should be. In fact, right where he wanted her, in the arms of a man perfectly willing to protect her and keep her safe, which meant she wasn't *his* own responsibility.

So there was no reason for his gut twisting, no reason at all.

While Andy was holding on to Dorie like he might never let go, Cadence and Brandy joined the group hug like *they* might never let go.

"Get in the damn boat!" Denny yelled.

Ignoring him, Brandy pulled back a bit and fingered the shirt Dorie wore over her clothes.

Christian's.

Dorie's lips moved, and given that Brandy, Cadence, and Andy all turned to look at him, Dorie was explaining exactly whose shirt it was, and why she was wearing it.

He wanted to turn away but there was the little matter of what they'd just seen below to discuss. Feeling like he weighed a million pounds, he moved closer to Dorie. "I need to talk to you."

"Later," Andy told him.

Christian gave Dorie a long look, trying to convey the need for them to talk *now*.

She closed her eyes.

Well, hell. He turned toward Denny, who was still trying to corral everyone into the raft. "Problem."

"No shit, Sherlock." Denny looked sincerely rattled, shaken to the core, and beaten down from the past twelve hours fighting the storm. "We're abandoning ship. Jesus, I've never had to do this with guests on board. Where the hell's Bobby?"

Christian opened his mouth, but Andy called out to them.

"Wait," Denny said to Andy, eyes locked on Christian. "Did you find him yet?"

"Damn it, this can't wait!" Andy pointed to the east, where the sky had lightened from purple to pink, where the horizon didn't just fall off the earth but hit a distinct black outline.

The outline of an island.

Denny stared at it. "Thank fucking Christ."

"Is it Fiji?" Cadence asked.

"I doubt it," Andy said. "Maybe it's Bora Bora."

Denny turned to Ethan and Christian. "We'll limp in."

They had little choice because without the sails or their equipment—all in complete shreds and tatters—they could do nothing but.

"Ethan!" Denny called out, on a mission now. "Starboard—"

"On it."

Christian leapt to help, directing the *Sun Song* to where it could be drawn in toward the island by the tide.

"Windward shore approach," Denny yelled.

Andy shifted closer, followed by the others. "What does that mean?"

"The windward shore is where the wind is blowing from," Christian explained.

"The waves'll be smaller because of the reduced fetch," Denny called, standing at the half gone helm.

Everyone turned to Christian for translation.

"Fetch is the distance of water that the wind is blowing over."

"Leeward shore harbor!" Denny called.

Again everyone looked at Christian.

"Jesus, Denny." He rubbed his forehead before meeting everyone's gaze, trying to tap down his own impatience. "The entrance is narrow. It might be difficult to enter. Especially the way we're crawling in."

"Oh, God," Cadence whispered, gripping Brandy and Dorie tight. "Can this get any worse?"

"Yes," Dorie said, her eyes on Christian. "Trust me. It can."

Christian tried to reassure her with his eyes but she turned away. With no idea what that meant, he worked the boat with Ethan.

"I hope the island has a big restaurant," Andy said. "I'm starving."

"You won't starve if we're in the American Samoas," Brandy said. "None of us will. Half the canned tuna sold in American supermarkets comes from the Samoa Islands." She lifted a shoulder. "I watch a lot of the Discovery Channel."

"Don't worry," Denny shouted down to them from the damaged helm, his gaze locked on the outline of the island. "We've made it this far, we're not going to do anything less than cross the finish line." He gestured Christian close. "Obviously we have no idea where we are but I think—hope—some Cook island just saved our ass."

The Cook Islands spread across 750,000 square miles. Christian wasn't sure how that translated to saving their asses, but not drowning was excellent. "About Bobby."

"It's going to be fine. In an hour this will all be a distant memory."

"I don't think so." Christian glanced back at Dorie. She was with the others, in a tight group, but looking right at him. Her eyes were huge and unwavering.

"We're still in serious trouble."

"Are you kidding?" Denny laughed. "Bullet dodged. Lawsuits avoided. By noon we could be in a bar, checking out the local ladies . . ." But when Christian just looked at him, his smile slowly faded. "Don't tell me. Ah, Christ, I don't want to know."

"You've got that right."

Dorie was still looking at him, waiting for him to do something about poor Bobby. Bobby, who was not on this boat. Bobby, who'd bled all over his bathroom, and who might have not have left this boat by choice. "Denny."

"Later. Over that beer."

"This can't wait."

"Denny?" Brandy called. "Is this island inhabited?"

Everyone shifted closer for his answer, dripping wet, exhausted, and just about as far from carefree vacationers as they could get, looking more like drowned rats instead.

And they were all within listening range.

Panicking range.

"I'm banking on a lux hotel," Denny said, charm intact. "Five star."

Christian stared at him. There was no way to know that, and in fact, with the hundreds and hundreds of islands in the South Pacific, a huge number of them uninhabitable or even uncharted, the percentages were against them. They were more likely to find wild boars than a five-star hotel. "You can't promise—"

With a laugh that didn't ring true, Denny slapped him on the shoulder. "Let's just get there."

Christian glanced at Dorie, who was still snuggled up to Andy. The guy was cupping her head close to his chest in his big home run hitting hand. Over her wild hair, Andy met Christian's eyes, his cool and assessing.

Had she told him about Bobby? Christian doubted it. But Andy had known Bobby before the cruise. They'd been friends, which meant one of two things. Either Andy was about to be completely devastated, or . . .

Or he'd had something to do with him going overboard.

Ethan and Bobby had known each other, too. They'd worked together all season, long enough for Ethan to be perpetually annoyed and frustrated at Bobby's lackadaisical work ethic.

Ethan hated lackadaisical.

But Jesus, hated enough to kill? It was hard to imagine.

"Did you see Bobby?" Ethan asked him.

"Later," Denny said, looking at Christian. "We'll get to Bobby later."

Which left Christian to wonder about the third man who'd known Bobby.

"Let's just get to land," Denny said. "Where I promise to make up this whole nightmare to each of you. We'll get a fancy hotel and meet in the bar for drinks on the house. But for now, since we're not going rafting, if everyone could go belowdecks while we bring her in, or even to your rooms—"

"Denny," Christian said softly, thinking of Bobby's room, and what would be found there, "the salon would be better than belowdecks."

"Perfect," Denny said without missing a beat. "Everyone to the salon as we bring this baby in. Andy? Could you get the women into the salon?"

"Sure." Andy guided the women inside. Christian saw Dorie go up on tiptoe, brushing her mouth to Andy's ear to say something. He responded, probably drawling in that soft accent he had, and shaking his head, tried to hold her back.

Dorie broke free, patting Andy gently on the arm, a comforting gesture that had always irritated Christian whenever it'd been done to him. But suddenly he wanted Dorie to pat his arm in that same sweet, caring, comforting manner.

Clearly, he was losing it.

Then he sucked in a breath because she walked right up to him, eyes bright, looking at him with that blazing inner strength and determination he couldn't help but admire, even when it doubled his worry.

"What can I do?" she whispered.

"Stay safe. That's your only job."

"I want to help, Christian."

"You can help by keeping a low profile."

"You don't want me to say anything about Bobby." Her eyes telegraphed her emotions on that very clearly. She was wondering *why* he didn't want her to tell.

"I didn't hurt him, Dorie. You know that."

"Actually, all I know is that *I* didn't hurt him. And that you don't want me to tell anyone that we suspect he's overboard."

"That's right. Because the very last thing we need right now is something new to panic about, when there's nothing, *nothing* we can do for him right now." He reached for her, but she backed up a step.

"Stay away," she said very quietly, though her voice quivered.

He stared at her, shaken to the core. "Jesus, Dorie. You can't really think I'd—"

"I'm going to save what I think for the police." Hugging herself, she lifted her chin to nosebleed heights. "Who I plan to call as soon as we touch land. If he fell on his own, then hopefully he's still out there, alive, waiting for rescue."

But if he hadn't fallen on his own . . . Neither voiced the thought that surely he was long dead by now. Christian glanced at the island, which was looming large now that they were close. Tall mountains jutted up into the shifting, changing sky. The mountains were covered in lush green jungle, and rocks.

Lots of rocks.

And unfortunately for all of them, not a single dwelling in sight, much less a five-star hotel. In fact, there was nothing at all.

The place looked completely deserted.

THIRTEEN

Still in shock, Dorie stood in the salon, flanked on either side by Brandy and Cadence. They were holding hands as they watched the crew take them toward a shadow of an island that kept rising and falling through the misty waves.

A crew minus Bobby, though Dorie seemed to be the only one to notice, which disturbed her. So did the way she kept looking at everyone, wondering if they'd been the one up on deck with Bobby.

"I don't see any hotels," Brandy noted, staring at the vertical mountainsides so steep they looked like they were exploding directly out of the sea.

"It looks pretty lush," Cadence said. "Maybe the hotels are hidden behind all that tropical rain forest."

She'd always wanted to see the rain forests, Dorie reminded herself. Now seemed like as good a time as any . . . except for, oh yeah, the missing crew member!

She glanced out the window—glassless now—to where Christian worked in silence next to Ethan. He might have hurt Bobby, but she didn't think so. Even only knowing him for a few days, she felt the temper and grief pouring off him in waves.

No one was that good of an actor. But was she willing to bet her life on it? Because really, all she knew about him was that he was a doctor. Oh, and that he kissed like heaven on earth. Let's not forget that part.

But little else.

Only . . . that wasn't actually true either. She'd watched him treat each of the guests with care and great attention, no matter his personal feelings. Plus, frustrated or not over whatever debt he owed, he seemed to take his oath as a doctor, to heal, to save lives, very seriously.

Which meant she could trust him. It also meant that until there was more information, he was the *only* one she could trust. She wished that came with some comfort, but it didn't.

Cadence and Brandy decided to sit, and pulled her down next to them. But sitting had her sucking in a breath because of the splinter. It was beginning to seriously hurt, maybe even getting infected as she'd been warned.

"Hon?" Brandy leaned in close and frowned in her face. "You okay? You getting seasick? You look green."

"Oh boy, you really do," Cadence agreed.

Brandy pulled out her flask. "The handy-dandy fix-all."

"It's barely morning."

"Yes, but somewhere in the world it's Happy Hour."

Dorie managed to smile. "I'm good." And good was relative, right? After all, compared to Bobby, wherever he was, she was exceptionally good.

Don't think about it now.

"Hold on to your seats, ladies," Brandy said just as a wave hit them, and everyone gasped as they rose and fell, momentarily losing sight of the island.

"Whew," Brandy said, somehow managing to still look gorgeous despite all they'd been through. Her short blonde hair was no longer perfectly spiky around her head, and she'd lost her gel or whatever magical hair product she'd been using, but it didn't matter, the short strands framed her face, making her look softer, sweeter. "Maybe there'll be some hot natives," she said, ever hopeful.

Okay, maybe not sweet exactly.

"I'd be fine with a hot shower," Cadence said. "This sea salt spray is hell on my fair skin."

Dorie would be happy just to see Bobby's scowl again. But because that thought nearly choked her, she forced another. The island got bigger as they drifted closer, but as the dawn lightened, she could see that her fears were true, that the island was indeed one big, craggy, rough, inhospitable rock. A volcano, hopefully a very, very dormant volcano, draped by that lush rain forest.

She glanced behind her to see if anyone else had noticed this unwelcome turn of events and found her gaze locked on Christian's.

He stood on the deck next to Denny, working hard to aim the boat into the channel, but he locked his stormy eyes on hers and didn't look away.

The boat hit another swell and next to her, Cadence gasped. Dorie tightened her grip on her hand. Only yesterday such a swell would have terrified her, too, but now she knew there were other things to fear.

Lots of other things.

Such as Christian, and the odd hold he seemed to have over her emotions.

He hadn't replaced his shirt, and still wore only those black board shorts, long to his knees and loose, hanging dangerously low on his hips. He wasn't muscle-bound like Andy, but long and lean and hard in a way that suggested food had never been all that important to him.

Lucky bastard.

She had the feeling that maybe nothing was all that important to him, and hadn't been for a long time.

"So where do you think Bobby is?" Brandy asked in a low voice. "I haven't seen him since he brought me a nightcap last night."

Dorie tore her gaze off Christian. "Bobby brought you a nightcap?"

"Sure did. And let's just say, the boy isn't quite the underachiever we thought."

Dorie stared at her as this sank in. "You mean, you two . . . hooked up?"

"Well, not quite. Denny interrupted us, needing the extra hands on deck. Damn greedy man. Just a few minutes more, and—"

"The captain," Dorie said, thoughts racing. "Denny called for Bobby during the night?"

"I don't remember that," Cadence said.

Brandy paused. "Why would you? You weren't there."

"No, but I was with Denny."

Now Dorie stared at Cadence. "You were with Denny? Doing what?"

Cadence blushed. "Uh . . . stuff."

"You slept with him?"

"Not slept with." Cadence squirmed. "Not yet . . ."

Dorie blinked. "So did everyone have some sort of *Love Boat* connection last night?"

"Not me." Andy plopped down next to her, sounding just a little bit baffled at the situation. "I didn't."

A loud crash interrupted this conversation, accompanied by a shuddering scraping sound as Christian and Ethan drove the bow of the boat onto the island's shore.

They'd arrived.

However, exactly *where* they'd arrived was another question entirely.

The water was only a couple of inches deep for what seemed like half a mile out. As the sun made an appearance, the palm trees cast mini islands of shade on the wind-rippled sand-sea. Where the sand ended began dense tropical growth, covering the surrounding rocks in sensuous greens. The sounds of the place were scary and somehow soothing at the same time—the rustle of wind through the trees, the songs of birds that couldn't yet be seen, the gentle wash of the shallow surf.

"Safe and sound," Cadence murmured.

Brandy nodded, clearly relieved.

Safe and sound? Dorie could only hope so.

*Day One on deserted island without an outlet
for the hair straightener.*

"We're all going to die of malaria," Cadence said when they stood on firm ground, staring around at their rain forest surroundings.

"I got the shot," Brandy said. "No malaria for me."

"I got the shot, too, but it's only 98 percent effective, so two out of a hundred of us are going to get it."

"Not a half-full glass kinda gal, are you?" Brandy said.

Dorie pulled the bug spray from her purse to ease her mind. "Here. Let's spray ourselves."

"Deserted." Andy still seemed in shock as he stood on the beach absorbing both Dorie's bug spray and their situation. "Who'da thought?"

"No worries." This from Denny. "We'll set up a day camp, and start a fire for the smoke."

Cadence moved close to Brandy and Dorie. "I want my money back." She held out her arms and closed her eyes as Dorie sprayed her.

"We didn't pay." Brandy shook her head, not wanting bug spray. "Don't waste it on me, hon. I never get bit. I'm not sweet enough."

"Well, then I want this week of my life back." Cadence waved her arms to dry them, looking to be an inch from meltdown. "Did you know I can't even watch *Survivor*? They use leaves for toilet paper. *Leaves*, people."

Dorie checked her cell phone for reception, of which there was none, and eyed the high volcanic mountain peaks with frustration. "At least there are lots of leaves."

"Where's Bobby?" This was Brandy's sixth time asking. Dorie knew this because she'd been counting.

Cadence studied the boat, listing to its side, half in the sand, half in the shallow water where they'd beached it. "What if—"

"Look." Andy gestured with his chin. "Ethan and Denny are back on board. He's probably with them."

Dorie's heart sank, and she opened her mouth to tell them the truth, but Cadence covered her mouth to hide a sob. Dorie hugged her tight, remaining silent about her suspicions on what had happened to Bobby so she didn't freak her out even more. Keeping silent didn't feel good either.

The sun continued to rise, bringing with it a heat index so high the air shimmered with individual heat waves, thick and salty and humid. They sat on the beach. Or the girls sat. Andy wandered

around, while the crew worked on the boat. Or that was their offered spiel anyway. Dorie knew the truth was they were working
on finding out what had happened to Bobby.

With nothing to do, they talked, mostly about men. They ate,
thanks to Ethan bringing them some goodies from the galley. And
they sunbathed.

Correction. Brandy sunbathed, Cadence covered up her pale
complexion the best she could and gathered seashells because
she couldn't sit still. "It is gorgeous here," she said, coming back
from the water with a handful of shells and rocks. "Wherever
here is."

"The sun is amazing," Brandy said, pulling her bathing suit
strap to the side to study her tan lines.

"You should cover up, too," Cadence told her. "You don't want
skin cancer."

"I'm going to die young anyway." When Dorie and Cadence
just stared at her, she waved off their concern. "It's just one of
those things. I've never seen myself growing old and sitting in the
rocker, you know? I am going out young, with a bang."

Which is what Dorie wanted to do. Not the going out young
part, but the bang part. Living life . . .

"Let's make a nice camp," Cadence said.

"Jesus, girl." Brandy patted the sand next to her. "Sit. I'll braid
your hair."

After she'd done that, she eyed Dorie's wild mop. "Honey."

"I'll tame it." It seemed incongruous to be worried about her
hair, but one could only stay freaked out for so long, so she dug
around in her purse for her anti-frizz, which had cost a bazillion
dollars but rarely worked. In high hopes that this would be the
time for a miracle, she smoothed it on and then corralled her hair
into a ponytail. "Better?"

Brandy rolled her lips inward.

Dorie sighed. "Never mind. It's hopeless."

"Here." Brandy moved behind her and pulled out the ponytail. "Just last month we used a bunch of poodles in our show, and I did their hairdos."

"So I'm going to look like a poodle?"

"You already do. But I'm going to fix that." She worked the tangled strands with her fingers, pulling so tight Dorie closed her eyes in self-defense.

"You have great hair," Brandy said.

"I thought I had poodle hair."

Brandy put more product in. "But it's healthy poodle hair. There."

When Dorie opened her eyes she found Christian standing in front of her, watching the whole spectacle.

"What do you think, Doc?" Brandy asked.

He considered. "Maybe a little more of that stuff."

Dorie rolled her eyes and watched Cadence, who'd started gathering fallen palm tree fronds for who knew what. With a sigh, Brandy went after her.

"You okay?" Christian asked now that they were alone.

"Define *okay*. If you mean alive, then yeah. I'm okay."

"Dorie—"

"Did you find Bobby on the boat?"

His eyes flickered grief. "No."

She closed her eyes. "Do you know where we are?"

"If we'd stayed on course we'd still be in Fiji."

"Okay. But we didn't stay on course."

"No. We were hundreds of miles off course when we last had a working compass."

Hundreds of miles.

"We could be in the Cook Islands," he told her in his blunt honest way. "Or the Samoas. No telling, really."

"So what now?"

"We stay calm."

"Yeah. Working on that." But she'd ended up on an island with a group of strangers including a baseball stud, a hyperactive artist, a stripper—er, *dancer*, a laid-back captain, an unflappable chef, the gorgeous grumpy doctor standing in front of her, and oh, a missing attitude-ridden boat hand.

"We stay very calm," Christian said again, as if sensing her impending breakdown. "I need to speak to you a moment."

Heart pounding, she let him take her hand and pull her away, beneath the shade of a palm tree whose fronds hung down around them, secluding them as if they were on their own island.

They were alone, at least for the moment. No more need for pretense. Knowing it, some of her rigid control drained, and with that came a flood of anxiety and despair. Touching her eyelids, she let out a sound and shook her head. "I'm beginning to lose it."

"I know," he said, and shocked the hell out of her when he pulled her close. She was certain he meant the embrace to offer comfort, not anything sensual, and it was soothing, but after about ten seconds, it was also disturbingly erotic as all the misplaced adrenaline rushing through her began to mistake the comfort for something else entirely.

"Goddamn," she heard him mutter against her hair, assuring her she wasn't alone in this realization, and then he tipped up her chin and covered her mouth with his, no warning, no asking, though if he'd asked, she'd probably have said *pretty please. Pretty please keep on kissing me . . .*

He did.

With one of those wildly sexy murmurs low in his throat, he hauled her tighter up against him and swept his tongue to hers.

Please keep touching me . . .

He did that, too, one hand tunneling into her "poodle" hair to palm her head, the other sliding low on her spine, then lower still, cupping her bottom—ouch, splinter!—before gliding up again, fisting in the material of her top, then slipping beneath to touch the bare skin of her back.

Oh yes, definitely keep doing that—

But then it slowly penetrated through her brain that someone was calling for Christian, and with what sounded like a very French curse, he pulled free.

"Christian, goddamnit. Where the hell are you?"

It was Denny. With a grim smile, Christian looked down at Dorie's mouth, sweeping his thumb over her wet lower lip before turning and ducking under the palm fronds, walking away without a word.

"Yeah, okay," she said. "I'll just . . ." She lifted her hands. "Hang in there."

FOURTEEN

Still Day One,
still waiting for Ashton Kutcher
to jump out and yell, "Punk'd!"

Dorie, Cadence, and Brandy sat on a large rock, their feet dangling in the water, the surf splashing rhythmically against their calves. Denny had forbidden them to go back onto the boat, saying it wasn't safe.

So they sat. They'd debated whether Brad Pitt was still hot or not, and had moved on to Josh Duhamel when Andy came back from his visit to the boat, mouth tight, eyes wet, looking openly destroyed.

Behind him came Denny, Ethan, and Christian.

"Bobby's dead," Andy said hoarsely.

"Now wait a minute, we don't know that for certain," Denny said, but his voice broke. "We don't know anything yet." He looked out at the water, so calm now. "He's an excellent swimmer. I believe he's out there, waiting for rescue, same as us. Hell, he'll probably be picked up first."

Ethan's eyes looked suspiciously wet as well, and he nodded. "Yeah. Picked up first."

"What?" Brandy demanded, reaching for Andy. "What's going on?"

"He's missing." Andy allowed Brandy to hug him, for a moment gripping her tight as if he needed the support. "Been missing since last night, and I don't see how he could still be alive out there . . ."

"He went overboard," Denny admitted. "Sometime during the storm. We don't know how it happened, if he fell, or . . ."

Ethan was shaking his head. "He wouldn't have just fallen on his own."

The silence filled with dread and horror, especially for Dorie, who was beginning to suspect she hadn't imagined the two figures on the deck, the ones who'd disappeared.

"Let me get this straight," Brandy said to Ethan, her voice shaking. "You think one of us . . . pushed him?"

Dorie replayed the scene in her mind. Not hugging, but fighting. But as much as she tried, she couldn't place the figures as any of the people standing before her, no more than she'd been able to at the time of the fight.

"Ohmigod." Cadence staggered back a step.

"Let's not panic," Denny said. "Let's talk this out. Who saw him last?" He looked at Brandy. "You were with him last night."

"No." She shook her head. "You called him away—"

"I did, but he never showed up." Denny jerked his chin toward Cadence. "And she can attest to that, because she was with me—"

"Oh, no," Cadence said quickly. "I was only with you for a short time, and then I played cards with Andy in the salon—"

"For an hour," Andy agreed. "And when you left, I helped Ethan for the rest of the night wherever I could."

"Because I went to bed," Cadence said slowly. "I was tired."

"That's true," Ethan said. "Because you called for some crackers for your upset stomach, and I saw you in your room. But I didn't see Dorie or Brandy—"

"Hey," Brandy interrupted. "I told you—" She stuttered to a halt at a piercing whistle.

Christian's piercing whistle.

He lowered his fingers from his mouth and leveled them all with that icy gaze. "Arguing about your various alibis, isn't going to help. We have bigger problems—"

"Alibis? None of us need alibis," Andy said.

"We have bigger problems," Christian repeated, turning to the east, where the sun had fully risen, blinding them with its brilliance as if the storm never happened. "We need protection from the elements, especially for tonight."

When it would get dark.

Very dark.

"Maybe we'll be rescued by then," Cadence said in a small voice.

The look on Christian's face spoke volumes about what he thought of that. "No way of knowing how long it'll take. We can't count on anything."

Dorie thought of the TV show *Lost*, and how they were still waiting for rescue after multiple seasons and counting . . . She staggered back a few feet with the intention of sitting down on the nice flat rock behind her, only the flat rock moved. Just walked off. "A turtle," she murmured in surprise, holding out her hand to see if it would let her touch. "Look how ador—"

The turtle stuck out his neck and nearly snapped her finger off.

"Snapper." Christian moved toward the turtle aggressively, waving his hands, until the thing turned and slowly meandered off.

Christian turned to face her. "Just one of the services we offer. You know, along with luring you all into the South Pacific, then terrorizing everyone with unexpected hurricanes and uncharted snapper-filled islands."

"Christian," Denny said in a warning voice.

"Uncharted?" Andy shifted uneasily. "So we're truly alone here then?"

"The island's huge," Denny allowed. "We'll have to search it before we know what's here. For all we know, we're only a hike away from getting the Coast Guard out there for Bobby, and a good vodka tonic, straight up, for the rest of us."

Andy narrowed his eyes. "You really have no idea where we are."

"Unfortunately, no," Ethan said, accepting a quelling look from Denny. "Hell, Den, they might as well know it."

Cadence let out another low sob, and Denny slipped a hand into hers, his voice low, hoarse. "Listen, no bullshitting, okay? we're stuck here for now."

"And Bobby's gone," Brandy whispered.

"And Bobby's gone," Denny agreed. "And we're all looking at each other differently. We can't call the cops. We can't call anyone. It's just us. We have to rely on each other."

"It's more than that," Christian said.

"Christian, don't," Denny said tightly.

"No, tell us." Andy looked at them. "I want to know all of it."

"The storm knocked out our instruments," Christian said. "And along with it, all communications. If we made it as far as the outskirts of the Cook Islands, we need to lay low and not advertise our helplessness."

"Why?" Andy asked.

"In case of pirates," Ethan said.

Cadence abruptly sat on the sand. "Pirates."

Christian shook his head at Ethan. "We just have to stay calm and smart."

"We'll get you out of this." Denny looked at Cadence. "I promise."

"Yeah, did you make that promise to Bobby as well?" Andy asked.

Denny's jaw tightened. "For now, I'll ask that you stay put and let us figure things out." With that, he nodded to Christian and Ethan to follow him back to the *Sun Song,* where they began to secure the boat to the shore.

Shortly afterward, Denny and Christian hauled out the luggage for everyone to go through their things. Cadence, Brandy, and Andy jumped right on that, opening their suitcases and hanging their belongings to dry in the sun, talking quietly amongst themselves as they did. There was a spot for Dorie to join them, and she almost did, but instead headed in the opposite direction toward the *Sun Song.*

Christian had appeared, and leaned against the hull, head bowed, shoulders tight and stressed. He'd put on his baseball cap but not a shirt. He was barefoot.

With absolutely no expression on his face.

"Hey," she said.

He looked up. "Do you need anything?"

"Other than a plane? No."

He nodded, then straightened. She realized he was holding a small backpack. "Where are you going?"

"Scouting. To see what there is on the island."

Oh, God. He was going to go exploring. She'd already seen Christian's work ethic in action. She knew he was damn good at both sailing and being a doctor, but now she was struck by his sense of responsibility. They'd been shipwrecked, which really pretty much derailed his job and responsibility to any of them. Out here, he was just like her, a survivor. Each man for himself.

And yet he hadn't stopped working, or shucked a duty. Maybe he wasn't sweet and kind, at least in the traditional sense, but he had loyalty down to a science, and carried more responsibility on his shoulders than she could even imagine, managing with a grace and dignity she could only dream of.

She tried to picture him in her world, walking the aisles of Shop-Mart, dealing with a boss like Mr. Stryowski, and it was almost laughable.

He'd never fit into her world, because he'd never let his life live him. He lived his life, doing whatever it took, and more. Even now, surrounded by tragedy and destruction, he was prepared to do what had to be done, no matter that a coworker had gone missing, or that maybe he was hungry, or hot. He stood there, all lean and muscled and tough, gorgeous enough to be on a movie set waiting for the director to yell "action," and yet he was no actor.

And this was all too real.

"You don't think someone's looking for us, or that we'll be rescued today then?" she asked.

"All I know is that it's too hot for us to be okay out here for days. We need to know what our options are."

That he'd neatly avoided her question didn't escape her, and she wondered how he did it: how did he keep the emotions in check? And who was there for him when he needed someone? She had the feeling she knew the answer to that—no one.

But she wanted to be. In a way that made no sense, she wanted to be there for him.

He adjusted the hat low on his face, so that all she could see was his jaw, covered in two days' worth of beard. His torso was damp with sweat and tight with tension as he walked away from her.

She glanced at the others. Andy had pulled out some chewing tobacco and was showing Brandy and Cadence how to spit. Cadence looked to be surprisingly good at it. She should join them and leave Christian alone. Instead, she followed her heart.

After a few feet, Christian stopped. Sighed. "Dorie, go back. It's safest for you on the beach with the others."

The no shirt thing turned out to be hugely distracting. Without her permission, her gaze lowered to her favorite spot on a man—his belly. It was flat, ridged by his six-pack, and . . . well, quite fantasy-inducing. "How about you?" she asked. "What's safest for you?"

He let out a harsh laugh and rubbed at his jaw. Then he turned and kept walking, not stopping, not even when they came to a huge outcropping of rocks that prevented them from going any farther on the beach. Nope, he simply turned and began climbing the rocks, movements steady and sure, his skin practically steaming, his muscles bunching and releasing with each step.

Huffing and puffing behind him, not nearly as graceful, she grappled to keep up with him. "Could we slow down?"

"Go back, Dorie."

"Sorry. I'm done doing what I'm told."

He let out a sound that managed to perfectly convey his frustration.

"You do realize you never answer my questions, right?"

Blessedly, he stopped. Swiping his arm over his forehead, he looked at her. "You asked me what's safe for me. But trust me, you don't want to hear that I'm safer anywhere far, far away from you."

Her stomach plummeted. "You think *I* hurt Bobby?"

With a huge sigh, he scrubbed a hand over his face. "No, I don't think you hurt him. I don't think you could hurt a fly. That's the problem, I want you safe. Safer than I can get you."

Sometimes when he spoke, she found herself caught up in the accent, with the meaning behind his words following seconds later. This was one of those times. She blinked as what he'd said sunk in. "What does that mean?"

"Forget it." He went back to climbing.

Her thoughts raced. He thought he was safer away from her. Because . . . because maybe he was attached to her. Maybe so much that it scared him. She scrambled to keep up. "Christian—"

"Look, I'm still on the crew. Which makes me in charge, for better or worse." Towering over her, face tense, sweat streaking over his chest, he pointed down.

He was afraid for her. He cared about her.

"Go back to the beach."

"First ask me again how I am."

"I already know the answer."

"Ask me, Christian."

He sighed, and took a good look at her, probably seeing the emotion spilling all over her face, because he stepped over the rock between them, coming toe-to-toe with her.

She resisted the urge to put her hands on his damp chest. She had no idea why it was so unattractive when a woman perspired, but just the opposite when a man did.

Focus. "Ask me."

"Fine." A muscle in his jaw twitched. "How are you?"

"Bad."

He grimaced. "Look, you've been through a lot. You've probably never dealt with anything like this before, much less worried about the threat of possible physical violence, but—"

"You don't know that."

He arched a brow.

"Okay," she caved. "I've never been in this type of situation before. Nothing even close, but that doesn't mean I can't handle it. But it's you I'm worried about—"

"Me?" He looked incredulous. "I can handle it. I can handle anything."

And probably had. "You know Bobby personally. It's different for you."

He folded his arms over his chest, so close yet still so closed off to her. "So you've decided that I didn't kill him then?"

"Will it go to your head if I say yes?"

He gave her another of those long, penetrating looks that had her wishing she'd managed to do something more about her bedraggled appearance.

As if reading her mind, his gaze slid slowly down her body and then back up, but before she could read his expression, he turned his back on her and once again began climbing. "Go back to the beach," he repeated.

She eyed the sleek sinew of his back, the way his muscles bunched and stretched, his entire body working like a well-oiled machine, recognizing the steady, unwavering motions for what they were—suppressed grief.

He'd helped her earlier, helped her deal, and now she wanted to do the same for him. Hurrying to keep up, she reached out to touch him.

"Don't," he said, those muscles jerking beneath her fingers.

"It's a lot to deal with alone—"

"Goddamnit. At least I *can* deal." Belying that cool, unfathomable voice, he whirled away from her. "Bobby can no longer deal at all. I should be counting my blessings." He glanced at her. "And you should be counting yours, too."

"What does that mean?"

"It means if someone offed Bobby for being annoying, you might consider yourself in mortal danger."

Fifteen

Forget Ashton,
send the Coast Guard (and chocolate).

Five minutes later, Christian climbed straight up onto a plateau.
Shit.

Not high enough to see past the mountains behind them or the other side of the island, and not low enough to see any other routes, it was a dead end. "We could go into the rain forest, see if it leads anywhere," he said over his shoulder to Dorie.

"Oh, God. Really?"

He let out a sigh. He'd come back on his own. "Back to the beach then." He turned to Dorie, and caught her oogling his ass.

The sheer lust on her face created his own, which was bad. Very, very bad. "Dorie."

She shut her mouth and closed her eyes. "Sorry."

Sorry. How much of a jerk had he become that he'd made a woman sorry for wanting him?

"I'm going back now," she said.

"Good idea. Come on." He took her hand and they walked in silence back to the beach. Brandy was sunbathing. Cadence was busy with the luggage. Andy was standing near the water's edge, his Abercrombie and Fitch cargoes rolled up, his head down.

Dorie let go of his hand and headed for Andy, and Christian had no choice but to let her. He looked at the boat and tried to get his mind off her and whatever connection she was making with Andy. He'd tried to get the galley appliances working, but the water damage had been thorough. They had no working lights, refrigeration, or running water.

They would have to eat cold cuts and anything else that could go bad in the heat. By his own calculations, they would last approximately one more day without having to go search out food.

He hated the thought of barbequed snapping turtle.

Dorie was still with Andy.

"You really are something," Andy was saying to Dorie. "Beautiful." He touched her jaw.

Dorie swallowed hard. Christian's stomach tightened.

Dorie smiled, but it was a little weak. "Um, I hath to go get thomething."

Andy blinked. "Huh?"

She appeared to bite her own tongue, but she backed away. "I'm thorry, but—"

"Are you all right—"

"Thine." She whirled then, apparently not as easy to seduce as Christian would have bet on, and ran—

Right into Christian.

"Oh," she gasped as he caught her. "Sorry."

He peered into her face. "What's the matter with your tongue?"

"Nothing. Nothing now anyway. Excuse me." Pushing away from him, she moved down the beach toward Cadence and Brandy, who were turning over their drying clothes on the rocks. It was like a Frederick's of Hollywood sale, with panties and bras and things all over the place. Dorie sat in the center of it and pulled a pad of paper from her purse. She began drawing, her tongue between her teeth, her brow furrowed in concentration. With the humidity, her hair had gone wild, barely contained on top of her head with curly tendrils hanging down in her face, which she kept blowing away with an irritated huff.

She was no longer wearing his shirt, a fact for which he was grateful because the sight of his clothing on her had given him an unwelcome surge of possession over her. Now she wore a light-weight skirt and two camisoles layered over each other.

The clothes clung to her body, outlining her, a situation he couldn't say was a hardship to take in. She was only average height, really, and he supposed average weight, more curvy than thin, which was a bonus if he'd been looking to hook up with her.

He was not.

Not going to mix business and pleasure. Not when he had other, more pressing things to do—like help them all survive.

Lifting her pad, Dorie showed Brandy and Cadence what she'd drawn. Then she grabbed a palm tree frond and began twisting it, maneuvering it into some shape . . . a visor, which she set on Cadence's head.

Cadence laughed and handed her another frond for Brandy, and she twisted that as well, and they all laughed. Bonded.

Christian turned away. Ethan was gathering wood for a fire, and doing it rather ineffectively. With a sigh, Christian joined him, tripling the stack of wood in front of the makeshift fire pit in minutes.

"Thanks," Ethan said, swiping sweat from his eyes. "I need a break."

"We need to build a shelter first." Between the two of them they used the palm fronds and sail remnants to create an overhang to protect them from the elements, the relentless sun, and later, the night, which would be darker than their guests could imagine.

Cadence immediately got busy making the shelter homey, keeping her hands busy. Christian understood the feeling. He needed to keep himself occupied as well. He glanced at Dorie, and caught her watching him. She licked her lips, a nervous little gesture that gave her away, but not as much as her nipples hardening, an impressive sight in those two thin, layered tops.

Andy wandered over there. Of course he did, blocking Christian's view, to show Dorie his pants, which were ripped at the seam.

Dorie opened her purse and pulled out a small kit of some kind, doing something that included scissors and a needle and thread, all the while engaging in conversation with Cadence and Brandy. He had no idea how women could talk nonstop like that for hours on end; it was just one of those phenomena he attributed to having more estrogen than testosterone. But Andy didn't appear to mind that, or having her hands all over him as she fixed the pants.

Andy leaned in to kiss her, and she surprised both men by turning her head and giving him her cheek.

Andy kissed her, sliding his finger over her shoulder, his gaze briefly dropping to her breasts.

So did Christian's.

Her nipples were no longer hard.

She didn't get turned on by Andy, not like she had for Christian. He really wished he didn't know that.

"Here he comes," Cadence whispered.

Dorie's heart thumped hard. "Christian?"

"Baseball Cutie."

She turned. Yep, Andy was back, looking determined. *Oh boy.* He held out a frond. "Do me?"

"Uh . . ." Once again her tongue swelled and stuck to the roof of her mouth.

"Make me a visor?"

"Oh! Sure." She began twisting the frond, concentrating on that instead of her tongue, but then he sat close enough that their thighs brushed.

She glanced over at Cadence, who moved away to give them privacy, and then back to Andy. "Andy, I think I've given you the wrong impression." She couldn't believe she was going to do this. "I think you're a really great guy."

"Uh-oh," Andy said. "The 'great guy' speech."

Oh, God. This was hard. But after the past few days, after the way her body had sort of taken over and reacted to Christian, she couldn't continue with Andy. "I just don't think I'm right for you."

"You're exactly right for me. You're beautiful, sweet, and un-jaded. You're like a fresh breeze, and I—"

"Andy." She let out a disparaging sound. "Crazy," she said to herself. "I'm crazy for doing this."

"It's the heat," he told her earnestly, looking so gorgeous it physically hurt to look at him. "It's getting to me, too."

"No." She covered her face, then dropped her hands and looked right into his eyes, determined. "It's not the heat. You're not right for me."

He blinked, the rejection clearly new and foreign territory for him.

"I'm so sorry—"

"No. No problem. It's okay, I understand." And with a baffled smile, he moved off.

"Don't feel too bad, honey," Brandy said, moving in close. "In his world, women throw panties and phone numbers at him, nightly. They wait outside his locker room to have him autograph their boobs and to tuck their hotel keys into his pants. They blow him in those hotels, they don't blow him off. So really, you've done him a favor by giving him this experience."

It didn't feel like a favor. "It's all my tongue's fault."

"Hey, a tongue knows what it knows."

Was that even possible? Because Christian wasn't what she wanted . . . or at least not what she wanted to want.

First night on deserted island—
Where's Jeff Probst when you need him?

As the day turned into the dreaded night and they weren't rescued, Denny announced that they'd scout out the other side of the island first thing in the morning, by whatever means they could.

In the meantime, faced with impending dark and the resulting helplessness, they got a rip-roaring fire going, then sat around it, eating a feast of leftovers from the boat, prepared by Ethan.

He hoisted a bottle of vodka and took the first swig. "To Bobby," he toasted somberly, and passed the bottle around.

They each toasted to their fallen ship hand, while Dorie looked around at all their faces, trying to see who felt the most panic at being trapped here overnight.

But if someone was jumpy—not to mention guilty as hell—they kept it close to their vest.

She eyed the thick, lush rain forest that seemed to rise straight upward in the falling night, covering the volcanic peaks, stretching so high into the dusk sky that she had to tip her head way back to see it all. From inside that dark jungle came a steady stream of sounds that upped her nerve factor, though Andy assured her most of the strange, eerie calls came from birds.

Most.

But not all.

The thought would have brought more terror to her gut if there'd been any more room for it, but on the fright scale, she was just about maxed out, something not helped by the low fog that rolled in, upping the creep factor. The wet grayness moved with shocking speed, slipping over the craggy cliffs, like that from a smoke machine on a horror movie set.

"Oh, God, another storm." Cadence held her hands out as the first drops of rain fell.

"It'll only last a few minutes," Christian assured her. "The clouds snag on the mountains. The trees on the top trap the moisture until it's too heavy, and it all drops."

"A self-watering forest," Cadence murmured, still looking unnerved.

"It'll be over as soon as the cloud passes overhead."

Sure enough, less than three minutes later, when the cloud had passed, so had the rainfall, leaving the sky clear again. It might have all been just a part of the adventure and romance of the cruise, if the *Sun Song* hadn't been on its side in the shallow water, permanently grounded. Oh, and if Bobby hadn't been missing.

After eating, Christian and Denny used material from the *Sun Song*'s wrecked sails to add strength to the frond overhang they'd erected, and as darkness fell, Dorie was grateful for the protection, meager as it might be. Cadence worked on the inside of the shelter like a woman possessed, smoothing out the sand floor until Denny made her sit down and relax because she was making him dizzy.

"I need to keep busy," Cadence whispered, and shivered even though it wasn't cold.

Worried about her, Dorie pulled her back to the bonfire, where she sat next to her new friend and stared at the flames. Gazing at the red glow, Dorie tried to put things in perspective. So they were shipwrecked, so what. This was the new millennium. There were no uncharted waters. They'd be found in no time. Besides, big picture? She was a Shop-Mart salesclerk who'd managed to get herself halfway around the world and was getting an upfront and personal experience on a South Pacific island.

And, bonus, she was living her life.

"Truth or dare," Brandy said, plunking down next to them. "I pick dare. Someone dare me to go skinny-dipping in the waves. I've always wanted to do that."

"How about a PG version?" Dorie asked, not wanting to get naked.

Brandy sighed. "Fine. Truth."

Cadence looked at her. "Truth? Why aren't you freaked out about being here?"

"Hell. Skinny-dipping would have been much more fun." Brandy tipped her head up to the sky, which was becoming littered with stars as night took over. "Maybe I'm enjoying the break from my life."

"You think of this as a break?"

Brandy laughed, but it was mirthless. "Believe me, Cadence,

when I tell you there are far worse things than being stuck on a gorgeous deserted island for a few days." Brandy nudged Dorie. "Truth or dare?"

She wasn't ready for truth. "Dare."

"Go kiss one of our resident studs."

"Did I say dare? I meant truth."

Brandy smiled. "Okay, then. If we *were* playing the X-rated version of truth or dare, which stud would you have kissed?"

Oh, God. There was only one. Giving herself away, she glanced at Christian and found his gaze on her, intense and hot enough to singe her skin. Matching heat flooded her from the inside out. "Uhm . . ."

A scraping sound in the sand had her glancing down, where she discovered that not three inches from her sandals crawled—

"*Alligator,*" she cried out.

The crew came running at her shriek of terror, Christian at the head of the pack.

Dorie didn't move, just stared down at the foot-long, dinosaur-looking creature strutting past all of them as if it was king, holding a still squirming frog in his mouth.

"Iguana," Christian said.

The thing had wide beady eyes with a vertical pupil that gave it an alienlike expression, not to mention the prickly spiked ridges over each eye that almost made it look like it was wearing glasses. It's teeth were disarmingly plentiful, gripping its prize.

"He's got his dinner," Ethan noted.

Dorie did her best not to lose hers. "That poor frog is still alive!"

"Not for long." Ethan offered the bottle of vodka. "Here, this might help." He also had the last bag of chips. "Anyone?"

Brandy took the alcohol.

Cadence wanted to share.

Dorie went for the chips, and wished they were chocolate.

Denny went back to brooding on the *Sun Song*, and Christian and Andy tended to the fire.

Ethan stayed with the women. "Pass the vodka."

Dorie offered to pass the chips around as well, but Brandy shook her head. "I might as well lose a few pounds while I'm here, because if we don't get rescued in a timely fashion, I'm going to get fired. Being fit will help me get a job somewhere else."

"If I don't get back soon," Cadence said. "I won't finish a painting I'm doing on spec for a customer, and I'll lose my rent money for the month."

"If I don't get back . . ." Dorie paused. If she didn't get back, what would happen?

Nothing.

Nothing would happen, and nothing would change.

Not such a great thought. "I think I have changes to make," she said softly. "Serious changes." She realized they were all looking at her. "It's that whole waiting for life to happen thing. I need to stop doing that, and *make* it happen."

"Well, you could always go kiss a stud . . ." Brandy took a big swig of vodka. "In the name of the game."

Dorie's gaze locked on Andy and Christian. Andy stood on the far side of the fire, staring in the flames. Christian moved from the pit, walking toward the water's edge.

"Actually," she murmured. "You might be on to something."

"She is?" Cadence asked, shocked.

Brandy smiled. "You go, girl."

"Wait." Ethan snagged the bottle from Brandy and offered it to Dorie. "You might need a shot of this first."

Dorie took a swallow, choked, then handed it off. She stood, grabbed her purse, and started walking.

"Which one is she going after?" Ethan whispered.

"Not sure," Cadence whispered back. "But she has her purse and the box of condoms."

"A *box*?" Brandy asked.

Dorie kept walking, past the fire.

She heard Cadence's surprised intake of breath, or maybe that was her own. But she was no longer unsure of her next move. There was really only one thing to be done, probably there'd always only been one thing. Actually, one man.

And she headed directly toward him.

Sixteen

As Dorie approached Christian, he looked up, his face streaked with sand, sweat, and a barely banked misery that pretty much ripped her heart right out of her chest. "What is it?" she asked.

He lifted a hat, which he'd clearly just pulled from the water, an Astros baseball cap.

"Bobby's," she gasped.

He hung the hat off the closest palm tree and shoved his fingers through his hair.

"Christian?"

Swiping an arm over his forehead, he waited for her to talk.

She swallowed hard. For whatever reason, she'd had some misguided idea that she could approach this tall, dark, and attitude-ridden man, and seize the day. *Her* day. Now she simply wanted to give him some comfort, but was suddenly at a loss. She glanced back at Cadence and Brandy, who waved her on. *Right.*

She could do this.

"Can we walk?" It was a procrastination strategy, but he shrugged and grabbed his flashlight. They headed up the beach, Christian not saying a word, Dorie's heart hammering so loudly in her ears that she couldn't have spoken to save her life. The long, dark beach curved around, and within a few minutes they could no longer see the glow from the campfire, could see nothing but the dark outline of the island jutting up to the heavens on their right and the glimmer of the faint starlight on the waves on their left.

Dorie had always imagined a deserted island would be silent, but she'd been very wrong. The water crashed onto the sand. Insects buzzed, and given the ear-splitting decibels of the hum, they were damn large insects. The small colorful, plentiful birds hadn't gone to sleep with the setting sun, and their cries were piercing. Haunting. And she'd have sworn that not all those screeches and hoots were avian based, but she didn't want to think on that too long.

At a sharp curve in the beach, they met the rocky climb they'd made earlier, and silently took it again.

Ten minutes later, the steep incline once again gave way to the plateau that provided a windy, sweeping view of the dark beach far below. Dorie stood there, panting for breath.

She really needed to get serious about exercise. Assuming she survived her vacation, that is.

"What are we doing?"

"Seizing my day. My life."

"Huh?"

"I . . ." *Want to jump your bones.* "Um—"

"Shh," he said suddenly. "Do you hear that?"

Cocking her head, she listened. She could hear the wind rustling the trees. More insects buzzing. And then the lone cry of a bird. Surrounded by the wet, dark rain forest that she couldn't see, the lushness of it dripped with moisture, and even by the moon's glow, seemed vacuous. "I hear lots of things."

"Water." He pulled her off the rock and into—big gulp—the rain forest.

It swallowed them up whole.

One moment she could hear and see the waves below, and above the slender moon and billions of stars, and then the next moment, nothing. *"Christian."*

Taking her hand, he tugged her along. Damp branches and leaves brushed her arms and legs. Something touched her cheek, and with a squeak, she glued herself to Christian's back.

"What?" he asked.

She brushed a hand over his pagan-god-like shoulder. "You had something on you."

Seeing right through her, he snorted, then continued on, but suddenly went still.

Oh, God, what now?

"Look," he said.

She realized she'd closed her eyes in terror, and with a brave swallow, she opened them to find herself standing before a cliff that zoomed so high up she couldn't see where it ended. From somewhere up there fell a waterfall, landing into a natural pool about thirty feet below them. Lit by the moon, the water shimmered like live crystals, but the pool, shadowed by all the lush growth, lay still as smooth, black marble. Still but not quiet. Here even more insects buzzed, and the birds continued to chirp and squawk. Coming in all around them was the damp, warm night air, making everything seem too close.

Too intimate.

"Fresh water," he marveled, their feet sinking into the heavy, wet growth beneath them.

It looked like heaven on earth, and drawn to it, she took a step forward, only her foot went right through the thick growth and sank into the sand at the edge of the water.

"Watch it."

Watching it didn't seem to be her forte, but instead of letting her fall, he tugged her back against his nice, hard chest, which was beginning to be very familiar.

"You need a keeper, you know that." Arms still around her, he leaned back, Spine to the tree behind him, chest damp and hard, he stuck to her everywhere they touched, which was in some very interesting places. "Tell me you didn't just twist your other ankle."

She took quick stock. *Nope.* In fact, held against him as she was, her spine to his torso, backs of her thighs to the fronts of his, her bottom snugged to his crotch, everything felt pretty darn warm and fuzzy and happy.

Very happy. "Ankle's good."

"And you didn't lose that purse."

"Of course not."

"Of course not. You didn't even lose it in a shipwreck, so what am I thinking."

She had no idea what he was thinking, but she was thinking damn, it felt good to be held against his body, good to forget, even for a minute, the hell they'd found themselves in. Twisting to face him, she opened her mouth to apologize for this whole mess. But he kissed her.

She'd figured maybe they'd talk through their grief, but as a grief release, this worked, too. This worked just fine. Their hands grappled for purchase on each other while their tongues did the tango.

When he slid a hand beneath her tops and found her nipple with his thumb, her knees buckled . . . "I can't stand," she gasped.

Without missing a beat he whipped her around so that she was pressed to the tree, held there by his body. "How's that?"

"Good." *Incredible*

"Good." And he kissed her again.

Her flashlight dropped to the ground and skittered away, the beam shining off into the distance as his hands claimed her breasts while his mouth attached itself to her throat.

A freight train of lust surged through her veins. It'd been a long time, too long. Over a year ago she'd gone out with a guy five times before he got this far, and in his haste to get to the good stuff, he'd removed only the essential clothing on both of them, and had touched her breasts almost by accident as he'd made his way to ground zero (which he'd missed by a good three inches), getting inside her with just enough time to go off like a bottle rocket.

Leaving her over-revving her engine at the starting gate, and once again faking it.

But Christian seemed to have a whole other agenda going on, and she didn't have to fake anything, certainly not her reaction. He wasn't panting like a lunatic, whispering "Oh God, please don't let me come too fast . . ."

In fact, he wasn't saying a word, but that might have been because his mouth had other things to do. As he kissed her, long and wet and deep, she felt herself slipping under his spell, her body coming alive so that it practically shivered with anticipation, humming with a pleasure she couldn't quite contain. The sound of it escaped her with every whimpering breath.

Truth was, he had her halfway to orgasm without doing much more than kissing her, which made her as pathetic as her last date.

She'd be mortified later, because right now her body had taken over and was demanding the rest. *"Hurry."*

God, again with the out loud thing, but he didn't make fun of her. Instead, he slid a big, warm hand up her back, his fingers encircling her ponytail so that he could lightly tug, better angling her mouth to his. His other hand curled around her breast, his fingers rasping over her camisole-covered nipple, coaxing another gasp out of her. *"Hurry,"* she said again.

"Why? Is there a race?"

"My body thinks so," she managed as he dragged his mouth along her jaw, to her ear, which he sank his teeth into, yanking yet another gasping moan out of her.

"Shh." He laved the spot with his tongue, then shifted, bending his head to her throat, her collarbone. "Unless you want to be rescued by the others."

She shook her head wildly. She did not want to be rescued, not from this. He glided his tongue over her skin, heading toward her breasts, licking her through the cotton, and she couldn't help it, she made a noise of sheer lust.

He lifted his head and looked into her eyes, his own dark, so dark with heat, his mouth wet from kissing her.

"Don't stop," she said.

"Are you sure?"

"Very, *very* sure."

He nodded with intent, a wicked, naughty intent that made her go damp. Or damper. "You still have that box of condoms?"

Oh, God. "In my purse."

"I'm beginning to like that purse."

She fumbled to get to it while he went back to what he was doing. She'd been holding on to him for all she was worth, but at the first touch of his tongue, she cried out. *Damn it.*

A man of his own means, he took her hands and gently pressed one finger to her mouth. She nodded. *Shh.* She really was trying, but— "Ohmigod," she whispered when he tugged the spaghetti straps off her shoulders so that his clever, talented mouth could have more freedom. *"Ohmigod."*

Without a break in the wet, open-mouthed kisses he was trailing over her, he pressed her fingers to her lips again.

Right. Quiet. She was doing her best, but she was only human here, and her body had shifted to high, hopeful alert status, quivering with it, in fact. She peeked down at his dark head, at the direction he was heading with purposeful intent—which were her nipples, covered only because her tops had snagged on them.

Then he tugged again and her breasts were bared to the night air and his hot, hot gaze.

She had to close her eyes. She slapped her hands to the tree trunk on either side of her hips, needing the handholds. "Christian."

Again, he stroked a finger over her lips, then *his* hand covered her mouth, because apparently she wouldn't possibly remain silent with him now crouching down before her, her camisoles gathered at her waist, his fingers slowly pushing up her skirt. Her hands dropped from the tree to his shoulders and dug into the muscles there, and when he'd bunched the entire skirt up past her hips so that he had an eyeful of her panties, she went utterly still, torn between wondering why she'd put panties on today at all, and what would have happened if she hadn't.

Then he slid his fingers beneath the elastic edging at her hip, tracing it down . . . His knuckles brushed her center and she jerked at the touch. "Um—"

He tugged and words failed her. Then her brain failed her as well when he leaned in and kissed her.

There.

Oh, God. All she managed was a squeak.

He grabbed both her hands, having to peel them off his shoulders, and reaching up, again put them to her mouth. He pressed gently, silently encouraging her to shut the hell up.

So she held her hands over her own mouth and panted for air while he stroked her with his tongue, her head thunking back against the tree. She saw stars, felt the earth move, heard fireworks going off in her brain, the whole shebang, and it was most definitely not from hitting her head, though she did spare a second to think that next time she had wild tree sex she should really wear a helmet.

But then he added his fingers to the mix, and she completely and totally burst right out of herself.

An orgasm.

With a man.

Without working at it, she was having a mind-blowing orgasm. This time when her legs gave out, he let her fall, though he caught her, yanking her onto his lap, covering her mouth with his, his hands urging her thighs open, wrapping them around his hips.

Then his pants were somehow open . . . okay, she opened them . . . and she straddled him right there on the bank of the natural pool, on the soft, still warm sand beneath a skinny moon. Gripping her hips, he slowly pushed up inside her.

"Ohmigod!"

He wrapped her ponytail around his hand and pulled her head back to his, kissing her hard, ensuring her silence as he arched up, seating himself deep within her, oh God, so deep.

She'd never felt such a bone-melting heat, never, ever, and starting from within, working its way out, making it almost impossible for her to do the quiet thing. "Christian—"

"I know." He whispered this against her mouth, moving in and out of her with a heart-stopping sensation that was not only unexpected, but suddenly as necessary as air.

Her eyes were open, locked on his as he rocked his hips in a glorious, maddening, perfect motion. She stared at him, thinking he was so beautiful, all hard angles and intense heat. She'd never kept her eyes open during such an intimate moment before. Never thought to, but this felt so real, so real she almost couldn't stand it.

"Okay?" he whispered.

"*So* okay."

His smile was reward indeed. Lifting his head, he glided his mouth along her jaw to her neck, tasting her as he slid into her, over and over, until she tightened her legs around him, until she, unbelievably, felt herself begin to go over again.

Two orgasms in less than ten minutes.

She couldn't believe it, but she didn't even have time to marvel at it because he shifted, gripping her legs as he subtly changed the angle to thrust even more deeply inside her. A soft gasp escaped her at this, mirrored by his own rough breath. Her name was on his lips when he groaned and came, and she spared the second to think that it was the most lovely sound she'd ever heard, before she exploded all over him, giving herself up completely to the mesmerizing, sweet, hot, glorious sensation of being lost.

Even as she felt found.

Christian didn't know how long he and Dorie clung to each other by the lagoon, breathing like crazy, serenaded by the island, which pulsed with life around them.

That wasn't the only thing pulsing.

He could still feel her body twitching, contracting around him, milking him dry, and the sensation kept him hard.

She was something, so much so that he was going to be ready for round two if he wasn't careful. Normally at this point of the evening's festivities, his mind would already be wandering, but his brain remained solidly on task—*do her again*.

Focus.

From his vantage point of being flat on his back, he could see the two cliffs high above the lagoon. Closer, hanging from the rock just above them, was a cluster garden of poinsettias, oleanders, and an assortment of fruit trees: papaya, sour sop, tamarind . . . "We're not going to starve to death."

She didn't respond. Or, for that matter, move. That couldn't be good. Sinking his fingers into her hair, he lifted her face from where she'd pressed it into his shoulder.

She was wearing those sweet, drown-in-me eyes. In spite of himself, his heart rolled over and exposed its underbelly. Her mouth was soft, and just a little swollen from his kisses. And her hair . . . all over the place, more than usual that is, including a strand stuck to his jaw and another stabbing him in the eyes. Her two camisoles were still shoved down past her ribs, her skirt rucked up around her waist, exposing her mouthwatering breasts and the treasure between her legs, which made his mouth water even more.

Except for that look in her eyes. The one that said she was falling for him, that said she was making plans which undoubtedly included a white picket fence and a set of hopes and dreams to boot.

Even that wasn't his biggest problem. He could fall as well. He'd been having sex since his fifteenth birthday, when a nurse from his father's clinic had seduced him beneath a Brazilian summer night's sky. He'd been with his fair share of women since, maybe more than his fair share, and he'd even managed a few good relationships out of the deal.

But nothing compared to the five-minute quickie on this god-forsaken island in the arms of a woman with the eyes that could slay him in less than a single heartbeat. "Dorie."

She smiled. "I know. Sand. Everywhere."

When he didn't return the smile, hers faded, her expression telling him she was already prepared for rejection. "Don't worry, Christian. I know what that was. A release of fear, tension, and adrenaline. I'd get up, but my knees are still knocking together and I don't think I can stand."

He closed his eyes. She slayed him, all the way through.

With a soft breath that spoke volumes, she slipped off of him and moved away.

Jerk that he was, he let her go. Or started to. Then his damn conscience rose up and bit him on the ass. "Dorie."

She'd turned her back to him as she fought with her clothing, which involved a lot of muttering as she attempted to right her two tops. Finally she yanked them both off and started over.

He rolled to his feet, ignored the undeniable fact that his own knees were still knocking together as well, and watching her bare breasts bounce in the moonlight as she dressed didn't help. "Listen—"

"I'd head back alone, but I'm pretty sure I'd get lost." She said this very quietly, still not looking at him. "So if you could just point me in the right direction, and maybe watch my back—"

He took her arm and pulled her around to face him.

She studied something over his shoulder. "If we don't get back soon, they'll wonder—"

"I don't sleep with guests."

"Except for tonight," she pointed out still not looking him in the eyes.

Good point. "And I'm not sure why."

"I know why," she whispered. "For me, anyway. It's . . . been a long time. Really long."

In the dark he could sense her embarrassment and imagined that her ears glowed, and he felt a tug in the region of his chest. "I wish I could say the same, but—"

"You know what's really funny?" She laughed, the sound more heartbreaking than amusing. "I actually wanted to comfort you. Over Bobby. Can you believe it? I thought I could." She sighed. "Look, don't worry." She patted his arm. "We're okay."

Then she walked off.

"Dorie?"

"Trying to have a dignified exit here," she called back.

"Wrong way."

"Oh. Right." She did an about-face, passed him, and kept going, heading through the forest by herself in spite of her fear and trepidation, reminding him yet again like a punch to the gut just how brave and courageous a woman she was.

She'd laugh at that. She'd say *he* was the brave one, considering his job and how he'd lived. But she'd be wrong. Because she wore her heart on her sleeve, leaving it out there to be treasured.

Or not.

Brave as hell.

While he, on the other hand, had buried his heart deep, refusing to open it up for much of anything these days. Which made *him* the coward. He scrubbed a hand over his face. He just needed to let her go, and keep his distance.

Ahead of him the branches rustled, and then came a muffled female curse. He tipped his head up to the star-riddled sky. For a brief moment he actually considered letting her go on by herself, letting her walk away and go back to the beach on her own, all to maintain that distance he needed.

Another round of rustling, and a soft cry of distress.

Ah, hell. Of course he had to go after her. If by any chance at all she was right about Bobby being pushed off the boat then they were all still in possible danger, and even he wasn't coldhearted enough to not care. He headed after her, through the clearing, skidding to a stop at the sight of her at the top of the cliff, standing so still he'd have wondered if she was breathing if it wasn't for the single tear making its way down her cheek.

His heart, the one which only a moment ago had turned over and exposed its underbelly, cracked right down the center. "What are you doing?"

"Nothing." She swiped at the tear. "Nothing at all."

"Don't." He'd froze at the sight of her and that single tear on her face. "Don't cry."

"I'm not." She sniffed and hugged herself. "I'm not doing anything, I'm just standing here."

The pit of his stomach contracting into a knot, he took a step toward her, but was surprised when she jerked away.

"Look, I'm not crying over *you,* all right? So stop looking at me like that, all pitying and worried that you broke the poor stupid passenger's heart. You probably break all their hearts, but you didn't break mine. I'm crying because my ankle hurts, and because my hair is frizzy, because I look like something the cat dragged in, and because we're trapped here without M&M's, and *damn it, because my splinter hurts!*" She slid a hand over her ass and gingerly rubbed. "But I am *not* crying over you! I would never cry over you."

Okay, that was good. "Um . . ."

"That's *my* word, remember?"

He found himself wanting to smile. Only a moment ago he'd wanted to cut off his own stupid dick, but now he wanted to smile.

No doubt, she was slowly but surely driving him over the edge. "We need to ice the ankle if it's still aching."

"Okay, I'll just call room service."

"I have instant ice packs in my gear. And as for your hair . . . it isn't that bad—"

She glared at him.

Christ, had he learned nothing about women at all? "Actually," he said very quickly. "It looks just fine, I swear."

She didn't move a single muscle but he'd have sworn her ear cocked outward slightly.

She was listening.

He raced on. "And for the rest of your problems, well, I think I just proved I can't keep my hands—or my mouth—off of you, so you can cross the worries about your looks off your list. You're sexy as hell, Dorie, and so goddamn beautiful I had to talk myself out of having you again."

There. Her eyes met his. Definitely listening.

"And I should tell you," he said softly, moving a little closer. "I have a secret stash of M&M's in my bag, though they're the peanut ones. Do those work for you?"

Her eyes practically shimmered, full of so much emotion it almost hurt to look at her.

"If you're lying about the M&M's," she finally said shakily, "I'll hurt you."

He lifted a hand to his heart. "I promise. They're yours, if—"

Her face creased into disbelief. "There's an if?"

"If you let me help you get that splinter out."

Both hands went to her ass now. "No."

"There's no need for this . . ." He waved a hand toward her splinter. *"Savoir-faire."*

"What?"

"False modesty. Look, I just got an upfront and personal view of every inch of you, remember?"

"It's not modesty." She bit her lower lip. "Okay, it is. But . . ."

"But?"

"I just had a quickie, and I don't do quickies. Worse, I did it with a guy who prefers to pretend it didn't happen. I really need to be alone with the M&M's."

"I can't leave you alone."

"Then don't. *I'll* leave *you* alone." And with that, she walked away. Luckily, she walked the right way, so he didn't have to do anything but follow at a respectful distance.

But as he did, he wondered at the odd sense of regret he felt, and the certainty he'd just blown the best thing that had ever happened to him.

Seventeen

Dorie made it back to camp, passing the fire pit to go directly to the makeshift shelter.

Cadence and Brandy sat on two pads, with a third between them, made up like a bed at a luxury hotel.

"Here, for you." Brandy patted the empty pad. "Ethan set us up. Four-hundred-thread-count Egyptian silk, can you imagine?"

There was even a chocolate on her pillow.

"Also Ethan," Cadence said. "Are you going to eat yours?"

"Knock yourself out." Dorie plopped down on the pad, and feeling Brandy's steady gaze on her, shifted uncomfortably. "What?"

"You gave up chocolate. Willingly."

"I'm not hungry."

"Now, see, that right there is a sign." Brandy looked her over some more. "Plus your hair is a little wilder than usual, and your skirt seems slightly twisted off to the side. Interesting."

Dorie tried to adjust her skirt.

"But most telling? Your camisoles were layered white over the pink when you left, and now the pink is on top."

Crap.

"Find what you need out there in the rain forest, hon?"

"Oh, you know . . ." Dorie lifted a shoulder and tried to be cool. "What are you guys doing?"

"Having a slumber party," Cadence said. "Which would be better with chips, drinks, and gossip."

"I've got the rest of the chips in my purse," Dorie said.

Brandy pulled out her flask. "And I've got the other two covered." She took a healthy swig and passed the flask to Dorie. "So. You got laid."

Dorie choked.

Brandy looked across the fire. Dorie followed her gaze to Christian, who'd reappeared from the forest and stood at the bonfire, staring into the flames. He still had the whole edgy, brooding thing going on, but there was something else, too. A definite lessening of the tension in his body.

Dorie knew what that came from, and felt her face heat.

Cadence blinked. "You had sex with Christian?"

"Okay, I need chips for this." Dorie opened her purse and the box of condoms fell out.

"Huh." Brandy fingered the opened box. "Look at that. Wonder how many are missing?"

Dorie snatched the box back and shoved it low in her purse. "I don't want to talk about it."

"Was he yummy?" Brandy asked.

Cadence was still gaping. "You. And the doctor. *Holy smokes.*"

Dorie found the chips and started shoving them in her mouth

even though she wasn't hungry. "I'm going to need that chocolate back, Cadence."

Cadence handed it back.

"Oh yes, he was yummy," Brandy decided, clapping in delight. "And of course he would be. I mean, look at him. He walks with that sexy confidence, the one that says 'I don't give a shit what you think of me, I know who I am.' Gotta love that in a guy." She sighed. "And then there's all that attitude." She shivered. "Yeah, I'd bet big money he knows exactly what he's doing." She leaned back with her hands behind her head and studied the stars. "So Cadence, does the captain know what he's doing, too?"

Cadence set down the flask and blushed beet red. "I told you I didn't sleep with him. Just . . . messed around a little."

Dorie grabbed the flask. "I guess we've all been a bit busier than I thought."

Cadence snatched the chips. "Don't take this wrong, Brandy, but I'd have sworn that if anyone was going to hook up on this vacation, it'd have been you."

"Fair assumption." Brandy accepted the flask back and toasted them. "But I'm taking over your penis embargo for a while."

"Why?"

"Someone's got to carry the torch. Besides, this is more fun."

Cadence laughed in disbelief. "Which part of this is the fun part?"

"Being away from my life is fun," Brandy said. "And though there's nothing remotely okay about what's happened to Bobby, I have to say, this is really nice, with you two." For the first time all night, she hesitated. "I haven't made a lot of time for girlfriends."

"Me either," Cadence said quietly.

"Or me," Dorie admitted.

"Well then." Once again Brandy lifted the flask. "To our friend-ship. And to whatever adventure is ahead of us."

They all drank to that, and later, after polishing off the chips, lay back and slowly drifted off to the island's own personal concert of night sounds.

But Dorie couldn't fall asleep, and restless, she moved to the fire. She figured it was well past midnight.

Not that time mattered here.

"Dorie?"

At the sound of Andy's low southern drawl, she turned. He'd gone to sleep beneath a palm tree but he was up now, walking toward her. She searched his face for a sign that he knew she'd turned him down only to have wild animal sex with Christian in the rain forest.

Oh, God.

She'd had wild animal sex with Christian in the rain forest.

She swallowed hard and looked at Andy intently, but if he knew, he gave no indication of it. "Are you okay?" she asked.

"That was my question for you."

"I'm fine. Go back to sleep."

"You sure?"

"Absolutely." Dorie watched him go, then turned back to the flames. The red glow was hypnotic and soothing. Or it would have been if she could shake the certainty that one of the people stuck here with her had hurt Bobby.

She walked to the water's edge, and with the water lapping at her toes, she looked at Bobby's hat hanging off the palm tree. "I'm sorry," she whispered to it. "So sorry."

"You shouldn't be out here alone."

Turning at the French voice, she looked up into Christian's fath-omless eyes, and then . . . and then closed them. "You're right." She began to walk back toward the fire. It was for his own good really, because if she stayed one more second, she'd ask for something he couldn't give her. A hug, maybe.

Or another round of wild sex in the jungle . . .

The night was dark, the sounds all around so alien and unfamiliar, but she flicked on her flashlight and kept moving down the beach, past the fire. It wasn't bravery, because she had a feeling she was better off alone, at least until she knew what had happened to Bobby.

She really could use that hug.

Christian was following her, she could hear him. Probably making sure she didn't get lost again. Damn, more evidence of that sweetness, the kindness she'd convinced herself he didn't have. She sped up, her silly sandals squishing into the sand. If she ever got home, she was going to design some seriously sensible sandals. They'd be beautiful, of course, but easy to run in.

Risking her neck, she burst into a run now, because suddenly she didn't trust herself not to beg for that hug, and if he gave it to her, she'd definitely lose her panties. "Ow, ow, ow . . ." Her damn splinter hurt like hell—

"Dorie."

Oh, no. Kicking it into higher gear, she turned the corner, away from the glow of the fire, away from the others, needing a private pity party, if only for a moment.

The rocks were stacked one upon another, making cliffs that jutted straight up, hundreds of feet into the sky. By day those cliffs had been green, teeming with lush growth, but now, at night, it was all black, looming, and suddenly terrifying.

Since Christian wasn't wearing silly sandals, and probably exercised more often than when someone gave him a gift certificate to a gym, he easily caught up with her and grabbed her arm, spinning her around to face him.

"I thought you said you don't do guests," she huffed, out of breath. "Now you want round two?"

"While that invitation is ever so romantic, no. I had something else in mind." He pulled out a small first-aid kit.

Opening it, he lifted a—

"Oh, no." She laughed, then shook her head at the gleaming pair of tweezers. "You're not going to come anywhere near me."

"Funny, you weren't saying that a little while ago." He still had a gentle but inexorable hold on her, and using that, led her to a large rock, upon which he sat.

She held her own butt, her gaze glued to the tweezers. "I'm not sitting."

"No. You're going to bend over and let me take care of your business." Unperturbed, he calmly fished through the first-aid kit for God knew what else.

"My business has been taken care of."

He looked up at her words. Met her eyes. His mouth quirked as if he wanted to smile. "Yes, and that was my pleasure, believe me. This"—he gestured to her butt—"this is my job."

She didn't budge. "Yeah, um . . . about that other."

His eyes heated. "Yes?"

She shifted her weight from one foot to the other. "My . . . *business* . . . doesn't usually get taken care of so easily."

Now he did smile. "Like I said, my *pleasure*. Now get down here."

"I don't think you understand what I'm saying."

"I understand English," he said. "Quite well, even though it's my third language. I understand analogies as well. You had an orgasm. Several, actually. I felt each of them, trust me. Watching you come, feeling you contract around me, was the highlight of a very fucked-up evening. Now come here."

The steel of the tweezers gleamed in the moonlight, making the muscles in her bottom twitch. "It's just that I don't understand what came over me, because . . ."

When she didn't finish her sentence, he arched a brow. "Because?"

This was simply too difficult with him looking at her. "Nothing. Forget it." She whirled to go, but he caught her hand. He looked up at her with a patience she would never have guessed at, and she let out a long breath. "I don't usually come like that . . . Well, I do, but only because I sort of . . . Oh, God." She covered her face.

"Just out of curiosity," he asked easily. "Are *you* still speaking English?"

"The last time I slept with somebody, I faked it."

"Faked it."

"The orgasm."

"Ah. *Now* we're getting somewhere."

Hands still over her face, she groaned. "Seriously, could you just not listen to me?"

"Did you fake it like the *When Harry Met Sally* fake it?"

"I don't think I was that good." She absolutely could not believe her mouth was betraying her this way. "The point is, I don't usually go so . . . wild."

He looked at her for a long moment. "Funny," he eventually said, looking a bit wicked and naughty and far too damn proud of himself. "You didn't seem to have any trouble with me."

EIGHTEEN

"You know what? We're not doing this," Dorie decided. But when she whirled away from Christian's far too gorgeous face, he once again caught her.

"Sorry. We're not done here." He clicked the tweezers open and closed.

Again her bottom twitched, and she quickly played the compassion card. "Seriously, Christian."

He put a mock look of fierce intensity on his face. "Seriously."

"It's just too embarrassing. I mean it's on my thigh."

"No, it's on your ass."

She felt herself get even redder. "Okay, yes. So you can understand why I'm feeling . . . awkward."

He grinned. "That's not what I'm feeling."

She drew a deep breath that did nothing for her nerves. "Sort of my point. Look, you're not going to get it out anyway, I tried. It's in there good."

"I can get it out."

"Not without a needle, and—"

"I'll get it, Dorie, I promise you."

"You can't, it's—"

"I'll bet you."

She blinked. "What?"

"You're so sure I can't get the splinter, I'll bet you. You name it."

"I . . . that's crazy."

"Not if you're so sure I can't get it. Come on, let's go for broke. If I get the splinter, you dance naked beneath the stars."

She laughed.

He just waited.

"You're kidding."

"What's the problem?" he asked silkily. "If I'm not going to get the splinter?"

There was no way he could, and yet that look on his face, that utter confidence, tripped her up. "What do I get? If you lose." Which he would. He had to, because she was not going to dance naked. No way, no how.

"If I can't get the splinter out, I'll dance naked for you."

Okay, now *that* might be worth the price of admission. "This is totally and completely crazy."

"Chicken?"

"Of course not." *Hell, yes.* "I just don't see any reason to worry about the silly splinter, that's all." She plopped down on the rock, let out a little cry when the stone hit the splinter, and bounced right up again.

"Okay, that's it." He clamped a hand around her wrist, this time an inescapable grip, and pulled her onto his lap. Slipping his arms around her, he leaned in and surprised her with a kiss. Because he was the most amazing kisser on the face of the planet, she helplessly sank into it for several long, delicious, mind-blowing minutes. By the time they surfaced for air, she had her hands in his hair, and was rubbing herself against the intriguing bulge at the vee of his jeans.

With a low murmur of pleasure, he pulled her in for yet another deep, drugging kiss, then slid out from beneath her, sinking to his knees beside her, pulling her down with him, turning her so that she faced the rock.

Oh, God. He was going to slip into her from behind, and her legs trembled because she was going to let him. Just to see if she could come again without any effort at all, she told herself. Call it research.

Or sheer, unadulterated, uncontrollable lust.

He bunched up the material of her skirt, pushing it high. But instead of skimming her panties down, he slid them aside, bunching them where no panties should be bunched, giving her a world-class wedgie. "Hey—"

"Shh."

She was just surprised enough to actually close her mouth, but then he flattened one hand on her bottom and ran a finger over the crease of her upper thigh, right where she'd removed the first splinter. "Good work," he said. "Where's the other one?"

"Don't you even *think* about it," she hissed, and began to struggle.

"Too late, I'm thinking." He whisked her panties down to her thighs, leaving her hanging out in the wind. "Ah," he murmured. "There it is." He might have said other stuff, too, but Dorie was too busy trying to get free in order to kill him.

"Hang on," he said.

Hang on. *Hang on?* Was he crazy? "Don't you *dare*—"

He spread his hand over her now bared bottom, holding her down. "I just need a light"—he rifled through the first-aid kit—"Perfect."

He'd found a flashlight. Which meant she was going to die of embarrassment right here. "We're not doing this."

"Not we," he corrected. *"Me."*

"I mean it, Christian—"

"Damn it, it's infected." He said this while still holding her down with ease, and she scrunched her eyes tightly shut because now that she wasn't blinded by lust, she could only imagine the picture she made for him, bent over the rock, her skirt shoved up to her waist, her panties pushed down to her thighs, exposing—

"This might hurt a little—"

"Ouch!" She yelped at the sharp prick, and would have whipped around except for that whole holding her down thing. Almost before she could draw a breath, she felt his finger stroke the spot with something cool and incredibly soothing.

"Topical antibiotic," he said. "Be still, you're squirming all over the place."

Her head was buried in her arms, her eyes still tightly shut. *Be still?* She was hoping to *die.*

"Relax, I've seen it all before. A million times."

Yeah, just what she wanted to hear. *Idiot.* She was an idiot. "Thank you," she managed, but the words backed up in her throat when his finger left the spot, replaced by— *"What are you doing?"*

"Kissing it better," he murmured, his mouth against her skin.

She jerked upright, which had the effect of bouncing his mouth off her butt, and whipped around, shoving her skirt down as she did. "Okay, thank you for the splinter removal, but—"

He sat back on his heels, his eyes gleaming with good humor. "Yes?"

"That was entirely inappropriate."

A full-blown grin left him at that. "You didn't say that the first time I had my mouth on your—"

"Okay, you have to stop that," she said, pointing at him. "Stop talking dirty."

"That's not talking dirty." He rose to his feet, a lithe, easy motion, and took a step toward her. "Now this is talking dirty . . ." And he pulled her into his arms, putting his mouth to her ear, whispering things that made her legs wobble.

Between them she could feel herself go damp. "Okay, yes that was dirty." She drew in a shaky breath. "But we decided not to do this again, remember? Now I'm going to bed."

His eyes were sleepy and sexy as hell. "Fine. But what about the bet?"

Oh good God. "I did not agree to dance naked."

"I took your silence as agreement."

"Well, it's a shame then that you didn't specify which night." Brilliant! "Because it'll be the night that hell freezes over."

His mouth curved in a little smile, but mercifully, he let her get away with it. Probably because when it came right down to it, he knew as well as she did that doing it again would be a colossally bad idea. So she faked a smile the way she'd faked orgasms—pre-Christian, that is. And then, with her pride intact—at least some of it—she turned and began walking back. She passed Bobby's hat—sobering—and went directly to the pad Ethan had set up for her earlier, no longer in a talking or eating or anything kind of mood. Curling up beneath the very late-night stars, she closed her eyes and attempted to get some sleep.

Instead, she lay there for hours listening to the waves crash against the shore, because sleep wouldn't come.

Day Two on deserted island—
Why isn't caffeine a staple of all emergency kits?

Dorie woke up at the crack of dawn to a symphony of birds and more of the waves pounding the sand. She tried not to let her brain kick into gear, because just beyond her grogginess she could sense a whole lot of stuff weighing her down, just waiting for her to remember.

But whether she liked it or not, it all came crashing back to her. Shipwrecked. Bobby gone.

Sex in the rain forest . . .

She sat up just as Brandy did the same next to her, and took a second to realize that for the first time in several days her bottom didn't hurt.

Fancy that. Still, it'd be a cold day in hell before she admitted it.

Or danced naked for a certain far too sexy for his own good doctor.

"Uh-oh," Brandy said, and looked at Cadence's empty pad. "Think she's okay?"

"Let's make sure."

They found her down the beach, facing the surf, talking to herself. Muttering, mostly.

"You had to go off the beaten path," she was saying. "You had to jump at this stupid vacation, just because it was free. Seriously, when will you learn to just stay home and relax in your own world—"

"Hey, girl," Brandy said.

Cadence whipped around, the stick in her hands coming up like a sword as she prepared to stab them, her eyes wild and full of violence. "Haaaiii–yaaaa," she screamed like a kung fu master, until she focused. "Ohmigod." Hostility deflated, she dropped the stick and stepped back. "I'm so sorry."

Dorie, shocked at the sheer aggression that had been inside Cadence's eyes, swallowed. "You know martial arts?"

Cadence sagged to the sand. "My therapist thought it'd be a great way to relieve stress. I've been taking classes for seven years, but it's not working."

"Seven years?" Brandy turned and looked at Dorie with a raised brow that said *holy crap, look at the meek one now.* "Impressive."

Dorie agreed but kept the thought to herself, still a little uneasy at what she'd seen in Cadence's eyes, because it drummed home the point that she didn't really know any of these people . . .

Or what they were capable of.

By mutual consent, they walked into the forest to handle their business behind different trees, but when Cadence let out a little scream, both Dorie and Brandy came running, Brandy with a knife in her hands at the ready.

Cadence pointed to a snake that slithered off into the forest, and sagged back against a tree. "Sorry, it startled me."

Knife gleaming, Brandy shivered wildly. "No problem. I hate snakes."

Dorie couldn't take her eyes off the blade. *Had everyone lost their minds?*

Since when had they all armed themselves?

"Hey, check this out." Brandy walked to a coconut tree and swiped the knife through the air, and a few coconuts came crashing down to the ground. "Man, that's satisfying." She did it again, bringing three more coconuts down. "This is what I should have done to my ex's family jewels."

"So," Dorie asked as casually as she could, "where did you get the knife?"

"Oh, this?" Brandy flipped it around like a Japanese chef, then stuck it in the waistband of her tiny Daisy Dukes. "I've been carrying it for protection. Turned out I needed it more than I thought."

"Have you ever used it?" Cadence asked.

Brandy's smile faded. "Not lately, if that's what you're asking."

They all walked back, silent now, each lost in her own thoughts. Dorie was certainly lost in hers. She thought she'd known these women, but it turned out, they were still basically strangers. Not a comforting thought.

Brandy kept fiddling with the tag on her top, which was a snug designer tee that read: *I don't mind that you are talking so long as you don't mind that I'm not listening.* "This thing is driving me crazy." Pulling the shirt off, leaving her in a tiny red string bikini top, she yanked at the tag . . . and ripped a nice hole in the shirt. "Well, shit." She thrust it into Dorie's hands. "You're a designer. Redesign."

They all sat on a large rock. Dorie set down her purse and ripped off the sleeves of the tee, then after a few more strategic tears began using her handy needle and thread.

"Oh, yes," Brandy said when Dorie tied her into her new halter top. "Very nice. You really ought to do this for a living, hon."

Yes. Yes, she should.

When they came out of the forest, Christian was dragging more wood to the fire. He nodded to Dorie, who didn't have it in her to just nod back. So she smiled. "Need help?"

Moving wood, taking off your clothes . . .

"I'm good."

Code for "don't talk to me." Got it. Luckily, Ethan had break-fast waiting, because nothing worked for awkward moments like a pile of food.

"This is the last of the meats I had frozen," Ethan told them, gesturing to the sausage and bacon, which he'd cooked over an open flame. "It all defrosted, so eat up."

Unsettling thought, eating the last of the protein. While they did, Denny stood up at the head of the group. "I thought I heard an engine this morning."

Everyone stopped eating and gaped at him.

"So we're going to divide and conquer. I'm going east. Ethan to the west, while Christian stays on the beach to keep the fire going for the smoke signal and to look after you."

"But what if we want to help explore?" Cadence asked.

"No. Your only job is to sunbathe, rest, and relax."

"What if we don't want to?" Cadence asked. "Relax, that is."

"Yeah. I'd like to explore," Brandy pitched in.

"Oh, no." Denny shook his head. "Too dangerous."

"No offense, Denny," Brandy said, "but you're not in charge of us on land."

From across the fire, Christian dropped an armful of logs, and locked gazes with Dorie, giving her a little zing of sexual awareness.

Damn it.

Swallowing hard, she turned her attention back to the conversation at hand.

"Sitting on the beach waiting to be rescued seems so passive," Cadence said to Denny. "I think we should all go, if we want."

All? Dorie wasn't in a hurry to hike/climb in the rain forest. "Maybe we should think about this—"

"We want to go," Cadence said. "All of us."

"Cadence, listen to me," Denny said. "It's going to be hot, sweaty, hard work—"

"We're going." This from Brandy, in a voice of steel.

New society, new rules, Dorie thought. Or maybe no rules at all . . . Fact was, they were all operating on sheer nerves at this point. And no matter how much she wanted to think otherwise, she was alone.

Once again her gaze collided with Christian's.

He looked back, his expression shuttered, but she could see past that, to the man beneath. No matter that they'd knocked their good parts together, no matter that they'd decided not to knock those parts together again, she could trust him.

Which mean she wasn't entirely alone after all.

Andy used a large stick to beat the branches away from his face as they walked. Ahead of him, Ethan did the same as he led them higher and higher up the rocky volcanic precipice.

Behind them both, Dorie gasped for breath and tried to keep up.

Andy slowed, and smiled at her. "You okay?"

"Terrific."

Denny, Brandy, and Cadence had gone in the opposite direction, with Denny determined to find the source of the engine he thought he'd heard.

Christian remained back at camp, manning the fire and watching for boats. He hadn't wanted to, but Denny had insisted. Dorie had wanted to stay, too, but if she had, the condoms in her purse would be calling her name about now, so she'd gotten off her tush, telling herself the exercise would be good for her. "I hope the other group is okay. I'm worried about them."

"I'm worried about us," Andy said.

"Why?"

"Because we're on a deserted island. Because rescue hasn't come. Because one of us is dead."

Her heart clutched. "We don't know that."

"Do you really think he hung on this long?"

"Maybe he was rescued."

Andy's face said what he thought of those chances.

Dorie swiped a scary-looking bug away. "What exactly are we looking for?"

"A lux hotel, darlin'. With all the amenities of a *real* vacation."

Dorie huffed out a laugh, then tripped over a fallen tree, managing to catch herself before she fell. "I've *got* to get better shoes."

Ahead of them, Ethan kept walking, the distance between him and his two charges getting bigger and bigger. "Go at your own pace," he called back.

Her own pace would be on her butt on the beach, which she could have actually pulled off now that she was splinter-free. Thinking about how Christian had removed it by flashlight brought a surge of renewed embarrassment.

Andy looked at her and stopped. "You're awfully red. Let's sit a moment."

"No, I'm good." Pulling away, she walked backward, smiling at him, thankful he couldn't read her thoughts—still on Christian, and how he'd kissed the spot. "Let's just keep—"

Andy's worry turned to alarm. "Dorie—"

"Going—"

"Dorie, watch out—"

Too late.

She tripped over another fallen log and tumbled backward over the huge stump.

Nineteen

She was on an island with a cabana boy leaning over her, the sun so bright she couldn't see his face as he offered her a cool drink—

"Dorie, wake up!"

No, thanks. The cabana boy shifted out of the sun, and turned into . . . Christian.

Her heart warmed. Not just her good parts, but her heart. *Huh.*

"Dorie, damn it, open your eyes."

She did, becoming aware of two things. One, she had a sharp pain in her head, and two, the face floating in front of her was blurry, the voice foggy because her ears were still ringing, but she smiled anyway because this made three times Christian had rescued her.

"Dorie? Darlin', say something."

Wait. No French accent. No low, husky voice that gave her

warm fuzzies, but Andy, and his adamantly hunky smile and sweet eyes. Only . . . she blinked to make sure . . . his eyes weren't look- ing so sweet at the moment, but . . . *uh-oh.* "Grandma," she said weakly, "what big eyes you have."

He smiled tightly. *The better to see you with, my dear.*

She swallowed hard. "And what big teeth you have."

The better to eat you with, my dear.

With a gasp, she sat straight up, then cried out at the dagger of pain between her ears.

"Jesus, Dorie, are you all right?" His hands settled on her shoulders.

To hold her down and eat her with. Those big fangs would help, too. With a little scream, she scrambled backward, cringing at the quick movement.

"Darlin', don't. Don't move."

"What did you say?" she asked hoarsely.

"Uh . . . don't move?"

"Before that. The eating me part."

The look on Andy's face defied description. "Nothing about eating you."

When she blinked again, he looked the same as always. Too cute for words, his eyes normal, teeth normal.

"You cracked your head," he said, clearly worried. "Let me—"

Unable to dispel the nightmare, she batted his hands away.

Stymied, he sat back on his heels. "Dorie? Do you know who I am?"

"Depends on whose teeth you've got at the moment."

"Uh-oh," he said.

"My head." She clasped it between her hands. "I think it's going to fall off." She touched her neck, to make sure it wasn't severed.

It wasn't.

Unwilling to keep sitting on the ground, she stood, then cringed. "Oh, dear," she whispered, her head spinning. Worse, so was her stomach, prompting her to go very, very still.

"Oh, crap." Andy leapt up, and out of her way, though she didn't actually throw up.

"I'm okay. I'm just . . ." She sat back down abruptly as her world continued to spin on its axis. "Going to sit right here for a minute."

"Good idea. *Ethan!*" Andy yelled, cupping his hands around his mouth. "Ethan where the hell are you? Dorie's hurt!"

So once again she'd shown her graceful side. *Nice.* Just like any minute now, she was going to show her ill side. She held her breath, willing to sell her soul to the devil rather than throw up in front of Andy.

"Dorie? Talk to me."

"Watch your shoes."

He backed up again, but she managed to keep her breakfast down. "Stop the world," she murmured. "I want to get off."

"Where the hell did Ethan go?" He slid his fingers gently into her hair, probing her scalp. "Ah, hell. You've got a huge goose egg here. Let me see your eyes."

She blinked at him. "Why?"

"I'm not sure." He stared into them. "But that's the first thing the team doc does when we get hit in the head with a line drive."

Her stomach pitched as if she was still on the *Sun Song* in the storm, and she clutched at his arms. "It's choppy out here."

"Oh, boy." He slid his arms around her. "You're screwed up, darlin'. Let me carry you back."

She wanted to say no, she was fine, except for one thing.

She wasn't.

He pulled something out of her hair—a stick. And then another.

"Get the bugs first."

"You don't have bugs." But he did pull out a leaf. "Hey, you don't seem so tongue-tied now, right?" He smiled into her eyes. "Maybe we could give this thing another shot after all."

"I'm not tongue-tied because I'm going to throw up."

"You're pale, but not green." His worried eyes searched her features. "Your skin's clammy and your eyes are glossy. But mostly, I'm concerned about the size of that lump."

"Really, I'm okay." Probably. Maybe. Hopefully . . .

The bush rustled again, bigger than before. Someone was coming. And not from the way Ethan had vanished, but from the direction they'd come from.

Andy got to his feet, his back to her, protecting her. She stood, too, and then had to cling to him for support because she was on an invisible roller coaster. She really hoped it wasn't a pirate, coming to pillage. "Get out your knife," she whispered. "Or whatever you have."

"What?" Andy twisted around and stared down at her in shock. "I don't have a knife."

So not everyone had armed themselves. Maybe he hadn't felt the need, because he'd been the one to hurt Bobby.

She set her forehead to his back, not because she wanted to touch him, but because she needed him to support her upright.

From out of bushes came . . . the other group. Brandy, Cadence, Denny, and . . . and *Christian*?

"Whew," Brandy said, swiping her forearm over her forehead. "Hot shit today, huh?"

"Too hot," Cadence agreed. "We went west forever, and came to one great big hike straight uphill, which led to nowhere except a bigger, sharper, more unclimbable cliff. We decided to try your way, and found Christian. Gorgeous Grumpy Doctor here thought he heard a cry for help."

"Gorgeous Grumpy Doctor?" Christian repeated. "What the hell is that?"

Dorie looked around for a hole to fall into. Oh, wait. She'd already fallen.

"I want some answers," Denny demanded.

"Yeah? I want a shower," Brandy told him. "And a massage."

"I want a real bathroom," Cadence said.

Christian didn't say anything, he just came straight at Andy, then reached around him for Dorie.

"It's okay," Andy said. "I've got her."

But Christian didn't let go, and for a moment, just a very brief beat really, there was a silent tug-of-war over her.

Dorie couldn't believe it. Two outrageously handsome men wanted her.

Her.

And she was going to throw up.

"Why are you green?" Christian demanded to know.

"It's my favorite color."

He pulled her close, then frowned down into her face. Without a word, he supported her while looking her over with a staggering intensity. *"Que s'est produit?"*

"Um, what?"

"What happened?"

Before she could answer, thunder boomed, and they all jumped. A storm had moved in so quickly they hadn't even noticed. As the clouds surged over the cliffs and opened up, Andy turned to Christian. "She fell." He had to yell this over the next boom of thunder, and the sudden drenching rain. "Bumped her head!"

Dorie went to nod in agreement. Not a smart move. A sharp pain that had nothing to do with the storm exploded behind her eyes. She heard a distressed moan—her own, she realized—and then her vision began to fade.

She'd fainted once before, in the Shop-Mart as a matter of fact, after a particularly nasty bout of the flu when Mr. Stryowski had made her come back to work too soon. The same warning signs had come to her then, a clanging in her head, her vision fading out, a funny metallic taste on her tongue . . . She opened her mouth to warn everyone, but the only thing she managed was "uh-oh."

And then everything went black.

Andy grabbed Dorie and sat on the ground with her in his arms. Christian sank to his knees next to them, pulling off his backpack to get to his first-aid kit, which he should rename the Dorie Kit. The rain was already moving on, and as he shook the water out of his face, he let a quiet calm wash over him, the calm that came whenever he was needed in a work capacity.

Because this was work, he reminded himself, and nothing more. "Dorie."

She didn't move.

Andy looked utterly shaken, though not shaken enough to stop him from touching her all over. He pulled his hand out from behind her head, his fingers dark with her blood, and went suddenly still. "My God. I didn't realize she was bleeding a little."

"Great," Denny said. "Just great."

"That's not a little," Cadence said, also clearly shaken. "Christian—"

He was on it. He ran his hands up Dorie's neck, feeling for injury there first before he carefully turned her head and found the source of the blood. An open cut, not deep enough for stitches, but oozing enough to look more shocking than it was. Still, in this heat and humidity, the chance of infection was extremely high. "Head wounds always bleed like a mother." He grabbed some gauze and pressed it against the cut with some pressure.

Dorie moaned but didn't open her eyes.

Andy looked down at the gauze, quickly going red with her blood, and went green himself. "Oh, God." Closing his eyes, he let out a matching moan to Dorie's. "Not so good with blood."

"Suck it up," he directed the baseball star. "When she opens her eyes, she needs to see you looking calm."

Andy nodded but still looked green.

Christian gently stroked Dorie's hair away from the wound. "The cut's superficial. The concern is the large contusion she's sporting." He looked up at Andy. "How long was she unconscious the first time?"

Andy swallowed hard. His color still hadn't improved, and Christian would guess he was close to passing out himself. Just what he needed. "How long, Andy?"

"She wasn't, not really. Just confused. She thought . . . I think she thought I was the big, bad wolf."

"Interesting," Brandy said, looking Andy over speculatively.

"Dorie," Christian said firmly, touching her jaw. "Wake up."

Her still wet eyelids fluttered, and then opened, and he took a deep breath of relief. "Morning, Sunshine."

"Hey." She tried to sit up. "Don't tell me I got another splinter, because—"

"Whoa." He held her down, then looked into each of her pupils. "Mildly concussed. You're lucky you didn't crack your skull open like an egg, you know that? Now just lay there a second, give your organs a chance to catch up. Took a good fall this time, did you?"

"Yeah." She closed her eyes again. "Because, you know, the last few weren't good enough." She went green to match Andy. "Oh boy."

He knew the signs. "Open your eyes," he instructed. "Look at a focal point until the dizziness passes."

Those killer eyes opened and landed on him. "I'm okay."

"You are definitely okay," he agreed. "Probably not ready for a mountain climb, but—"

"A flight home would be great."

He gave her a grim smile and pulled her slowly upright to a sit. "Well, that answers that. You know where you are. Tell me who you are and what year it is, and we'll be in business."

"I know who I am." Her eyes met his, and in them was the knowledge of what they'd done last night. "I'd like to stand up. Because I think there might be ants crawling in places they have no business crawling."

He got her up, noting that Andy kept an arm around her, acting as her crutch. Not that Dorie seemed to mind. Nope, she leaned on him, even smiled a sweet thanks into his face.

While Christian tried to remember why he'd ever wanted the two of them to find each other.

"Actually," Dorie said after a moment, looking shaky, "the ground was good. You guys go on ahead and finish your exploring, I'll just take a little nap."

"No nap," Christian said, catching her before she lay back down. "In fact, no sleeping for you, not with a concussion."

"You said mild."

"No sleeping," he repeated firmly. "Not until I say so."

"She needs to get back to camp," Denny said.

Brandy slipped an arm around Dorie's waist. "We're done exploring today."

"So where the hell's Ethan?" Denny turned in a slow circle, looking.

Andy nodded down the way they'd been walking. "He kept going."

Denny shook his head. "Idiot. Let's go back."

"And what, just leave Ethan out here?" Cadence asked, looking horrified.

"Ethan's a big boy," Denny said. "He can take care of himself, trust me."

They all began the trek back, each of them taking turns helping Dorie so that Christian didn't have to.

Which should have worked for him.

Except it didn't.

"I really thought I was cut out for this whole outdoor life adventure," Andy muttered at the halfway point. "Turns out I'm not. I need a vacation from my vacation."

At the shakiness of his voice, Christian looked at him. "You starting to lose it?"

"Yes. Yes, I believe I am."

"It's going to be okay."

"Really? So you think there's a Ritz on the other side of this island?"

"We'll be found," Denny said. "You'll get your Ritz."

"Yes, but when? A day? A week? We'll all be dead before then."

"Nah," Christian said. "We have plenty of fresh water, and it'd take a lot longer than a week to die of starvation."

"Good to know." But Andy's voice said it wasn't good to know at all.

When they finally staggered back to the beach, Denny handed out water, fresh fruits, and bread. The cheese and meats were gone, and though no one complained or said a word about it, Christian knew by tomorrow people would be panicking.

He hoped like hell Ethan found people on the other side of the island. And a working radio. He watched Dorie very carefully, which was how he knew that though she pretended to, she didn't drink and she didn't eat. He waited until Cadence and Brandy went with Andy to the water to cool off and then he crouched at her side.

"Are you going to ask me how I'm doing?" she asked without looking at him. "Because I'm not sure I could summon up a good lie right now."

"I want the truth."

"I want to take a nap."

"I know, but—"

"No, I mean I can't keep my eyes open, Christian." She put her hand on his arm and looked into his face, her own imploring. "I'm not trying to be a whiner here, but my head hurts like hell and my eyes are closing, and if you need me to stay awake, then help me."

He considered calling Andy back to get on babysitting duty, but that thought only pissed him off, so he rose to his feet and gently pulled her to hers. "Come on."

"Oh no," she said when he walked her back to the edge of the rain forest.

"Trust me."

She didn't say a word to that, so he assumed she did trust him, which he didn't want to think about. He remained silent, keeping an arm around her waist, guiding her, until they stood before the natural waterfall, where they'd had the most erotic, sensual, hottest sex of his life only the night before.

He pulled her into the cool water up to her calves, and immediately saw a change in her eyes. More alert, more aware.

Good.

Why he then pulled her against him, gently cupped her head, taking care not to touch her injury, before leaning in and kissing her, he'd never know. But he immediately sank into the kiss, into the feel of her doing the same with that sweet, soft sigh, and when she slid her hands up his back as if she couldn't help but touch as much of him as she could, he thought his legs were going to buckle.

Then she pulled back just a little and stared at his mouth in surprise.

He was just as surprised.

"What was that?" she asked.

With a shake of his head—which didn't help clear it—he stepped back. "Not a clue."

"I thought we weren't going to do that anymore."

"Like I said, not a clue."

She was still looking into his eyes, her own curious. "You said that it was just adrenaline. But that didn't feel like just adrenaline."

"I know."

Again, she looked at him for a long beat. "I'm going to make this easy for you, Christian." She staggered back a step, then held up a hand when he would have reached for her. "If you don't know how or why that just happened, then you need to keep your hands off me. And your mouth." She pointed at him. "Especially your mouth." With that, she turned and very carefully and very slowly began to leave.

He followed, and when she glanced at him, he raised his hands. "You want to go back. Fine. But not alone."

"I'm feeling better."

"Great, even if you're lying. But there's still the little problem

of whoever made Bobby bleed all over his bathroom, remember?"
He could see by her face that she did. "Don't ask me to let you go
back alone."

She stared at him, then slowly turned and began walking again,
allowing him to follow. Because apparently, he could do little else.

TWENTY

*Night Two on deserted island
without modern conveniences,
which sounds much more romantic
than it really is.*

For some time now, Dorie had had this recurring dream. It changed a little each time, but it came in some variation of finding herself seventy-something years old, complete with gray hair and white orthopedic shoes, moving up and down the aisles of Shop-Mart, still shelving for an even older, meaner Mr. Stryowski.

This time she was in the geriatric aisle trying to reach the Depends, and Mr. Stryowski was coming after her waving his cane.

When she awoke with a start, she was covered in sweat. "I am *not* going to be shelving adult diapers when I'm seventy," she said out loud, then shut up because her head hurt like hell.

"Well, that's good."

She gulped in air but kept her eyes closed. His voice was low, already unbearably familiar, and just the sound of it, French as ever, was so comforting she felt the burn of tears behind her eyes.

"Dorie? Look at me."

"No, thanks."

"*Dorie*."

Fine. She'd look at him, even if doing so always, *always*, did something to her belly, and it wasn't completely pleasant. She opened her eyes. Pitch-dark under their shelter, and pitch-dark outside except for the glow of the ever-burning camp fire.

Turning her head, she focused on Christian crouched at her side. Behind him, she could hear Brandy breathing deeply and evenly. Cadence was behind her, most likely asleep as well, though she wasn't making a sound. Andy, she knew, was closer to the beach, but was still in plain sight, or had been when they'd all gone to sleep.

She knew Denny had settled near Andy, with Ethan as well, who'd returned with no news. She could only assume that Christian had slept with the guys.

When he wasn't waking her up, that is.

He'd been waking her up every few hours. She had no idea what time it was, but guessed dawn was still a long way off.

"How many of me do you see?" he asked.

"Same as the last time you asked me that question, and the time before."

"Dorie."

She sighed. "I see one of you. Do you have an evil ex-wife?"

"What? No."

"Just checking, because you're always looking at me like you're waiting for me to bite you or something."

"I've never been married, and I'm definitely not afraid of a bite. What's my name?"

"Grumpy Doctor. Which reminds me to ask you, why are you a doctor anyway, if you grew up hating being dragged around the world with your father?"

"I never said I hated it, and what happened to the gorgeous part?"

"Huh?"

"I thought the nickname was *Gorgeous* Grumpy Doctor."

She rolled her eyes. Big mistake, because that hurt like hell. "Okay, why do you *look* like you hate being a doctor?"

His gaze cut to hers. "What I hate, if anything, is—*was*—being on a sailboat and healing paper cuts and sprained ankles."

"And splinters."

A very small smile curved his lips. "Actually, that was a nice perk."

"That's my butt you're talking about."

"Like I said, a perk."

"Well, thank you. I think." She studied him a moment, and he let her. In reverse, she'd be squirming, but he wasn't much of a squirmer. He was extremely comfortable in his own skin, an appealing trait, she had to admit. "Why aren't you working at a hospital then, healing much more serious problems?"

He looked away.

Interesting. He'd never hidden a thing from her, not his annoyance, his arousal, nothing.

"Christian?"

"It's complicated."

She understood complicated. She lived complicated. "Like working at Shop-Mart instead of designing clothes because you're afraid kind of complicated?"

"I'm not afraid. Of anything."

Somehow, she believed that. "Then what?"

He drew in a deep breath as if reaching for patience, and it occurred to her, he was trying to scare her off. Except after being shipwrecked and concussed, she'd learned something about herself.

She didn't scare off easily. "Spit it out."

He shot her a half-amused/half-incredulous look. "Spit it out?"

"American saying for 'get to it, buster'."

"Ah." He looked into her eyes, checked her pupils. Then slid his talented hands through her hair to feel the goose egg on her head. "Are you in pain?"

"No. You've fixed all my sprains and splinters and aches, thank you very much." A big, fat lie. Her head hurt so bad she could hardly breathe. "Good thing you're not billing me—I couldn't afford you."

"Your head still hurts."

"Okay, yes, it hurts like hell. Now get back to the subject. The subject of you."

"Isn't there anything else we could talk about?"

"Humor the patient, Doctor."

He sighed. "Fine. I'm here because I'm indebted to Denny for another year. After that, I'll go back to France, or wherever I end up, and practice where I've always wanted to, in an ER."

"Indebted? What do you mean, indebted?"

His fingers were at her temples now, and began some sort of massaging motion that felt so incredibly soothing and pain-relieving, she actually moaned. "Oh my God." His hands were the most amazing, talented hands that had ever been on her. And it didn't matter that he wasn't touching her sexually, she felt that happy little switch inside her click on. Basically, he turned her on by just looking at her.

How embarrassing was that?

She squeezed her thighs tight and tried to come up with ways to distract herself. She thought of her unpaid bills at home, for instance. And then the fact that she was hungry but if she tried to eat, she'd probably toss her cookies. "Tell me about the indebted."

"One-track mind."

"I've been told. Are you paying off school debts?"

"Not really. My father's mission in life was to help impover-ished villages by making doctors available. He went wherever he felt the calling the most, using connections for donations."

"Connections?"

"He was a master at getting what he wanted. With one hand he worked with the villagers, while with the other he cultivated friends in high places."

"That's quite a fence to straddle."

"Yes, it is. Especially when not all those so-called friends were on the up and up. He ran into financial trouble a few years back and a friend had to bail him out."

"Denny," she guessed. "Oh my God, your father sold you to Denny to cover his debts?"

"It's the twenty-first century, not the Middle Ages," he said dryly. "And it wasn't Denny, but the owner of the *Sun Song*, Den-ny's partner."

"So you're working to pay off your father's debt?"

His silence was her answer. She couldn't help it—the thought bowled her over. Her own parents were a little bit clueless when it came to her—okay, a lot clueless—but she couldn't imagine them ever expecting her to step in and help them fulfill a debt *they'd* in-curred. Unless . . . "They were going to rip off his kneecaps, right? That's why you had to step in and work on the *Sun Song*?"

"Shh." He dug his fingers in, deepening the massage, and it felt so good she nearly passed out. She wanted to concentrate on him, on what he'd just told her, and how it completely changed the way she saw him. He'd given up two years of his life to help his father, had put everything on hold to honor a debt that wasn't his. But he kept at the massage, and it was putting her brain cells into a pleasure coma. "You're doing this on purpose, luring me into a state of ecstasy." Her words were actually slurred because of the bliss coursing through her.

"Stop squirming and relax."

"Are you kidding? I can't relax when your hands are on me."

His fingers went still for one telling beat. "What did I tell you about saying things like that?"

"That you could take advantage."

"That's right."

The thought of him doing just that made the tingling worse. Not that he was amoral, or dangerous, at least not to her physical being. But he was a man who could push her to the edge of her comfort zone without even trying, and though he'd stop if she asked him, the bigger concern here was . . . would she ask him to? The answer to that was a big, fat, humiliating no. "I'm not the one who decided that this thing between us was . . . what did you call it? Oh, yes. Asinine."

He sighed, then rose to his feet. "I'll be back to check on you later."

"Yeah. Okay, great." She lay there listening to him walk away until Brandy rolled over and slid her sleep mask up to her forehead.

"You should have gone for it again, hon. I wouldn't have watched. Okay, I might have peeked, but that's all."

Dorie let out a huffing laugh. "Oh my God."

"Hey, I'm not here to judge."

Dorie turned over, and found Cadence gone from her pad.

"Uh, Brandy?"

Brandy came up on her elbow. "Huh. Looks like someone else is going for it."

"So much for the penis embargo."

"Honey, sometimes a woman just can't help herself."

Unfortunately, Dorie could identify with that.

It didn't feel like she slept, but the next time she came awake, she sensed it was much closer to dawn, though the sky was still dark.

Only a week ago, her nighttime fantasies had run along the lines of, say, Matthew McConaughey, but now as she lay on the long, golden stretch of beach, staring past their shelter to the star-riddled night sky, she fantasized about chocolate chip cookies.

Make that double chocolate chip cookies.

Sorry, Matthew, but priorities were priorities. Stuck on a deserted South Pacific island without cookies? Serious suffering going on.

All around her came the sounds that people tended to buy those nature CDs for: the waves gently hitting the shore, crickets chirping, an exotic bird squawking . . .

Her stomach growling.

She put her hand on her belly, thinking she'd give her right arm for an entire bag of cookies all to herself. Maybe even her left as well.

"How's the patient?"

Ah, there he was, the bane of her existence. She knew this because just his voice made her nipples go all happy.

Damn nipples.

She felt him sit in the sand at her side but she didn't look at him. Nope, looking at him was a really bad idea because then her brain would begin that painful tug-of-war.

Want him.

Hate him.

Want him.

Hate him.

She sighed. "Go away."

"Ah. You're feeling better." He lay next to her so that his arm brushed hers, the one she would definitely sell for that bag of chocolate chip cookies.

"Question," she said.

"Hit me."

"Do you ever think about chocolate?"

He turned his head and looked at her. He was all hard, lean, sinewy lines to her soft, curvy ones. She imagined if she pointed out how different they were, he'd say he liked those differences very much. "I think about other things," he said.

"Like?"

"Things."

His arm shifted, just barely pressing into the side of her breast. And more than just her nipples got happy. *Bad. Bad body.* "I'm tired."

"Here's something to wake you up." Instead of taking the hint and leaving, he rolled to his side, facing her. "Our bet."

Oh, no. "We are not going to talk about the bet." No way.

"That's because you lost."

"You cheated."

He was silent, letting that lie live a life of its own as she remembered the details . . .

As if she could forget.

"You could just pay up," he suggested.

That thought shot tingles of excitement directly into certain areas of her anatomy that had no business getting excited. She closed her eyes, a bad idea because her other senses took over. How did he manage to smell like heaven on earth while on a deserted island? "I don't know what you're talking about."

He just laughed softly.

Bastard.

"You didn't hit your head that hard," he said. "You *know*."

"You're not going away. Why aren't you going away?" she asked desperately, knowing *exactly* what he was talking about, exactly what bet she'd made, and what she now owed him, which involved her.

Dancing.

Naked.

Beneath this very starlit sky. "If you were nice, you'd go."

He lifted a broad shoulder. "Never claimed to be nice."

Also true. *Damn it.*

"Plus we're stuck on an island," he pointed out. "Just how far away do you think I can go?"

Keeping her eyes closed, she sighed again. She really hated it when he was right.

The next time she opened her eyes, the sky was just beginning to lighten in the east, and she was left to wonder. Had his visit been a dream?

"You okay?" Brandy asked, looking at her from her pad.

"You mean other than we're shipwrecked and I have sand in parts where no sand should ever be?"

"It's good for your skin."

"You said sex was good for the skin."

"Sex is great for the skin." Brandy looked Dorie over from head to toe. "And if we had a mirror, I could show you your reflection and prove it."

She felt her face heat. "I don't know what came over me."

Yes, you do. A tall, earthy, passionate, amazing man came over you.

And beneath her . . . "Brandy?"

"Yeah?"

"I have to ask."

"Shoot."

"Well . . . Cadence's worried about her job. Andy's worried about getting hurt and losing his contract. I can't stop thinking about the life I should have lived instead of the one I am living, but you . . ."

Brandy's smile turned serene. "Yeah?"

"You don't seem worried about much."

Brandy looked away, and something within Dorie tightened. She hadn't forgotten, not for one minute, that one of them had hurt Bobby, and that it could be any one of them.

Including this woman.

"You're going to think I'm crazy," Brandy finally said.

"Try me."

"My life in Vegas? Not quite my dream life. I mean I make plenty of money, don't get me wrong, but I turned twenty-nine this year." She grimaced. "Okay, thirty. I turned thirty. Three years ago." She sighed. "And I'm not going to look this hot forever, you know."

"Are you sure? Because you're pretty hot."

"Ah, thanks, hon, but it's all downhill from here for me. And I'm tired of trying to keep up. Out here, I don't have to try at all."

Dorie stared at her. "Are you telling me you *like* being here?"

Brandy lifted a shoulder.

"You do," she marveled. "You like being here."

"What's not to like? It's warm and very beautiful . . ."

"And deserted."

"Right. And because it is, money doesn't matter."

"Deserted. Did I mention *deserted*?"

"I know you think I'm crazy, but trust me, in Vegas, I'm on borrowed time. I don't want to dwell on regrets here, but on an island like this, who cares about lengthening mascara, or how high I can kick on stage?"

Dorie thought about working for Mr. Stryowski for the rest of her life. "Yeah. I guess you're right."

They were both quiet a moment, and Dorie lay there listening to the surf, her thoughts drifting.

"I think someone pushed Bobby," Brandy whispered.

Dorie's heart stopped. "What makes you think that?"

"I went to his room to find him, and I saw—"

"What?"

"Blood." Brandy closed her eyes. "Lots of it."

"Why didn't you say anything?"

"Same reason you didn't. I was afraid. Still am." Brandy's gaze was steady when Dorie looked at her. "You saw. I can tell you saw."

"Are you looking at everyone," Dorie asked quietly, "wondering who did it? Who hurt him?"

"Yeah."

"For whole moments at a time I can actually convince myself I imagined this whole nightmare."

Brandy let out a low laugh.

"I know. I blame my upbringing. My whole family is this together, organized, successful unit. I'm the black sheep, the romantic. The illogical one."

"The dreamer," Brandy said quietly. "Nothing wrong with that." She shook her head. "I guess I was born cynical."

"No one's *born* cynical."

Brandy's smile was somber and just a little sad. "I've decided it's not you, you know."

Dorie appreciated that, she really did. And she knew Brandy's expectant silence said she was waiting for Dorie to repeat the favor to her. But she couldn't help but remember how comfortable Brandy had looked brandishing the knife that no one had even known she carried.

Extremely comfortable. Almost as comfortable as she'd looked while recalling how she'd wanted to cut off her ex-husband's family jewels. "You really thought I hurt Bobby?"

Brandy lifted a shoulder. "If it makes you feel better, I considered Cadence, too. But she jumps at her own shadow, so I can't see it being her. Christian takes his doctor duties far too seriously to ever break the physician's oath, and then there's Andy."

"Who can't handle the sight of blood," Dorie said quietly. "Yeah, I noticed that today."

"Sort of shrinks our options, you know? Because there just aren't that many of us left now, are there?"

"No." She hated this. She sat up, then held her head while it swam for a moment. "Not many options at all, except for the remaining crew. The very people Bobby trusted the most."

"Trusted?" Brandy shook her head. "I don't think they trusted each other at all. They work together, that's it."

Dorie looked over at Cadence's empty pad. "And right now, Cadence is with one of them. Probably alone."

"Yeah." Brandy stood up, then offered Dorie a hand.

Dorie let her pull her up, then stood very still waiting for her world to stop spinning. "We're going to check on her."

"Uh-huh."

"Even though she's undoubtedly busy. Very busy."

"Honey, she's undoubtedly naked. We're still going to check on her. It's what friends do."

Friends. Dorie wanted that to be true. They walked to the beach, and got yet another unwelcome surprise.

The *Sun Song?* *Gone.*

Twenty-One

Third day of no chocolate.
(72 hours, or 4,320 minutes . . .)

The sun rose over the craggy cliffs, bringing a new day, and what should have been renewed hope. Instead, the morale in camp had sunk to a new low.

The boat had vanished, and no one knew how, or why.

Dorie looked around at the glum faces. Ethan poked at the signal fire, his movements jerky. Denny stood on the beach, the water lapping at his knees, staring at the spot where the *Sun Song* should have been as if he could bring it back by sheer will.

Andy dragged wood to the fire log by log, as if they'd be here for a while.

Dorie could only hope not.

Cadence was actually sitting. She had her head in her hands. Dorie and Brandy had run into her coming back to the pads, and she'd said nothing. She stood now. "I'm going for a run."

Brandy, who'd been sitting by the fire reading the *People* magazine Dorie'd given her from her purse, looked up in disbelief. "Honey, you're stranded on an island without a mall. There's no reason to walk anywhere. And that's the good news. Come read about the latest bitch fight that broke out in Hollywood last week between the two blonde It-Girls."

"No, you don't understand. I have to run."

Brandy leaned in a little closer. "Didn't you already get your exercise with . . ." She jerked her head toward Denny's back. "You know."

Cadence winced. "No. Actually, I didn't." She lowered her voice to a whisper. "We didn't get that far."

"Why not?"

Cadence glanced at Denny's back, then lifted a shoulder. "Something stopped me." She shook her head at the questions in their eyes and stood. "Sorry. I've really got to run."

"Stay where you can be seen," Denny said, and when everyone looked at him, he turned to face them, looking unusually tense. "For safety."

Right, Dorie thought. Because their boat had vanished. Oh, and one of them might be a whack job.

"I'll stay in view," Cadence said, and took off running on the sand.

Dorie felt as restless as Cadence, and she left the campfire, too, walking toward the forest, where she'd seen Christian vanish a few minutes prior.

"Hey," Denny called out.

"Waterfalls for a shower," Dorie called back. "I'll scream if I need saving."

Brandy's gaze said she knew exactly why Dorie was going to the "shower" and who was already there, but that didn't stop Dorie from making the climb up the rocks anyway, following the now obvious trail to the waterfall. Beneath her feet, the earth was soft and springy. No crunching leaves. Here, everything was wet and giving. Lush.

She'd come here to shower yesterday after her fall. But she'd felt too out in the open, so she'd slipped behind the waterfall. Either that hadn't occurred to Christian, or he didn't care, and she had to admit as she came into the Eden-like clearing and took in his long, leanly muscled body, gleaming from the soap he was spreading over himself, he didn't have reason to care.

The man had it going on.

Being a doctor wasn't particularly physical, but being part of a sailing crew was, and he'd honed every single muscle on his body to hard, sinewy perfection. She could have looked her fill forever, watching him gliding the soap over his torso, up and down his arms and legs, and—

She should look away, to give him his privacy if nothing else. If someone had been watching her, she'd have been mortified, but she couldn't move, she could only stand there, tongue hanging out.

When he caught a glimpse of her, he tossed the soap to the edge of the water and put his hands on his hips. She tried to turn away, she really did. But her gaze had a mind of its own, and took itself on a happy little tour down the front of him, past his soapy, glistening shoulders, past those six-pack abs . . . The man really did have a world-class bod, and asinine or not, she wanted him. She could tell herself it was simply a physical reaction, or even more understandably, an adrenaline rush because of all they'd been through, but it was so much more than that.

Without a word, he turned and dove into the water, just beneath the waterfall, and she let out a long, shaky breath, fanning her face.

Didn't help.

Then he unexpectedly surged out of the water near her feet like a merman, making her squeak in surprise and fall backward to her butt into the shallow water.

"If you wanted to join me," he said. "You only had to say so."

Sputtering, the cold water seeping into her clothes, she shoved her hair from her eyes. The water was only a foot deep, but sitting in the soft sand beneath it like she now was, it lapped just beneath her breasts. "You scared me."

"Really? Because you don't look scared, you look turned on." He glided in, only his head out of the water as he slid his hands up her legs, opening them so that he could swim between them, gaze level with her belly.

She opened her mouth to remind him that hey, they weren't doing this, but he spoke. "Your head okay?"

"Better."

"Where is everyone?" His shoulders held her legs open to him as his hands skimmed up to her waist, then up her ribs . . .

"Um—"

"Occupied?" Dipping his head, he used his jaw to nudge down the skinny strap of her top, while his hands slid beneath, warm against her drenched skin.

"Um . . . yes. Occupied."

"Good." His fingers fisted in the thin material of her tank, and then tugged.

Her breasts popped out. Palming them, he smiled, then gently scraped his beard-roughened jaw over a bared nipple.

He opened his mouth on her, his tongue hot, a sharp, sensual contrast to the cool water.

"Look at you," he murmured, bending his head to take in his own long, tanned fingers on her pale, pale breasts. "So beautiful."

As she'd noticed before, when angry or aroused, his French accent deepened, and she had to admit, his voice alone could make her weak in the knees. She was so weak in the knees now, she couldn't have stood to save her life.

But apparently, standing wasn't going to be necessary. Mouth still on her breasts, his hands slid down her legs, and then back up again, taking the material of her wet and clinging skirt with them.

"Christian."

He didn't answer. He was too busy scooting her back so that only her legs were in the water, then slipping his thumbs in the edging of her panties.

Oh, God.

He tugged, then tossed her underwear aside, where they landed next to the soap.

"Christian."

He lifted his head and met her eyes. "Yes?"

At the look in his eyes, her toes—still in the water—curled in anticipation. "Um . . ."

Again he bent his head, kissing her inner thigh, her hip.

Low on her belly.

Then ground zero. Her eyes rolled back in her head and she gave herself up to the sensations of being taken . . . cool water, warm sun, hot tongue . . .

And when he'd drawn her right out of herself with shocking ease, she lay back on the bank of the lagoon, blinking up into the sky, blown away by what he did for her.

To her.

She rolled to her side and found him lying next to her on his back. Turning his head, he met her gaze, his own hot and hungry.

"I still have the condoms in my purse." He was hard, jutting straight up into the sky she'd just been studying. *Oh my.* She'd done that to him. The knowledge, the power of it, surged through her.

"I'm really starting to love that purse."

"I'll get them, but first . . ." Smiling, she leaned over him.

He stared at her. "I like that expression."

"Good." Bold in a way she'd never ever been before in her life, she ran a finger down the chest and abs she'd wanted to nibble at. And then indulged herself, replacing her fingers with her mouth.

As in most things, she felt clumsy. A little uncertain. But bolstered by the way Christian's chest rose and fell, as if he'd been running for miles, she thought maybe she was doing okay, so she kept going, spreading open-mouthed kisses from one hip to the other, and then . . .

In-between. She ran her tongue down his hot, silky length and then back up again, and with a low, rough groan, his hands embedded in her hair, he rocked his hips to her rhythm.

He liked it. Good to know. She decided to see what else he liked, and opened her mouth on him.

Another one of those low, rough groans escaped him, and again his hips lifted.

He liked that, too.

Maybe she was getting the hang of it after all . . .

Still Day Three, and maybe there are
better things than chocolate . . .

"So much for not doing that again," Dorie managed.

Christian's response was a wordless groan.

They were both lying beneath the waterfall. He'd pulled on a pair of board shorts. She'd straightened her wet clothing. Her heart was finally slowing to its normal pace after a very aerobic workout that hadn't involved exercising so much as more of that yummy wild, island sex.

Which, she figured, was even better than a typical workout, because it'd left a stupid grin on her face. No gym ever did that.

Christian came up on his knees, then leaned over her.

"Again?" she asked breathlessly, her body tingling in shocked but hopeful anticipation.

He probed the bump on her head and checked her pupils.

"Oh," she said, greatly disappointed. "That."

Still kneeling over her, his hands holding her head, he looked into her eyes, his own amused. "Did I not satisfy you?"

"No," she lied, then waited for him to rectify that.

He leaned in so that his lips were just brushing hers. "So were you faking it then?"

"Um . . ."

"Twice?"

"You counted?"

"You were wrapped around me like plastic wrap." He grinned against her lips. "Panting my name. *Christian,*" he mimicked softly. *"Oh, Christian, don't stop, please don't stop, Christian . . ."*

She felt her ears begin to heat up.

He sank his teeth into her lower lip and tugged lightly. "Sexy as hell."

"You made noises, too," she managed.

"Did I?"

"Uh-huh. But more of a rough groan . . ." Like he'd been in heaven and she'd put him there. Even thinking about the way he'd sounded made her thighs tighten.

She wanted to hear it again. But most of all, she didn't want him to shift away from her, to go back to camp, to stop talking to her, smiling at her in that way he had that made her feel so special.

She was tempted to say it all out loud but didn't want to scare him, this man who claimed not to be scared of anything. She knew, given the life he'd led and all the things he'd seen and done, he truly believed himself fearless.

But she also knew, on some core level, in a way he wasn't ready to admit, she did scare him.

Big-time.

He had a three-day growth of beard on his tanned, rugged face, and she was fairly certain he hadn't bothered to do much more than finger comb his hair in days. He wore those black board shorts and that was it. He looked very . . . island. Exotic.

Primal.

Maybe he'd deny being scared, but her? Terrified, especially given that she was the one who was going to get hurt in this deal. Because this thing they had going on, as wonderful, as incredible, as amazing as it was, couldn't last.

She didn't fit into his world, which wasn't going to make it any easier when they were rescued. But when that day came, she'd lift her chin and smile, and watch him walk away. It would hurt, but hey, the pain would remind her that she was living life, right? "So how does a sailboat vanish anyway?" she asked, desperate to have a conversation rather than continue thinking too much.

"It couldn't have sunk in the shallow water."

"And it couldn't have sailed away."

"No."

The silence filled up with their racing thoughts she'd hoped to avoid. "So. Guess we should ration the rest of the condoms. Or are we back to the no more sex thing, which if you've noticed, hasn't worked so well this far."

She hadn't meant to ask, but she'd never been all that good at controlling herself.

He sighed.

At the sound, she got to her feet. "I should get back."

He pushed to his feet. "Dorie—"

"No, really. They'll worry about me."

"I'll walk you. I'll feel better if you stay in sight."

"Of you?"

"Yes."

"Really? Because you strike me as the kind of man who craves his freedom."

"I do value my freedom. Greatly, but—"

"I know you don't need anyone in your life. You don't have to worry. I knew that when we—" She looked at the spot where they'd made love. "I know."

"My life isn't suited for a relationship," he said slowly. "I had another year on the *Sun Song*—"

"But that's over now."

"And because of it, I'm jobless. Homeless. I have no idea what will happen."

"I know that, too." She forced a smile. "It's okay, Christian. I'm okay."

A muscle in his jaw twitched, but he didn't say anything else.

She was still smiling, mostly because her muscles were stuck. Tired of it, and tired of herself, she reached for her sandals.

"Dorie?"

She shoved one foot into the shoe.

"Stick close. *Oui?*"

Damn, she wanted to say no, but close worked for her. Far too much. *"Qui."*

TWENTY-TWO

Afternoon of Day Three—
So how does a girl get
voted off the island?

Dorie watched Ethan stab at the fire with a large stick. His mouth was carved into a tight grimace. "A chef without food to cook," he muttered.

"Don't forget a sailing crew without a sailboat."

"That, too." The afternoon sun was beating down, and his face was streaked with perspiration. His hair stood straight up in spots, and not so straight up in others.

Under normal circumstances, Dorie would think he was a man on the very edge of his sanity, but these weren't normal circumstances, and she had the feeling that they all were looking a little crazy.

But which of them looked crazy enough to kill? She eyed each and every one of them, slowly and carefully. Cadence was sitting on a rock, a stack of coconuts in front of her. In her usual frenetic, unable-to-relax fashion, she was cracking them open and cutting out the meat.

Brandy sat on a rock as well, painting Andy's toenails.

"You have polish remover, right?" he asked warily.

"Right. Want a flower on your big toes?"

"How about a baseball?"

Christian came into the clearing, shirtless, damp with perspiration, dragging a large log for the fire.

Denny was still stalking back and forth along the beach, every few feet stopping to stare in disbelief at the spot where his boat had been.

Dorie shook her head. She'd have figured they'd have discussed the boat vanishing in detail, and they damn well should have, but no one brought it up. "It didn't just sail away."

Everyone looked at her.

"Well, even I know that much," she said.

"The boat's lost," Ethan said. "Story over."

"Yeah, but how do you lose a sailboat?" Brandy countered.

Ethan laughed harshly and went back to poking the fire. "It's Bobby's ghost, haunting us."

"Why?" Cadence asked softly. "Because someone did this to him?"

Finally. Maybe they'd all been in shock from what they'd been through, and things were just now sinking in. But it was time to deal with it. Past time.

"I think someone pushed him," Cadence said. "One of us." Her voice wobbled, and her eyes were wide. She was losing it.

Dorie moved to her side and took her hand. "Honey—"

"No, it's true. I heard you and Brandy talking about it, about the blood in the boat, and now the boat's gone so there's no proof." Cadence pointed at all of them. "I've been thinking about it, trying to be logical, and you know what logic says? That it could have been any one of us, because we each had motivation!"

The silence became heavy, like a two-ton elephant standing on the beach between all of them, chewing on a secret.

"Whoever's responsible," Cadence continued, "Bobby is going to haunt you until you admit it!"

"Cadence," Dorie said softly, nervous. She didn't know how smart it was to stir that pot with no exit plan.

Cadence turned on her. "It could have been any of us, Dorie. Isn't that driving you crazy? *Any of us!*"

"Stop." This from Denny, who came toward her, crouching at her side to take her hand. "The situation sucks, but—"

"Yes, it sucks! He worked for you, and you talked to him like he was nothing but a stupid kid—"

"He was lazy as shit, yes. But not stupid."

"Then why, on our first day out, when he hoisted a sail wrong, did you say 'I'm going kill you, Bobby'?" She gulped hard. "I heard you."

He looked around him, clearly blown away by the accusation. "That's just a figure of speech."

"Bad choice of words?" she asked. "Is that it?"

"Christ, yes. You don't really think I could have—"

"I don't know what I think."

Denny took a step back, obviously hurt to the core.

Cadence shook her head again. "It's not just you. Ethan called him"—she closed her eyes—"a 'fucking moron.' A couple of times."

Ethan choked, but Cadence went on. "And then Bobby retaliated by using Ethan's toothbrush to clean their toilet. When Ethan found out, he told Bobby he was going to kill him."

Ethan was looking like all his brains were leaking out his ears. "How do you even know this?"

Cadence shrugged. "I have good hearing. And there's more."

She looked at Andy. "Bobby owed you a lot of money, and he wasn't going to pay you. You were really mad."

"Well, yes," Andy said. "But I never—"

"That first night on the boat, after all those drinks we all shared. You said you could 'kill that little shit.' "

"Do you have a photographic memory or something?" Denny asked.

"Yes, which is how I remember exactly when Brandy also said she was going to kill him." Cadence turned to Brandy with apology in her eyes. "The night of the storm, when he took you to your room. He offered to help you undress."

"No, what I said was, I'm not sure whether to fuck him or kill him."

"But see? All of you said it at one time or another, and then he ended up dead."

"Not me," Dorie said. "I never said it."

Cadence just looked at her.

"I didn't."

"Yes, you did. That first day, when he didn't help you on board and you nearly lost your luggage."

Oh, God. She had. "But I didn't mean it . . ." She really hadn't, but realized that *none* of them had meant it.

All but one of them . . .

Dorie glanced around. Everyone was silent, each of them with mixed emotions on their faces: horror, regret . . . and if she wasn't mistaken, guilt.

How could *everyone* be feeling guilt?

Denny turned to each of them. "There's no proof anything suspect happened to Bobby, so I think we all just need to relax—"

"No." Cadence stood up. "I can't relax anymore or my head is going to blow right off my shoulders." Sticking her hands in her hair, she turned in a slow circle, eyes wild. "Eat. Relax. *Can't.*"

Worried, Dorie looked at Christian, who spoke in a calm voice directly to Cadence. "Taking a moment is a good idea—"

"You only think so because you're doing Dorie."

Shocked, Dorie stared at Cadence, who covered her face with her hands. "I'm sorry. I am. It's just that I'm so uptight and scared, and I don't have the benefit of multiple orgasms to release the tension!"

"Oh! I have my vibrator," Brandy offered. "And even some spare batteries—" She broke off when Cadence only groaned again.

"Just ignore me," Cadence begged. "Please, just ignore me. I'm just overwhelmed with the shipwrecked thing, and then the boat vanishing, and now Bobby's ghost—"

"I'm not crazy about ghosts either," Brandy said, looking around her.

Again, Christian met Dorie's gaze, his own hooded and unreadable. "I'm doubting it's a ghost."

"Yeah? So then what happened to the boat?" Cadence demanded. "And please don't insult my intelligence and tell me it simply vanished. I might be stuck on an island, but I'm not stuck on stupid."

"It doesn't matter what happened to it," Denny said. "Because we're going to be found today. I feel it."

"Oh, you feel it, do you?" Ethan jabbed a stick in the fire. "Do you feel what's going to happen to your crew as well?"

"What do you mean?" Denny asked.

"Well, we're basically homeless now, and jobless to boot. It's not like we've set up job security."

"You're worried about job security?"

Ethan just kept stabbing at the fire.

Denny sighed. "Okay, listen. All of you. If I had ropes and some climbing equipment, I could get to the other side of the island, where I *know* there are people."

"And you know this how?" Cadence asked.

"I feel them. And I told you I *heard* them."

Ethan's mouth tightened. "Do you feel food in our near future?"

"We'll be okay," Dorie said. "There are coconuts and pineapples. And fish, if we can catch them, right?"

"How should we catch them?" Ethan asked her. "Ship gone, remember? Fishing poles gone. Hope gone."

"Stop it." Dorie pointed at him. "We need positive thinking here." She looked around them, saw the defeat and exhaustion sinking in, and felt her heart catch. "We can't give up." She looked at Christian. "We can't."

He met her gaze straight on, his steely eyes filled with depths she hadn't imagined that first day when she'd bumped into him on the dock. More strength than she could have imagined. Passion. Intelligence. And a surprisingly sharp, quick wit that could make her smile even while on a deserted island with a bunch of quirky strangers and a missing crew member. "We can't give up," she said to him.

He nodded. He wouldn't give up. Ever. It wasn't in his genetic makeup. But then he straightened, staring out at sea. "What the—"

She whipped around, then felt her jaw drop in disbelief. There, on the horizon.

A boat.

"Oh my God," Cadence cried, jumping up and down. "Here," she screamed. "We're here, we're here, we're here—"

Dorie put her hand on Cadence's arm. "It's okay, they're coming."

Cadence stopped jumping to hug her. "We're rescued. Ohmigod, we're saved!"

It was a sailing yacht, definitely heading toward them, and Dorie turned with a smile to Christian, but it slowly faded. He hadn't relaxed. In fact, there was a stillness about him now, one that suggested he was prepared for whatever came his way, including battle.

Cadence and Andy were too busy hugging each other to notice, and yelling and laughing and crying. Brandy stood right next to them, quiet, lost in thought.

Denny and Ethan were eyeing the ship with a watchfulness Dorie didn't understand. "What is it?" she asked. "What's the matter?"

Christian stepped closer to the water, so that it lapped at his feet as he watched the boat come into the cove. "Denny."

"On it." Denny turned to Andy. "Stay where you are, back from the water. If I tell you, take the women into the rain forest, behind the waterfall—"

"*What?*"

"Just listen to me. If we tell you to run, do it."

Dorie's heart began pounding hard and heavy and fast. Why would they have to run from anyone with a boat? "Could they be . . . bad guys?"

The answer was all over the crew's faces. *Oh, God.* They were worried about modern-day raiders who crept up on unsuspecting boats—or in this case, shipwrecked passengers—and took whatever they wanted.

Pirates.

Did they still rape and pillage? Dorie held hands with Brandy and Cadence and watched the boat moved in closer, then closer still, but wasn't able to make out how many people were on board.

Or if they were smiling.

Not that that mattered. Pirates smiled. Or they did in the movies. "Friend or foe?" she whispered.

Cadence had finally gone still, the happiness faded from her face. "This never occurred to me."

"It occurred to me." Brandy patted the back pocket of her Daisy Dukes. "But don't worry. I'm armed."

Dorie wouldn't worry.

Much.

Christian stood shoulder to shoulder with Denny as the boat came in closer toward them. That was the good news.

He just hoped there wasn't any bad news.

"A fifty-eight-foot Hatteras," Denny noted, eyeing the boat. "Nice."

About half a million dollars worth of nice. On it stood two men, watching them as carefully as they were being watched.

"Two of 'em," Ethan said quietly, coming up on Denny's left.

"I see."

"Might be more below."

Christian tried to get a read on the men, but the sun was in the wrong position, casting their faces in shadows. He'd been out on these waters a damned long time, a lifetime it seemed, and for much of that, it'd been the friendliest place on earth.

But they'd run into trouble before. They'd been held up three times actually, always out in the middle of nowhere, once while on an island such as this one. He glanced at Denny, who nodded.

Christian drew a deep breath, and then, as he had on that other island, reached into his pocket for the knife he'd tucked there, knowing damned well the women behind him could see exactly what he was doing.

It wouldn't be a stretch for their overworked nerves and adrenaline to focus on his weapon. Except for one interesting fact—plenty of them seemed to be armed in some manner or another as well. Funny, that. On the surface they were a group of people brought together to a closeness only achieved by sharing near death.

But he knew the truth, that beneath that surface closeness, they were all perfect strangers. Well, not all perfect strangers, because he'd let Dorie in a lot more than he'd ever intended. He couldn't claim *not* to know her, or that she didn't know him. Risking a glance at her, he found her eyes wide on his.

She'd seen the knife. "It's going to be okay," he told her, told all of them.

Denny glanced at him in surprise. Yeah, yeah, so he wasn't exactly known for his gentle bedside manner. That was usually Denny's area of expertise, babysitting the passengers. Just another example of how far Dorie had wormed her way into his heart. So much so that he'd been awake all last night trying to figure out how to make a go of this thing with her. A real relationship. A long-lasting one. He'd come up with nothing. But he didn't want to think about that now, not with his heart pumping and adrenaline flowing as the boat came closer.

Normally, he had only himself to think about, worry about. That had changed, and wasn't that just the crux of his problem. For the first time in far too long, he had something to lose.

Someone, to be exact.

TWENTY-THREE

Dorie's gaze stuck on Christian's back, and the knife he held there, so that she nearly missed the huge, beautiful sailing yacht come closer. One of the men on board waved to them as conflicting emotions battered her.

Why did Christian have a knife?

"Ahoy!" one of the men on the boat called out.

Denny lifted a hand in greeting.

"Can I be of any service to you?" the man asked through cupped hands.

He had a British accent, Dorie noted. He wore baggy white linen pants and a matching white shirt with some sort of saint's medallion at the base of his throat, held there by a thin piece of leather. He had a thin tattoo around each wrist, a diamond in one ear, and a smile on his face. He was dark from the sun, with melting dark eyes and darker hair, sun kissed on the ends, which curled to his collar. He could be a drug runner—a successful one. Or just a successful man.

He took them all in, including the fact that there was no boat anywhere near them, and raised his hands as if to say *what happened*?

"We limped in after the storm," Denny called out. "And lost our boat."

"Ah." The man handed his helm over to the man standing at his right, and hopped down into the water without regard to his clearly expensive pants. Water splashed up to his knees as he stepped onto the shore, holding out his hand to Denny. "Michael Phillips."

"Denny McDonald," Denny said, and the two shook hands.

"So you're in a bit of a bind," Michael said in that expensive British voice.

"You could say so."

Ethan and Christian were behind him, tense and very watchful.

"Men," Brandy whispered in Dorie's ear. "They're playing the who has the biggest dick game." The Vegas dancer stepped closer. "How did you happen on us?" she asked.

Michael turned his head and looked at her. "I didn't just happen on you."

Denny and Ethan went very, very still.

Christian didn't move either, and Dorie could almost see him mentally wielding the knife she knew he held.

"I own this island." Michael studied each of them in turn. "We saw smoke from your fire yesterday and figured a boat had stopped for some beach fun. When we saw the smoke again today, I decided to come check it out."

"You own the island," Brandy said in a *holy shit* voice.

He smiled. "Along with a very exclusive getaway on the north side. You didn't see that, apparently."

"No," Denny muttered. "We didn't."

"We tried," Ethan said, "but we couldn't get over there."

"Which is what makes it exclusive. We don't usually have more than a single guest at a time, for privacy's sake."

Uh-oh. Dorie knew what that meant. Either he was catering to the rich and famous, or he was a drug runner. God, she hoped it was the rich and famous.

"So you're stranded," Michael said calmly. "Stuck here."

"The guy's a genius," Denny muttered, and Dorie wondered if he was put out because he was no longer the only captain on the island, or if it was because he was the only captain on the island without a boat.

Michael didn't seem concerned with either possibility, or with the fact that the men still hadn't relaxed. He walked up the beach like he did indeed own the place, and smiled at the women. "Are there any injuries?"

Their matching smiles faded in unison as they remembered.

Bobby.

"What is it?" he asked, his voice low with obvious concern as he took in each and every one of them. "Who's hurt?"

"Not hurt," Denny said. "Missing. We lost one of our crew."

"In the storm?"

They all looked at each other, and Dorie was right there with them. What to say now? Yes, in the storm, but one of us might have assisted that loss? The ramifications of saying anything close to that hit her like a one-two punch. The authorities would be called, and each of them who'd been on the *Sun Song*, including herself, would be held for questioning.

They'd be *suspects*, one and all. And worse, suspects outside of the United States and its authority, which meant they'd be held in a foreign prison.

"It's complicated," Christian said calmly. "But we'll need the authorities."

Michael lifted a brow. "Is there a crime scene?"

The silence became weighted until Christian spoke. "The crime scene was on the boat."

Michael just looked at them. "So there are . . ." He counted. "Seven of you."

"Yes," Christian said.

"Been a rough few days, I imagine?"

"Actually," Brandy said. "If it hadn't been for poor Bobby, I wouldn't have minded any of it."

"A noncomplaining woman." He gave her a second look. "What a refreshing surprise in a guest. I have radio communications and a telephone line. You can call whoever else you need to. Consider yourself rescued. You could be out of here by nightfall."

His boat, aptly named *Elegance*, was every bit as beautiful as the *Sun Song* had been. Even more so, if that was possible. The ride wasn't long, but Dorie took in the crystal chandeliers, the brass fixtures, the wealth and sophistication in every inch of the yacht and felt bowled over by all it represented. "Do you sail often?"

"Used to." Michael served them all champagne. "But then I built my place, and . . ." He lifted a shoulder. "Now I'd rather be on the island, if I'm not working."

"Working?"

"Writing scripts. Producing."

Cadence blinked.

Brandy gasped.

So did Dorie. "Are you . . . *that* Michael Phillips?"

Michael smiled.

"Oh my God," Cadence said. "I saw you get your third Oscar

this year. I love you. I mean—" she stuttered when everyone laughed. "I love your work."

"The elusive, hermitlike Hollywood big shot," Andy said slowly, sitting forward, flashing his million-dollar smile. "Hey. Someone more famous than me."

Michael laughed and topped off their flutes. "I don't know about that. Ah, here we go. Up ahead."

His place was quite simply the most amazing thing Dorie had ever seen. The mansion was cut into the mountainside as if a part of it, all wood and various levels with walls of windows and so many decks she couldn't count, shaded by lush growth and flowers in every hue.

Michael's crew maneuvered them to the dock with hardly a bump, and when they tied off, they all stepped onto the wood and stared up the grassy cliffs with amazement.

"Wow," Cadence said, speaking for all of them.

"Let's go inside." There were two sets of rock stairs cut into the mountainside, leading straight up the cliff to the house. Michael gestured for them to take the left route. At the top, Dorie turned in a half circle and realized she could see nearly half the island, and what looked like the entire ocean and horizon. She'd had her breath taken away before but this cut right through all that and stole her heart.

Completely.

She stood at the top of the world it seemed, the house behind her, the entire ocean in front of her, and simply couldn't breathe.

"There's a phone just inside," Michael said.

Right. Back to the real world. She looked at Christian and realized the truth. She wasn't ready to go.

*   *   *

Christian walked through the room he'd been given, stripping as he headed to the bathroom. It was done. The authorities called, loved ones notified, nightmare over.

The only negative—and it was a big one—Bobby's body had been found, so the rescue had turned into a retrieval.

Christian hated that.

Given the situation, he knew there'd be a circus of authorities descending on the island as quickly as possible.

They all had mixed feelings about what would happen next, him most of all. Naked, he stepped into the shower and stood beneath the spray of the water, letting it pummel his exhausted body.

Lifting his hands to the wall, he bent his head, letting the water beat down on his shoulders, working at the tension knotted there. His home, for what it was worth, was gone. He had no idea what that meant for his life in general, but at least he still had a life, and was breathing, which he doubted could be said for Bobby.

From the time they'd shipwrecked until this very moment, Christian's own survival had taken precedence over Bobby's disappearance. He hadn't really had the time to get past the surface of what had happened, but he did now. One of the people he'd just spent four days with, eating, talking, working, *surviving* . . . one of them had done this to Bobby.

Denny could be a first-class asshole but when it came to violence, he *always* backed down. It was why Christian had had to hold the knife when Michael's boat had first shown up. Besides, Denny needed crew members around him. It made him feel important. It was why he'd sailed with three instead of the customary two. For him to get rid of Bobby was totally and completely out of character.

As for Ethan . . . Christian was maybe the only person on the planet who knew the chef had harbored a secret crush on Bobby.

Not just a crush but something deeper, which had both baffled the younger man and driven the kid crazy, because Bobby was as straight as an arrow. Even though Ethan had a lot of drama in him, he was a self-proclaimed pacifist. Imagining Ethan hurting Bobby made even less sense than Denny doing it.

Then who?

Andy was the logical choice, because Bobby had owed him a helluva lot of money that Andy was never going to see. And yet the sight of Dorie's blood had made the baseball player want to pass out.

Which left the women.

Brandy, with her cool eyes, cool smile, jaded ways . . . and heart of gold. Cadence, a little hyperactive, a little OCD, and a whole lot of heart as well.

Then there was Dorie—

Who, he suddenly realized, had let herself into the bathroom and was standing on the other side of the glass shower door looking her fill. "You have a thing for watching a man take a shower," he noted.

"Would you believe I got lost?"

Just looking at her standing there, indeed looking a little lost and a whole lot uncertain, beautiful without even being aware of it, grabbed him by the throat and held, squeezing the air from his lungs. She could destroy him with nothing more than her eyes.

"Lost," she repeated. "And you know what?"

Suddenly it hurt to breathe, much less talk, so he just shook his head.

"I've also, somehow, found my way," she whispered, and there was something in her eyes that made his chest hurt even more.

Her heart.

Oh, God. Not that. Not her damn heart. He told himself to

turn away. To just continue on with his shower and his very rare, very private moment of reflection. In fact, he reached out to shut the shower door, blocking her, but somehow his brain didn't get the message to his hands because they fisted in her top and hauled her into the shower with him.

She gasped, a sound he swallowed with his mouth, and he realized almost immediately that this kiss was different than their others.

Not just sex.

Ah, hell. If he could just get her out of his head, but she'd been stuck there since he first laid eyes on her at the dock in Fiji, alone and just a little bit bedraggled, a little bit bewildered, and a whole lot sweet and sexy.

Not.

Just.

Sex.

God. Pulling her in, he softened the connection. Not as wild now, not as out of control. Not as new, but no less necessary.

Sweet. Slow. Hot.

Deep.

Deeper than any kiss he could remember, and then he wasn't thinking at all because she let out a soft, helpless little murmur that he inhaled and felt as his own.

She undid him. Completely undid him. He didn't know how that would translate in the real world, but right now as he turned her, pressing her back against the tile, holding her there with his body, so his hands could roam over her wet, hot one, he didn't care.

"I want you," she whispered. "So much."

Stopping nearly killed him, but he lifted his head. "I want you, too, Dorie." He closed his eyes and touched his forehead to hers. "So damned much it hurts, but—"

"But it doesn't change anything. I know, Christian."

When he opened his eyes, her were shiny, too shiny, but she was smiling. "It's okay." Then she kissed him. Kissed him until he could do nothing but wrap her in his arms and moan her name. Only when air was necessary did he pull back, looking into her eyes, those amazing, mesmerizing eyes.

"I know what's in store tomorrow, Christian," she said softly. "And I still want today."

God. He pressed his forehead to hers. He didn't deserve this, didn't deserve her, and for her sake, he needed to stop the madness. "I can't do this to you. I—"

"I'm a big girl, Christian. Now love me. I want to remember this. You."

Lifting his head, he stroked his fingers over her jaw. "I'll never forget you."

"I intend to make sure of that."

Then she put her mouth to his again, and pulled him under.

TWENTY-FOUR

When Christian came up for air, Dorie's lashes were wet, sticking together, the shower water running down her face and into her clothing, which was plastered to her every curve. He'd never seen anything so sexy. "Do you always take a shower with your clothes on?"

She smiled. "It's becoming a habit."

Taking the hem of her top in his hands, he lifted. Raising up her arms, she let him pull it off over her head and toss it out of the shower. Her eyes filled with arousal and trust and so damned much affection and need he nearly had to close his.

Don't need me. Christ, don't need me. At the end of the day, he never had anything left in the tank to give to someone.

At least that's what he'd always thought, what he'd believed, and he'd lived his life by it. He healed others, that's what he did, the end.

A little breathless, she smiled again, the one that clenched his gut tight and knotted him up, all in good ways, ways he hadn't believed possible. Her bra was pale peach and sheer, revealing everything to him, including the fact that he turned her on every bit as much as she turned him on. Flicking open the front clasp, the blood drained from his head for parts south at the low, sexy catch in her throat. Then the bra slipped and fell to the shower floor, and he couldn't think at all.

She had tan lines, her limbs darkened from the last few days in the sun. Her breasts were perfectly outlined as if she was still wearing her bikini top, the skin there pale and glistening, her nipples hard and pebbled.

With water running over them.

"I've had a lot of firsts this week," she said very quietly, her voice husky as her arms slid up his chest and around his neck, one of her hands sinking into his hair, her fingers tightening. "All life-changing firsts."

Life-changing. He opened his mouth to ask her to clarify, but then her gaze dipped to his lips and he knew she wanted another kiss.

With their mouths already lined up, only a breath away, with her breasts smashed up against his chest, it was going to happen. But he forced himself to hold back a beat, to make sure he could, and it was just hard enough that he knew the truth. He wanted her more than he'd wanted any woman in a good long time.

Maybe ever.

The enforced wait had anticipation flowing through him, he slid his hands down her sides, barely grazing her breasts, her ribs, hooking his thumbs in the waistband of her skirt, which was clinging to her hips and legs like a second skin. He knew he had no right to this, but neither could he summon the strength to stop. "You should really walk away from me."

Instead, she pressed her body to his. "Don't say no," she whispered.

Was she kidding? It'd have taken a bigger man than himself. He slid her skirt down her legs until it pooled at their feet on top of her bra.

She was wearing a tiny scrap of green silk with tinier yellow daisies embroidered on the edging, which for some reason made him smile.

"I know I don't match. I'm not the most organized—"

When he tugged them off, she shut up. With the water hammering his back, he slid to his knees and pressed his mouth to her hip.

"Oh," she breathed.

Her other hip.

Her fingers sinking in his hair. "What if someone comes?"

He ran his tongue along the edge of the cotton. "The only person who's going to come is you."

Her head thunked back against the tile as her fingers tightened in his hair, hard enough to make him wince, but instead he smiled. Smiled as he drew her into his mouth and made her cry out his name. Smiled while driving her over the edge and into his arms. Smiled as he stood up, lifted her up and thrust into her.

He couldn't remember ever grinning as he took a woman before, and couldn't have imagined it, but then her creamy heat surrounded him, pulled him in, and his amusement faded away. In its place came that ache in his chest. A physical pain.

"Christian," she murmured, her hands cupping his face. Pressing her forehead to his, she panted softly as he moved within her. "I never knew—"

Him either. By her own admission, he had more experience than her when it came to sex, and he'd still had no idea. This wasn't simple sex, and in a flash of clarity, he recognized it for what it was. Not just pure attraction. Not just companionship, or an adrenaline rush.

But he didn't want to put a name to it.

Instead, he took her mouth and her body, and when she came apart for him with his name on her lips, he felt his already racing pulse kick into an even higher gear. Hell, his heart nearly burst out of his damn chest, especially when he thought about this being the last time. Because it hurt to even think the words he thought he'd wanted, he kissed her—a long, deep, wet kiss designed to make them both forget everything but what they did to each other, only even that backfired, because in the forgetting, he remembered how perfect it really was . . .

Dorie tossed back her wet hair and walked down the decadent upstairs hallway, marveling anew at the sharp contrast between the past few days with no luxuries, and now, surrounded by the most gorgeous house she'd ever seen. She caught sight of her own reflection in a long gilded mirror and stopped short. Her skin was glowing, her eyes sparkling. Seemed being shipwrecked agreed with her.

That, or the sex.

Actually, Christian. Christian agreed with her.

The hallway was wide, tiled, and cool, thanks to the lush plants and openness of the layout. The colors were definitely South Pacific, bright primary colors splashed on the walls. Everywhere there were plants, big and small, all moist and green and swaying in the light breeze provided by all the opened doorways and windows.

The balcony was lined in clear glass so that she could see down to the huge open room beneath. She came to a stop at the top of the stairs, aware that her body was still humming with carnal pleasure, and that most likely she wore a grin from ear to ear that screamed Just Satisfied.

Multiple times.

God, she felt alive, and had since Christian had pulled her into the shower and stripped her out of her clothes.

Actually, she'd felt this way from that first moment in Fiji when she'd stood watching him board the *Sun Song*, utterly at ease with himself and everything around him.

Being with him, especially when she was naked, was heaven. Leaving him, which she would do far too soon, was going to feel like hell on earth.

Later, she told herself. *Go there later . . .*

But she couldn't help herself. She'd told him she could handle this, and logically, she understood. She did. They came from two entirely different worlds. Not to mention he lived on the complete other side of the planet, pretty much the definition of geographically undesirable.

But she had fallen anyway.

She had no idea how that could even happen after only a few days. Maybe it was because of the intensity of it all, and what they'd been through. Perhaps it had sped up the process. Regardless, fact was fact.

She loved him.

TWENTY-FIVE

Uh-oh," Dorie whispered, staggered at the realization. She *loved* him. "Not good."

"What's not good?"

He'd come up behind her. She glanced at him in the mirror, wondering if what she'd been thinking was all over her face. When she'd left him only a few minutes ago, he'd been wearing nothing but a smile. Now he wore faded Levi's and a T-shirt, his hair still wet and finger combed off his face. At the sight of him, her body gave one hopeful little shiver of anticipation because it wanted more of what he'd just given her.

Also not good.

"Why are you looking at me like that?" he asked.

"How am I looking at you?"

"I'm not sure," he said slowly. "As if maybe you're seeing something you're not all that thrilled about."

Well, she wasn't all that thrilled that she'd gone and gotten her heart involved, because it was going to hurt. Big-time. "Christian, I—"

He pulled her around to face him and put a finger over her lips. "Wait. Listen."

She cocked her head. "I don't hear anything."

"Exactly." He walked past her. Three bedrooms, all opened and all empty.

"Where is everyone?"

"No clue."

The silence, which she might have noticed before now if she hadn't been in a sexual fog, was almost eerie. "Um, how long were we in that shower anyway?"

His eyes cut to hers, holding a flash of amusement.

"Just wondering," she said, and felt her ears heat.

He stroked a finger over one of them, a rare smile crossing his lips, slow and soft and sexy, and—her heart leapt—filled with genuine affection and heat. "We weren't that long."

Together, they moved down the stairs and through the wide, open living room, to an adjoining room that looked like it had every entertainment setup known to man, complete with a wall of television sets, all on, several turned to sporting events from what Dorie assumed was across the world. Two huge side-by-side screens were showing American baseball. Surely this would have drawn Andy out of wherever he'd been, and yet the room, the entire house, reverberated with an undeniable silence.

"Weird," she said.

"Very." He looked around them. "Let's—"

A scream pierced the air, and though Dorie took a second to process the shocking, startling sound, Christian did not. He was running before she could blink, and all she could do was follow him, through the house, down a hallway, and then another, through what looked like a library because of the miles and miles of shelves filled with books and more books.

But she was too busy keeping Christian in her sight to take in much. Without him, she knew she'd be hopelessly lost in the labyrinth of hallways, and she didn't intend to get lost.

Not with the scream that had sounded like Cadence.

"This way." Christian barreled through a set of double French doors that opened onto a wood deck, and a set of stairs that appeared to vanish into thin air.

Not vanish, she realized with a gulp as she blindly followed Christian, but led straight down at a dizzying pitch at least three hundred feet to the beach, and the deck.

She moved as quickly as she dared, but her sandals really had to go. Her purse banged into her hip, threatening her balance with every step. Halfway down, Christian pulled out his knife, which made breathing all but impossible, but she couldn't concentrate on that when she could see what lay ahead, which had her nearly apoplectic with terror.

Michael's boat was still docked. On the dock itself, his back to them, stood Denny. He was holding Cadence against him and gesturing to Brandy and Andy, who stood in front of him.

The knife he held gleamed in the sunlight.

"Stay back." His words came over the water with an eerie clarity.

"Jesus, Denny," Brandy said softly. "No wonder you can't keep a woman."

"I'm a man on the fucking edge!" he yelled at her. "You're supposed to be sweet-talking me, not pissing me off!"

"I don't—" But Brandy broke off, looking up at Christian as he flew down the stairs.

At her movement, Denny whipped around, and when he did, Cadence let out a loud, screeching "hi-yaaaaah" and karate-chopped him in the back of his neck.

His eyes went wide with surprise for one beat before they fluttered, revealing the whites rolling up. Letting go of Cadence, he hit the wood dock face-first.

Andy dove on the top of him, presumably to hold him down, but Denny was out cold and not going anywhere.

Brandy grabbed the fallen knife. Christian skidded down the last step to the dock. "Are you hurt?" he asked Cadence.

Looking shell-shocked, she shook her head, then glanced down at Denny. "I almost gave up my penis embargo for you!" Then she kicked him in the butt.

Denny stirred and lifted his head. "Hey, that hurt!"

"So would that knife if you'd have used it on me!"

"Kick him again, honey," Brandy directed. "Just for the hell of it." She sneered down at Denny with disgust. "I should have known you were evil from the moment I saw you treat Bobby like your slave boy. A person who is rude to the hired help is not a nice person."

Dorie got onto the dock and reached for Cadence, who looked like a good wind might knock her over.

"Thanks," Cadence whispered, squeezing hard, her eyes a little wet.

"I wasn't going to use the knife on you," Denny said, still flat on the deck.

"How am I supposed to believe that when you used it on poor Bobby!"

Denny nearly choked. "I did not—" He tried to get up but Andy was sitting on him so he gave up. "Let me up!"

"Don't think so."

"Listen to me. I did not hurt Bobby. And I wasn't going to hurt Cadence."

"Still not letting you up," Andy said.

"Goddamnit!"

Cadence let go of Dorie's hand and crouched at Denny's side. "Maybe you should just relax," she suggested.

Denny didn't look like he appreciated the irony. "I am telling you I did not use that knife on Bobby!"

"Then who did?" Cadence demanded.

Christian went very still, then whipped toward the boat. "Ethan."

Ethan, who'd managed to get onto the *Elegance* unnoticed, had pushed off from the dock. Already a good hundred feet out, he started the small motor and lifted a hand in a wave. "Ahoy!" he yelled as he sailed away.

In Michael's boat.

Without Michael.

Without any of them.

"Oh, Christ," Andy said, his foot still on Denny's back. "He's the one who—"

"Goddamn, you're brilliant." Denny looked furious. "Now can you get off me so I can swim out there and nab his sorry ass?"

Andy removed his foot from Denny, but when Denny leapt to his feet and whipped around, Christian was still standing there, tall and tense, and very much in Denny's way.

"Move, man."

Christian didn't budge, didn't even blink as he spoke. "Someone needs to go after Ethan." He put a hand on Denny's chest when he moved to do just that. "Not you."

Michael came down the stairs and absorbed the situation in one glance. "*Shit*, I'll get help—" His hand went to his belt, but his face slackened in disbelief. "My radio's gone."

Denny laughed but it was mirthless. "Yeah. Ethan used to be a pickpocket."

Michael swore, and turning, went running back up the stairs.

Brandy grabbed Dorie, and they raced after Michael to help however they could. At the top of the stairs, Dorie would have liked to double over and gasp for breath, but Michael didn't stop. He ran around the back of his huge mansion, toward what looked like a one, two, three, *four*-car garage directly in front of . . . a moat?

And another dock.

Moored there was a small motor craft. Michael hopped in, and the girls did the same. The engine leapt to life, and Michael tossed them life vests. "Put them on!"

Dorie was still buckling in when he punched the gas, and after a moment of following the small waterway to the open water, they were faces to the wind, heading after Ethan.

"What are we going to do when we catch him?" Brandy yelled.

"Depends on if he's hurt my boat." Michael spoke evenly enough but there was underlying violence there. Dorie wouldn't want to be the one crossing him or his million-dollar boat, that was for sure.

"Why didn't you use this thing to take us directly to Fiji?" Brandy wanted to know. "Instead of putting up with us in your place?"

Michael glanced over. "This is just a ski boat. You do know how far from Fiji you are, right?"

"No idea."

"Let's just say it's going to take Ethan days to get anywhere close to a place he could possibly even think about hocking my boat."

"How long for us to catch up with him?"

Michael pointed, and as they came around a sharp, craggy curve of the island, they saw a white dot that was the *Elegance*, a few miles out on the horizon. It didn't take them long to get closer. Ethan wasn't having the easiest time sailing the huge yacht by himself.

Dorie looked back. She could just barely make out the vague outline of Michael's house high on the rocks, and far below, the beach where though she couldn't see them, she knew the others were with Denny.

Ethan tried to cut left, out to open sea, and got tangled up in a sail, which allowed them the precious seconds they needed to get closer. He was on deck struggling with the lines, swearing the air so blue it blew his hair back.

"Need a hand?" Michael asked politely, cutting his engine to be heard.

Ethan whipped toward them, and it wasn't the glint of a knife that stopped Dorie's heart this time, but the flash of a gun.

Going off.

Michael flew back against Brandy, who was propelled off her seat to the floor, with Michael in her arms. He rolled off of her, gritting his teeth before he could say anything. "It's just a knick. Duck, now, before he shoots again."

But Ethan had lost interest in them and was battling with the yacht, trying to hoist a different sail.

"Take the controls, Dorie," Michael commanded. "Quickly."

Gulping because his white shirt was covered in blood, Dorie whipped around and look at the controls. They might as well have belonged to a spacecraft.

"That's more than a knick," Brandy accused him, panic in her voice.

Dorie didn't look. She was trying to figure out how to make the boat go. At her elbow, something squawked, making her jump.

A radio.

"Base to Phillips," came a very French voice. "Tell me that wasn't a gunshot we just heard."

"They're at the other dock." Michael's face was shiny with sweat, tight in a grimace of pain. "Tell him to get out my Stryker. It's an offshore runner. He can catch Ethan on that."

"He's not going anywhere because we're bringing you straight there to him," Brandy said. "Do you hear me?"

Michael's face was cushioned between Brandy's two very expensive and beautiful breasts, and he didn't look as if he minded. "Hard not to hear you," he said. "You're shouting."

"Goddamnit, answer me," came Christian's voice over the radio, sounding very unhappy.

Dorie eyed Ethan. He was making headway, moving away from them with alarming speed. She lifted the radio to her mouth. "Yes, that was a gunshot. Ethan's getting away and Michael's shot and I'm trying to get back to you but I don't know how—" She ended this with a scream when a large swell slapped at the front of the boat and splashed her right in the face.

"Hit the throttle," Michael yelled at her. "Steer *into* the swells, not *with* the swells!"

Damn it. Maybe *he* could operate the radio and drive at the same time but she could not.

"Base to Phillips," came Christian again. "Pick up your goddamn radio or I'm going to kick some serious ass!"

"What the hell is his problem?" she shouted back to Brandy and Michael. "I answered him!"

"Hon, you have to push the button when you talk." Brandy had ripped off her shirt, and was pressing it to Michael's wound, leaving her in nothing but a tiger-striped bra and those hot Daisy Dukes. "Now forget the radio and drive this sucker home."

"I swear, I'm trying."

"Push the throttle all the way down," Michael told her.

When she did, the boat leapt to life. Okay, that was good. Speed was good, because her flesh was crawling, flinching in anticipation of a bullet tearing through it. She risked a look behind them.

Ethan had figured things out and was beginning to really move.

"First-aid kit," Brandy yelled. "Where is it?"

"Forget that." Michael said this through gritted teeth, sitting up with Brandy's help. "Dorie, keep going. Circle around him, he's going to ruin the—"

"Oh, you are not going to be a guy about this," Brandy told him. "Screw Ethan and your damn boat. You're going straight back. Christian's a doctor, the best. He'll patch you up—"

But Michael wasn't listening. His eyes had changed. Grown heavy.

Closed . . .

"Michael!" Brandy cried.

He didn't open his eyes but nodded. "Still here."

Both Dorie and Brandy sagged in relief, but he was bleeding like crazy, and Dorie began to worry that he could actually bleed out. "You have to stay with us, Michael."

He didn't answer. He didn't move.

Oh, God. There was a shocking amount of blood pumping from his shoulder, soaking into Brandy's shirt, and Dorie did the only thing she could. She faced the terrifyingly choppy water and pushed the throttle all the way to the metal.

Twenty-six

"Faster," Brandy cried. "We've got to get him back faster."

"On it." Dorie looked down at the swells barreling into the boat. "But I don't want to kill us."

"Circle around." Michael spoke without opening his eyes. "Head into the swells, hit them perpendicular, so we don't capsize."

Right. No capsizing. She whipped them around, the boat nearly tipping up on its end when she hit a swell too hard.

"Into them," Michael ordered again.

Into the swells. Into the swells. Into the swells. Dorie repeated it to herself like a mantra. She could see the house, the little canal they'd come out of, the dock that she was going to pull up to—if there was a God—and a figure standing on that dock.

Legs apart, radio up to his mouth, hair whipping around his face in the wind, Christian looked right at her from hundreds of yards away. "Are you hit?"

The button. God, she'd forgotten Christian still hadn't heard a word she'd said. She picked up the radio and pushed in the button. "Michael was shot! We're coming in—theoretically. Because I don't know how to park this thing."

"I can't hear you, you're breaking up. *Are you fucking hit?*"

"Not me. *Michael.*"

"*What?*"

Jesus! She looked up, screamed at the swell she drove straight into, nearly flipping them over, and tossed the radio aside to use both hands on the wheel. *Sorry, Christian.* She had to concentrate to turn into the canal.

Only she missed. She actually missed. "Oh, God."

"Gentle," Christian's voice said, and she realized he was speaking to her through the radio lying on the seat. "Gentle on the wheel, that's all." His voice came soft and easy. Laid-back. As if they had all the time in the world. "Make a wide turn and come back, try it again. That's it," he said as she followed his directions, and this time made it into the canal. "Don't worry about anything but this," he said. "Denny's tied up, and I've still got Ethan in sight. You're doing great, Dorie."

Bullshit, she was doing great. She was hyperventilating. Her heart was in her throat and her legs were sweating. "The steering on this is stupid!"

He couldn't hear her, but he responded anyway. "Ease up on it, there you go. Ten more feet and I've got you."

In five, he took a flying leap from the dock and landed like a cat right next to her, pushing her aside to maneuver the boat into the slip with an extremely irritating ease. "Tie us," he called to Andy and Cadence, who were running toward them to help.

Then Christian let go of the wheel and hauled her up to her toes.

"Thank Christ," he said, looking her over. "Jesus, I thought—" He shook his head, his breathing hard and uneven.

At the sound and feel of him, her heart sort of swelled, and then jammed in her throat, which didn't explain why her eyes began to burn. Strong as she'd had to be the past few days, she felt strongest right here, right now, surrounded by him. What she felt for him was so, so much bigger than she'd even imagined, and, more shocking, couldn't be contained. "I love you," she whispered, the words escaping without permission.

He went still, staring at her.

Oh, God. That thinking out loud thing really had to stop! "Michael's been shot."

As a diversion, it worked. He blinked, and very carefully put her down before moving to Michael's side.

She stood there a moment more, swaying in the breeze, wishing for one good wave to just rise up and swallow her. *Yeah, that would work.*

But somehow she managed to draw air into her lungs, and then turned to see what was happening behind her. Christian had dropped to his knees at Michael's side, where he'd pulled Brandy's shirt away from the wound at his shoulder.

"How bad?" Brandy asked him tightly.

"Not bad," Michael said.

"Shut up," Brandy told him, eyes on Christian. "Tell me."

"Not bad," he said, echoing Michael's words. "Bullet went through. Let's get him up to the house."

"My boat," Michael said, looking a bit pasty. "We have to get my boat."

"Oh my God!" Brandy exploded. "Will you stop being a stupid boy for a freaking minute? Jesus Christ, you're going to bleed to death and you're worried about a stupid toy, like a . . . a—"

"Stupid boy?" Michael's lips twisted, in a combination of good humor and pain.

Brandy glared at him. "This isn't funny. Nothing about this is funny." And she burst into tears.

Michael went immediately contrite, reaching for her.

"No, no, don't do that," she sobbed. "I'm okay. Delayed stress. That's all."

But Brandy couldn't stop crying. And because Dorie felt like crying, too, she hugged her tight, and together they watched as Christian and Andy helped Michael out of the boat and up to the house.

"He's going to be okay," Dorie said to Brandy.

"Yes, he is," Brandy agreed. "The son of a bitch. Of course he is. It's us I'm worried about." She sighed and wiped away her tears. "So. You love the gorgeous doctor?"

"Heard that, did you?"

"Honey, the whole world heard it."

While Christian stitched up Michael, his brain whirled so hard it hurt.

Dorie loved him.

How had that happened?

"Shouldn't he stay lying down for a while?" Brandy asked when he was done, hovering like a mother hen.

"No," Michael said.

"Yes," Christian said.

"No," Michael said again, and got up. He wobbled, swore, then stepped to the door.

On the other side of it stood Dorie, Andy, and Cadence.

Dorie had been pacing, but she jerked to a stop. She looked at a spot over Christian's shoulder instead of meeting his eyes. "Hi."

"Hi." He wanted to haul her up against him and hold on tight. He wanted to yell at her for nearly getting shot. He wanted to kiss her. But mostly he just wanted to look at her.

The others had circled around Michael, urging him to sit. Christian went directly to Dorie.

"Um, about before." She shifted her weight back and forth on her feet. "You know, when my mouth got the case of the runs? If you could just forget everything I said, that would be good."

She wanted him to forget that she loved him. He'd work on that.

Fat chance.

"Christian?" Brandy called. "Michael's insisting on talking to Denny. Tell him that's a bad idea."

"Colossally bad," Christian said, his eyes never leaving Dorie.

"Where is he?" Michael asked.

"On the dock where you last saw him. Tied up."

Michael headed out.

"Goddamn," Brandy said, and grabbing Cadence and Andy, followed him.

"We've got to go with them," Dorie said, and walked out, too.

"Goddamn," he said, repeating Brandy's sentiment and went after her.

Three minutes later, Dorie was on the dock with the others, standing in front of a trussed-up Denny.

Denny eyed them all. "Ethan get away, huh? Told you." His laugh was unpleasant.

"Premature elation," Christian said. "Might want to see a doctor about that."

Denny's smile faded. "Fuck you."

"I want answers," Michael said, looking pale but strong enough. "Now."

Denny tucked his lips into his mouth.

Christian sighed. "It's about the insurance claim, isn't it."

"What insurance claim?" Dorie asked.

"On the *Sun Song*," Christian said. "We had a claim on our last cruise. One of the passengers lost a bag overboard. She claimed all her jewelry was in it, half a mil worth. The insurance wouldn't pay out and the woman is suing Denny and the owner personally."

"Bitch," Denny said. "Her insurance would have covered it, but she wouldn't make her own claim. She wanted me to pay out, even though I didn't take her damn jewelry."

"That's what happens when you sleep with so many passengers," Christian said.

Cadence's mouth fell open. "You . . . sleep with passengers?"

"At least one each cruise. The oddest thing is," Christian mused, "that it should have been the owner's problem, not yours."

Denny turned his head and looked away.

"Unless . . ." Christian glanced behind him at everyone standing there. "See, I've never met the owner directly. Denny's always said the man's too busy to be bothered. I always found that incredibly strange." He turned back to Denny. "You're the owner, aren't you?"

"No."

"Working closely with him then, insurance scam, right? Yeah. I'm close." Christian stared at him. "No, it's not you, it's . . . Ethan?"

Denny's expression gave the truth away.

"Unbelievable."

"He never wanted anyone knowing," Denny admitted. "He likes the anonymity of it."

"So you, what, sleep with the passengers and then he steals from them? Is that how this works? And then you split the profits?"

"You think you're so righteous and moral," Denny said, "but if you'd been in my position, you'd—"

"What? Never have stolen in the first place? Sure as hell never murder someone to keep my secrets?"

"I didn't kill Bobby!"

Dorie's mind whirled, back to that first day on the *Sun Song*, when she'd overheard that odd conversation . . .

"I'm innocent!" Denny yelled at them.

Christian shook his head. "Then why were you holding a knife on Cadence?"

"I was holding her. And the knife. I wasn't holding the knife *on* her! I was trying to flush out Ethan! I followed him down here, hoping to get a confession out of him for killing Bobby."

Christian crossed his arms in disbelief. "So you didn't know. Is that what you want us to think?"

"Look at me," Denny told him. "Do you really think me capable of hurting Bobby?"

Christian looked at him for a long moment, then shut his eyes and shook his head. "I want to say no."

"Thanks, man. Untie me."

"Don't thank me. Because I won't be untying you. Here's the thing, Denny. I wouldn't have been able to say it about Ethan either."

"I didn't do it!"

"Maybe not Bobby. But you're in on the insurance scam. On the theft."

To Dorie, it was all making sense, terribly horrifying sense. "I heard you talking that first day," she said slowly. "It was you talking to Ethan, you said seventy-five/twenty-five but then you settled for fifty-fifty." Her heart stopped. "And then you told him to . . ."

She swallowed hard, understanding. "Take care of the mess. Bobby was the mess."

Denny closed his eyes. "Killing Bobby was not my idea. But then the kid caught Ethan red-handed and threatened to talk. Threatened to expose us. Ethan . . . he lost it."

They were all quiet for a long moment as it sank in.

"But why destroy the ship?" Brandy finally asked.

"Not planned," Denny grated out. "At least not on my part." He stared out at sea, his jaw tight. "I'm thinking Ethan had a different agenda altogether. He must have been worried about evidence."

"So where did Ethan take my boat?" Michael asked in a tone that suggested his yacht had better be safe.

"I don't know, but I could help find both Ethan and the yacht if you let me." Denny tried to stand but Christian put a hand on his head.

"Come on, Christian—"

"Where is he, Denny?"

"I told you, I don't know."

"See, here's the thing. I don't believe you."

"It's the truth!"

Christian's gaze scanned the horizon. "Michael, how many years in jail would you say he's looking at so far?"

"Without his cooperation? Ten to twenty, easy."

"Yes, I'd agree," Christian said thoughtfully. "Too bad he won't cooperate, I'm sure he could cut a deal."

"Hey!" Denny shouted when they all turned toward the stairs, leaving him there.

No one stopped.

"You can't hold me, I didn't kill him!" he yelled to their backs.

They all kept walking.

"I didn't do anything wrong!"

No one stopped at that either.

"Fine! So the whole insurance scam thing was a little shaky, but I didn't do anything else wrong!"

Still walking . . .

"All right. *Fuck!* You win! I thought Ethan was going to screw me out of the money so I sabotaged the damn boat for the additional claim. This is before I knew Ethan had offed Bobby, so don't link me with *that* crime. You happy?"

They all turned and looked at him, and at their expressions, he deflated like a balloon. "Okay, so you're not happy."

"Look at that, a captain *and* a genius," Christian said.

"I only did it so we could make a claim and pay off that bitch and still keep our livelihood. Tons of people do shit like that every day. Yeah, it makes me greedy and selfish, and yeah, we pulled the scam as often as possible to line our pockets and buy the boat outright, but I did not kill Bobby. I am not a murderer, and you can't just leave me here. I didn't do anything to any of you."

"Except sabotage the boat," Andy said.

"Which caused us to shipwreck," Brandy said.

"That's attempted murder," Christian said.

Denny practically choked on that. "Are you kidding me? We were never even in danger! Jesus Christ, did anyone so much as break a damn nail?"

In unison, everyone looked at each other, then began walking again.

"Wait! I didn't mean that. Stop. Jesus, stop! All I meant is that being on the island wasn't so bad, right? And look where we are now, in paradise!"

"Except none of us wanted to be on this island," Dorie pointed out.

"Damn A straight," Andy said.

"Duh," Cadence said.

Brandy looked at the sky.

"Um, Brandy?" Cadence said. "Back us up?"

"Maybe none of us planned for the island thing . . ." Brandy glanced at Michael. "But not all of us are having a bad time."

Michael, so rich he could have bought God, not to mention had been shot only an hour ago, smiled.

Dorie blinked, then looked at Christian. He met her gaze, with no outward sign of what he was thinking—except for the slight flicker of heat. And suddenly she was vividly reminded of the absolute *not* bad time she'd had right here on the island.

With him.

In the waterfall, on the beach.

In the shower, only a hour and a half ago.

He arched a brow, and if she wasn't mistaken, his lips curved. Was he thinking about when he'd tugged off her wet clothes and hoisted her up, pushing inside her until she'd cried out his name?

Of course not. He was more disciplined than she, and could control himself.

Plus, he hadn't done the unthinkable. He hadn't been stupid enough to fall in love with her, and then, oh yeah, let's not forget, admit it in front of everyone.

At least it was almost over. Soon she'd be home.

She'd thought that she'd be going back with a tan, maybe some beautiful pictures. Instead, she was going home with much more than that. Such as the knowledge that maybe she was far stronger than she'd ever given herself credit for. Good to know. And also that she needed to go after her dreams, which meant no more Mr. Stryowski . . .

But had all this newfound self-knowledge been worth risking her life for?

Yes.

And wasn't love also worth the risk?

She had no idea where the hopeful little voice came from, but yes, love should be worth the risk—if it went both ways. Too bad it didn't in this case.

"Well, *I'm* glad to be getting out of here," Cadence said, then glanced at Michael. "No offense."

"None taken."

"I can't wait to get back and kiss home plate," Andy said. "I think I'll write a tell-all about our adventures here."

Michael nodded. "Retain those movie rights, and maybe we'll make a deal someday." He looked around. "You'll all be home soon, and happy for it, I imagine." His eyes cut to Brandy. "Right?"

She didn't look at him, so he pulled her around, and in front of everyone, tipped up her chin and looked into her eyes. "You could stay."

"I have a job."

"Work for me instead."

"I don't do private shows."

"My assistant got married last week. Replace her."

Brandy's mouth fell open, speechless for what Dorie suspected was the first time in her entire life.

"Interested?" Michael asked.

"I don't do sex. Not for a job. Not for any job."

He arched a brow. "I said assistant, not piece of ass."

"You are serious."

"Of course I'm serious."

"Oh my God . . ." Brandy looked bowled over.

"Come on," Michael coaxed. "Take something good out of Denny's stupidity."

"Hey," Denny objected. "If good stuff happens, I should get the credit for it."

Michael didn't take his gaze off Brandy. "What do you say?"

"Yes," she whispered. "I'll be your assistant."

Michael's smile was slow and pleased.

"Hey, why don't you offer *everyone* a big life change," Denny said. "Then no one can blame me for anything."

"Not to let him be right or anything," Brandy said to Michael. "But did I mention Cadence is an artist?"

"Do you have a portfolio?" Michael asked.

"Why, are you going to put my art on your walls?"

"If you're any good."

Cadence stared at Michael. "I'm really good."

"My idea," Denny said. "Remember that. And for Andy's book, and the subsequent movie. I want credit for all of it, because you're all good to go now."

"Wait. Dorie," Brandy said. "She's—"

"A designer," Dorie filled in for her, saying it out loud and proud, feeling it warm her from the inside out. "But I'm going home to get started on my own."

Michael smiled. "Good for you."

"See? Slate clean," Denny said.

"What about me?" Christian asked more than a little wryly. "How are you going to appease me?"

Denny laughed. "Like I could appease you."

"You could."

"How?"

"I've given you two years of my life. You're going to be lucky to sail away from this and keep your own freedom. So give me mine. Forgive my father's debt."

"I can't, the deal wasn't mine, but—"

"Ethan's, as I now know. But you could make it go away, you know damn well you could."

"How? I'm trussed up like a turkey on Thanksgiving."

"Say it, goddamn you."

Denny stared at him, but let out a long breath. "Fine. It's done."

"Spell it out."

"I release you from your father's debt."

"Entirely."

"Entirely. We're even. Congratulations, you're now the best doctor in the South Pacific to be both homeless and jobless at the same time, you bastard."

Christian's mouth split in a grin that was so beautiful, Dorie felt her heart swell, and then rip wide open. She grinned back, and stepped into his arms for a tight hug.

"You don't have to be jobless," Michael told Christian. "After what you did for me, I'd be glad to help you get a job."

"Thanks." Christian squeezed Dorie, then let her go. "And the islands have been great, but I'm ready to get back to it."

"Back home?" Dorie asked with remarkable calm considering the train wreck occurring between her heart and soul.

"Yes."

To France. She'd known this. She'd expected it. And he hadn't made her any promises so there was no reason for her to feel like the bottom had just fallen out of her world, no reason at all.

"Do you hear that?" Brandy asked. They all went still to catch the humming that was getting louder and louder.

"A helicopter?" Cadence shielded her eyes. "A helicopter!"

This was greeted with such excitement that Dorie made herself smile along with the others. Because rescue was good. Great actually, because now she could put her new epiphany to the test.

She was going home to live her life. To design clothes, which had been her dream for a very long time. This trip halfway around the world had given her that, if nothing else.

Yep, any second now she'd feel the joy . . .

TWENTY-SEVEN

By the time the helicopter had refueled, Christian had gotten word via the radio that the authorities had caught Ethan. He'd run adrift on a ridge of coral and had given up fighting the sails. He willingly surrendered to the authorities and confessed in exchange for rescue.

Denny was hauled off, still trying to get everyone to say that he hadn't done anything wrong.

He'd be telling it to a judge soon enough, Christian knew.

Then the helicopter was ready to leave. Cadence had decided to go home with only what she wore on her back. She didn't want her bag, didn't want anything from the island. "Going home to make a fresh start," she said, and hugged everyone, even Dorie, though they were traveling together. "Friends forever," she whispered fiercely, smiling when Dorie repeated it back to her with tears in her voice.

Christian watched them, not surprised at the deep bond that had formed between them. They'd been through a lot in five days.

Andy lifted his bag. "I'm not leaving anything behind. I want to remember." He hugged everyone, too, and like Cadence, held on to Dorie for just a little bit longer than the rest.

Christian resisted the urge to step in, reminding himself what he'd always known, that there was just something about Dorie, something different. Special. She pulled back, smiled, and watched Andy get onto the helicopter. Then she looked at Christian.

He was staying to watch over a stubborn Michael for the night, since he refused to go to the hospital.

Which made it good-bye.

"My turn," Dorie said with false cheer. She hugged Brandy, then carefully did the same for Michael, then turned to join Cadence and Andy on the helicopter.

Christian stood there, poleaxed by a swamping rush of emotions. She was going to walk right out of his life. And since that's what he'd wanted, there was nothing he could say.

Dorie reached for the hand of the man squatting just inside the helicopter. He wore a headset and was talking into it, but all she could hear was the roar of her heart.

She was leaving.

Then someone tapped her on the shoulder. "What about me?" Christian asked. "No good-bye for me?"

At least that's what she thought he said. She couldn't hear him over the chopper, or her own heart. She certainly couldn't talk. Didn't he know how hard this was for her? Couldn't he just let her go, without making her lose it entirely? "Christian—"

"We need a minute," he said to the pilot, then pulled her aside.

"Listen, I'm really sorry about earlier," she broke in. She had to say this. "I didn't mean to blurt it out. I think it was just a remnant from all that adrenaline, from the shipwreck, from being back in a boat, from the gun—"

"When I heard the gun go off," he started, then closed his mouth. His eyes were shiny with some fierce emotion when he finished. "I didn't breathe again until I saw you."

God. The look in his eyes. She really wished he wouldn't look at her like that, like maybe it would have killed him if it'd been her to get shot.

"It was the longest minute of my fucking life, and then you wouldn't get on the goddamn radio—"

"I wasn't pushing the button down—"

"I love you back."

She just stared at him. "I'm sorry. I think my brain just hiccupped. Could you repeat?"

He let out a rough sound and rubbed his eyes. "Okay, but you're risking my organ failure, and I don't think you know CPR—"

"Look, I think I heard you correctly, but I've been really wrong about this stuff before, so—"

"I love you."

She swallowed, her eyes locked on his. "Just to clarify, this has nothing to do with us not using a condom in the shower, right?"

"*What?*" Brandy shifted closer, sticking her head between them. "Sex without a condom? Are you kids *crazy*?"

Dorie closed her eyes. "Crazy. *That* would explain everything."

Cadence hopped out of the helicopter. "What's the matter?"

"Well, they had sex without a condom, for starters," Brandy said.

"Just the once," Dorie said weakly.

Andy hopped out of the helicopter, too. "Hey, what's up?"

"Hey!" The pilot yelled out to them. "We're on the clock here!"

"Just one minute." Dorie hadn't taken her eyes off Christian. She couldn't.

"I've never felt like this before," he told her in front of everyone. "This can't-eat-can't-sleep sort of thing."

"It could just be indigestion," Andy said ever so helpfully.

Dorie twisted around and glared at him.

"Just saying," he muttered.

Christian took Dorie's hand and stared down at her fingers for a moment, before lifting his head. "I thought I wanted to go back to France, because that's the last real home I remember. I wanted to go there, work in an urgent care clinic, or the ER, because I figured that's what would make me happy."

"I know." And it would be okay. Somehow, it would be okay. If only she could keep breathing, but she couldn't seem to do that.

Out of the corner of her eye, she saw the headset guy tap his watch. She refused to acknowledge him.

"But I realized something," Christian said. "Home isn't a place. It's a who."

"Aw," Cadence murmured. "That's the sweetest thing I've ever heard."

"A who?" Dorie repeated.

"You." Christian cupped her face. "I never thought I'd feel this way, never wanted to, but I want you with me, Dorie. Smiling that smile, the one that snags my heart every single time. I don't care if we're in France, or at the damn Los Angeles Shop-Mart, or this island. The where doesn't matter."

"It doesn't?"

"Not a damn bit. Not as long as I'm with you."

They heard a sniff. Cadence was smiling with tears on her cheeks. "That's beautiful," she said, and sighed.

"Romantic, too." This from Brandy. "Especially with that French accent."

With an apologetic smile, Michael tugged both Cadence and Brandy away, and even though they were still surrounded by people and the damn helicopter, Dorie felt like they were the only two people on earth. "I can design clothes from anywhere," she said.

"I like the sound of that." Christian stepped close and hauled her up against him, smiling at the cheers around them but not letting her go. She hoped not ever letting her go . . .

EPILOGUE

Six months later,
with all the French chocolate one can eat . . .

The night sky was city, not island, and therefore the stars weren't quite as bright as they'd been in the South Pacific, but Dorie didn't care. Her view from the twentieth-floor balcony—which if she leaned out just right included the Eiffel Tower—was gorgeous.

Next to her, Christian was flipping through the day's mail, and came across her *Vogue*. "Mrs. Dorie Anderson Montague." He lowered the magazine. "I didn't realize you were going to add my name to yours."

"That's what American wives do, take their husband's name." She grinned and admitted the rest. "Plus, I married a doctor. My mother would never have forgiven me if I didn't take your name."

"So glad to oblige." His slow, warm, sexy smile was never ever going to stop making her want to jump him. She'd been doing plenty of that this past week, on their honeymoon, which was not on an island, thank you very much, or a boat.

Nope, after a small, intimate wedding with only her family, Cadence, Brandy, Andy, and Michael in attendance, they'd honeymooned right here in Paris, where they were going to buy a place and live, where Christian would do what he'd wanted to do forever, work in an ER, where she could be in the fashion center of the world.

She loved this world, Christian's, hers . . . theirs. So much that she been attempting to learn French—*attempting* being the key word here.

Tossing the paper aside, Christian leaned back in his chair. He looked so good, all long and toughly muscled, sprawled out without a care.

With a smile, she stood and slipped out of her sweater. Beneath, she wore only a pale lace bra.

"Too warm?" he asked.

"Not exactly." She began to work the long line of buttons down the front of her skirt.

His brow shot up. "You going to take a bath then?"

"No." Any second now he was going to realize she was currently commando. "There's a matter between us, something that was never settled. I don't like to leave things like that."

"Is that right?"

She let her skirt slip to the floor before she went still. "Damn, I forgot the music." Maybe he wouldn't mind.

His breathing was satisfactorily uneven now, more so when she reached for the hook of her bra, and she thought maybe he didn't mind at all.

"What do we need music for?"

"The dancing." She sighed. "I was going to dance for you. Naked." She pointed to the balcony. "Beneath the stars."

"Ah, the bet." With a thrilled grin, he stood up and kicked his chair aside. He was out of his clothes so fast her head spun. "Don't worry, I don't need music." And then he snatched her close, up against that body she knew she'd never get enough of. "All I need is you."

He looked so damn sexy. And happy. She made him happy. The thought made her heart soar. "Then you're in luck," she whispered, holding him fiercely, "because you have me, all of me . . ."